THE
BEST
BAD
THINGS

Cover design by the incomparable Hang Le
www.byhangle.com
Editing and formatting by: Elaine York, Allusion Publishing,
www.allusionpublishing.com
Copy editing by: Bethany Salminen, Bethany Edits
www.bethanyedits.net

THE
BEST
BAD
THINGS

An Unusual Standalone Romance
A Point Companion Novel

JAY CROWNOVER

AUTHOR'S NOTE

Hi.

I'm going to keep this intro short and sweet: this book is weird.

I know it. And that's what I love most about it. I also know the weirdness won't sit right with everyone, and I am perfectly fine with that. This is the first book I felt compelled to write in a long time. I got an idea and couldn't stop thinking about it. Inspiration like that has been hard to come by the last few years, so I'm prepared to embrace the good, the bad, and the ugly.

This is a different kind of novel than I usually write, but I think if you're a long-time reader, you will find many of my favorite, familiar bits and pieces scattered throughout. And if you are a new or newish reader, I promise you cannot base my work on this single title. This book is a beast that stands on its own.

With all of that out of the way, all I can say is hold on for the ride. Nothing is as it seems. You can't trust anyone on these pages. Everyone is unreliable... including me. And if you think you read something as one way in one chapter, and it's suddenly different in another chapter, that is intentional. Lol... I admit that my memory has gotten worse post turning forty, but it's not *that* bad.

As always, for those who are willing to read whatever I decide to write, I appreciate your bravery and adore your willingness to dip your toes into the strange and unusual.

Love & Ink,
Jay

Dedicated to
the usual suspects...

PROLOGUE

THE WORLD AS I KNOW IT

It was unfortunate when bad things happened to good people, but I'd learned the hard way that they inevitably would. Naïve people were bound to stumble into bad things and bad situations. The same was true for innocent, trusting people.

However, my biggest takeaway was that bad things were going to happen to *stupid* people, no matter what. They should've seen those bad things coming right at them, but they ignored all the warning signs.

I had fallen into all those categories at one point or another.

I was innocent and trusting right up until I was arrested under the suspicion of murdering my father. I was naïve to an embarrassing extreme when I was a teenager. I didn't believe my best friend and the boy I was obsessed with would ever turn their backs on me. But they did. Their words and accusations against me almost sealed my fate with a jury that was already eager to put me behind bars.

And I was stupid. So goddamn dumb. Every bad thing I'd been through the last few years was as clear as day in front of me, but I had walked into disaster anyway. When everything started to go so wrong, I had no idea how to navigate the bad things. I tried my best to be the perfect young adult so I'd be rewarded with a bright, exciting future. I foolishly thought that since I'd done everything right, goodness and truth would eventually win. They didn't. Goodness wasn't worth a damn.

Bad luck. Bad timing. Bad friends. Bad choices. Bad intentions. I couldn't escape the bad things once they got their claws into me. My misfortune seemed endless and unrelenting.

The day all my bad luck really caught up with me was my birthday. I had just turned twenty-five. But I felt one hundred. I was world-weary and disenchanted. I'd grown numb to tragedy and despair. Disappointment and discontent were so much a part of me that I'd long forgotten how to feel any other type of way. Long gone was the clueless, carefree teenager I'd once been.

I wanted to believe that the constant struggle over the years had made me smarter. That I'd grown a little bit harder, and I'd shed the wide-eyed innocence that had landed me in such a sorry state in the first place. I no longer trusted anyone. Though, no matter how much I'd been forced to toughen up and endure, I couldn't quite shake being an inherently good person.

That goody-two-shoes streak was annoying and dangerous considering the life I'd been forced into. I was surrounded by the kind of people who had no use for anything good in a place where bad things and bad people thrived. So, I kept my head down and my mouth shut at all times. It was best not to be noticed, because if I ran across the wrong person, they would take utter delight in burning that last bit of stubborn goodness out of me.

Unfortunately, I couldn't always keep a lid on the bright spots that still dotted my darkened soul. Good intentions still managed to leak from my heart even though I'd done my very best to bleed them all out.

These days, I had an obvious weakness: I couldn't help myself from worrying about the two young children who lived in the dilapidated room next to mine in the rundown motel I called home. In my memories, my concept of home was a large house with a sprawling lawn, filled with parties and people. The fridge was always full. The temperature inside was always just right. Everything was always clean without me having to lift a finger. My room was professionally decorated, and my clothes were designer. I went to a private school and had a future planned out that was as brilliant as my expensively straightened smile. It was an idyllic, privileged existence. It was too good to be true.

In my life now, my home was a place that rented rooms by the hour or the week. My younger self would've considered my humble accommodation a nightmare. Nowadays, I was often grateful to have the stained, often leaky roof over my head. But even if I had no choice but to settle for the less than stellar digs, I knew it was no place for the kids in the room next to me to grow up. The little boy and girl lived there before I moved in. I couldn't help myself from befriending them, since their mother often left them unattended, and they regularly showed up at my door looking for everything from food to basic affection.

I wanted to protect them. The desire ran so deep, I knew it came from feeling like no one had been around to protect me when my life went to shit. I was projecting, but I couldn't stop myself.

Their mom was a drunk. She often seemed to forget she even had kids. I did my best to check up on them at least once a day, even though I was barely scraping by. It was saying something that I was their best option for a caregiver, considering the disastrous state of my own life.

It was late that night. My birthday was almost over. Today passed like all my previous birthdays since my life turned upside down. There was little to celebrate aside from surviving another year in the wasteland of a city the locals just referred to as *the Point*.

I always came home from my shitty job, at an even shittier diner, well past the time it was safe for anyone to walk alone on the streets in this part of town. I'd had more than one terrifying run-in with the typical type of predator who used the shadows to lurk and hunt for prey. Luckily, I learned pretty quickly what it would take to survive in those circumstances and came away unscathed, mostly. Plus, it didn't hurt that for as long as I'd lived at the motel, there was a guy who spent his nights working on an old, broken-down car in the parking lot from dusk till dawn. I had no clue what he did during daylight hours, but as soon as the sun went down, he was making a racket right outside my unit's door as he banged around in the engine and tinkered with the car. He intervened more than once when I was harassed on my walk home. Almost as if he was watching to make sure I made it back safely every night. The guy looked to be around the same age as me, but he didn't talk much and didn't seem interested in striking up a conversation or friendship when I profusely thanked him for keeping the creeps off my back. Whenever I tried to offer a friendly greeting, he grunted in acknowledgment but never returned it.

He wasn't friendly, and he looked scary, but he made sure I got home in one piece, so I tried not to judge him.

On that night, he was out front, head buried in the rusty compartment of the car like always. He was working by the faint light from the almost burned-out bulb that hung in front of the kids' unit and a flickering flashlight. I didn't bother to say anything as I walked past him, but my nose twitched as I caught the overwhelming scent of gasoline coming from the car. The guy often had a cigarette dangling from his mouth. If I was anywhere else, I might've warned him not to smoke around such a flammable chemical. However, I resolved to keep my good intentions in check, so I said nothing.

I rubbed the end of my nose as it burned from the fumes. I stopped in front of the room next to mine and lightly knocked on the door. It would be awful if the kids' mom was still up and deep in the middle of a bender. She hated me looking out for her kids, often accusing me of trying to take her place in their lives. She was so unhappy. Even more so than me. I was uncomfortable around her for many reasons. I always reminded her I was the one who made sure the kids had something to eat most days. If I wasn't worried child protective services would separate the brother and sister once they were in the system, I would've turned her in the first week I moved into the motel.

4

Fortunately, the little girl, Tobi, opened the door with a big smile. She took the takeout container in my hand and called over her shoulder to her little brother that it was time to eat. I didn't know how old Tobi or the little boy, Jordan, were. They were both old enough to be in school, but I hadn't seen either of them attend anything that remotely looked like an educational institution. They were happy, fun little kids. They deserved so much more than a life locked in this dismal situation.

I patted Tobi on the head and blinked fiercely as my eyes watered once the door was pushed fully open. The overwhelming scent of rotten eggs filled the inside of the tiny room. I grabbed Tobi by the shoulder and pulled her outside as I peered inside the darkened interior. The kitchenettes in each room had rusty old stoves and barely working radiators that ran on natural gas. It wouldn't surprise me if one of the appliances was leaking, but it had to have been going on for a while for the smell to be so strong.

"How long has your room smelled bad?" I waved frantically at the little boy who was playing on the dirty carpet with a toy car and barked, "Jordan, come out here and stand with your sister."

Tobi cocked her head to the side and considered my question as I pulled them away from the room that I was positive had a serious gas leak. Out of the corner of my eye, I noticed their mother passed out on one of the two beds that took up most of the room.

"Vesper, it smells really bad. My head hurts, and so does my tummy. Jordan threw up earlier. Mommy said to ignore it." She shook the to-go box at me and begged, "We're hungry now. Can we go to your room and eat?"

I grabbed Jordan by the arm when he was close enough and tugged the kids into the parking lot, looking at the outside of the shabby, dilapidated motel with cautious eyes. If their room had a gas leak, and it was bad enough that the kids were experiencing physical symptoms, it was serious enough to filter into other rooms via the cheap, old air ducts. The entire building was like a ticking bomb waiting to go off. One stray spark was all it would take to blow us all off the face of the earth.

Trying not to panic, I gave Tobi and Jordan a little push toward the street. I frantically looked between the guy who was still buried in the engine of his car and the kids' oblivious mother. I wondered how I was the only adult in this absolutely fucked-up scenario who realized something was very wrong. I wanted to yell at the smoker to be careful. I wanted to scream at the irresponsible mother who put her kids in a perilous situation with her carelessness. I didn't want the kids to freak out or try to go back into their unit, so I bent down and looked directly into Tobi's wide, startled eyes. She looked like she was about to cry.

"You need to take Jordan across the street." I dug in my pocket for the handful of cash I made in tips during my shift and shoved it at the little girl. She didn't take it fast enough, so I shoved it into one of her dirty pockets. "Go wait for me at the gas station on the corner. Get something to drink and buy some candy. You can have whatever you want, but don't come back home until I come and get you. Do you understand?"

The little girl looked frightened, but she still reached out to grasp her brother's hand.

"Candy is too expensive. Mommy says it rots our teeth, and we don't have any money for a dentist."

The young boy nodded in agreement but looked longingly at the gas station.

I nudged Tobi in the direction I wanted her to go while muttering, "I'll take you to the dentist. I promise. Now hurry up and go across the street. Remember to look both ways and stick together. Be good, okay?" I was practically pleading with the children at this point, but it worked.

Pouting slightly, Tobi finally dragged her brother across the parking lot. I waited until the kids were out of sight before taking a step toward their unconscious mother. I faltered, wondering if it was the right choice to save her instead of the guy who had protected me repeatedly, even though he gained nothing from it. I felt like he was the type of guy who did something good for someone else despite himself. Like he wanted to let me suffer, but he couldn't help himself from intervening when bad things happened right in front of him. We had that in common. It would be a real shame if I let an almost good guy in this awful place get blown up without at least attempting to save him.

However, I also knew what it was like to lose a parent at a very young age. My mother disappeared when I was just a little older than Tobi. Losing her was the first bad thing I had to navigate, and the first time I realized it didn't matter how good of a girl I was; things weren't always going to be perfect. Life wasn't fair, and it felt like fate really wanted to hammer that point home.

The kids might be better off without that woman, but I knew they wouldn't see it that way. So, I had to do something to try and save their mom and my reluctant savior. That damn streak of wanting to do the right thing that still flowed within me made it so I couldn't simply focus on saving myself after the kids were out of harm's way. No good deed went unpunished.

"Hey, there's a gas leak!" I shouted at the guy working on the car and moved a few steps toward the open unit where the kids' mom was still unmoving on the bed. "Be careful." I wish I knew his name so he would pay attention to me.

I wasn't sure if he heard me, but my neighbor didn't move a muscle. I tiptoed closer to the dangerous room and held my breath as the horrible stench of sulfur got stronger. I couldn't imagine how the kids had endured it while it built to this level. It was unnerving that they were so accustomed to keeping their complaints to themselves that they suffered in silence.

I was almost at the door to my neighbor's unit when I caught a movement out of the corner of my eye. The guy working on the car straightened, his silvery-lilac hair popping up as he looked over in my direction. His hair was purple at one point and faded to the pretty violet hue. He always had his hair dyed a bright color. He stood

3

out like a peacock in a flock of pitch-black crows in this dreary city. The cigarette in his mouth dangled precariously between his lips. I gulped in a nervous panic, trying to shout a warning, but tripped over my words.

I was too late.

I wanted to save everyone. In the end, I couldn't save anyone. I always knew there would be a big, bad thing I couldn't escape. I knew that damn lingering goodness I couldn't get rid of was going to be the end of me.

I was right.

The guy flicked his cigarette away, right toward the puddle of gasoline I'd passed earlier; my neighbor shifted listlessly on the bed and swore at her missing kids. I couldn't yell a warning out fast enough to stop either of them. Right before the explosion blew me back and obliterated everything, my eyes met the startled gaze of the car guy. I could see that he belatedly realized something was wrong. He stumbled back a step and reached out a hand as if he wanted to pull me to safety. But we were both as good as gone. The cigarette hit the gasoline. I stood frozen and helpless in the middle of impending disaster. I wondered where exactly I'd gone wrong and pondered what heinous crimes I'd committed in the past to deserve such a sad and pathetic ending. On my birthday, for God's sake.

If only I'd run to safety with the children. If only I had a better sense of self-preservation. If only I hadn't been so fucking stupid to lose everything I had in the first place and end up in this tragically ridiculous situation. I had no clue why fate enjoyed playing games with me. I didn't know where I'd gone so wrong that my destiny was doomed.

The night lit up with an explosion that rocked the entire block.

It took a lot to get the people of the Point to take notice. The fireball that shot into the sky when everything combusted was powerful enough not only to catch the attention of those living rough and rowdy in this part of the city, but also impactful enough to alarm the people living pretty up on the good side of town. They called the nice neighborhood in this city the *Hill*. That's where I dreamed of growing up. I only had fuzzy memories left of opulence and wealth.

I doubted anyone there would remember me when I was gone. But I would never forget just how far and fast I'd fallen when someone I trusted and loved, someone who was almost a sister, decided she wanted my spot at the top of the hill. She couldn't betray me fast enough, and I couldn't have walked into her traps any quicker if I tried.

My last thought before fire and flame obliterated my entire being was...*why me?*

Hadn't I suffered enough?

After everything I'd already been through, wasn't this ending a bit underwhelming?

There was no revenge.

There was no absolution or awakening.

There was no remorse.

Trust me, there were plenty of days in my previous life that deserved recognition for being the worst day of my life. So now, the whole idea of dying by being accidentally blown to bits seem almost comical. If I could've laughed, I would've.

I wasn't going out in a blaze of glory.

Nope. It was a blaze that could've been prevented had I been anywhere else and if I were someone else. If only I'd given in and become the kind of person who embraced the awful and leaned into the terrible when my life turned upside down.

The heat that engulfed me was overwhelming. And so were my regrets.

If only I could go back and do so many things over again. If I had another chance, a shot at making sure I never ended up standing in front of this dreadful motel in the first place. Maybe I could finally save myself. I could save everyone.

I had saved the kids, not only tonight, but every night since I moved in. That had to count for something, didn't it? Karma needed to step up to the plate.

Asking for a redo didn't seem like too much, considering just how thoroughly fate had fucked me over.

The powers that be owed me one.

That was my final thought before the world around me blurred into a fiery red haze that obliterated everything, even the unbelievable pain that wrapped around me and stole my last breath.

Weirdly, dying felt a lot like falling.

Only there was no place to land, and the sensation of flying with no way to catch myself, or brace for impact, was much scarier than knowing I was caught in the center of an inevitable explosion.

ONE

BE KIND AND REWIND

I rapidly blinked my eyes and lifted a hand to block out the glaring sunlight. My entire head felt like it was being squeezed in a vise, and all my muscles were shaking. I felt like throwing up, but a hand landed on my shoulder and squeezed. The grip held me upright, making it impossible for me to bend over and gag.

"Get it together, Vesper. I know you're pissed my mom insisted on having the wedding the same day as your birthday, but you can share the spotlight for once in your life." Long, fake nails dug into the bare skin of my shoulder to the point I wondered if I was going to bleed.

I blinked as the girl standing next to me came into focus and I felt my stomach drop. She was pretty—otherworldly pretty. I remembered thinking how opposite we were the first time we met when she transferred to my school at the beginning of sophomore year. Addison Martin had long, straight, golden blond hair, bright blue eyes, and cute little dimples that made her appear soft and delicate. In contrast, I kept my pitch-black hair cut in a sharp bob that sat at my chin, with heavy bangs that rested right above my eerily pale gray eyes. She looked like a Barbie. I looked like Wednesday Addams all grown up. We were about the same height, but I was on the lanky, almost too-skinny side. Addison was perfectly curvy and fit. We were the same age, shared all the similar advanced classes, and became fast friends. It wasn't until our parents eventually got married that I realized things weren't quite what they seemed with Addison and her mother. I was too slow on the uptake to see that every single move from the moment we met until the moment my life was ruined, had been meticulously plotted and planned by the two of them.

If what I was seeing was correct, today was my eighteenth birthday and the day of my father's wedding. It was the day everything started to go wrong for me. I couldn't believe I was back in this botanical garden, wearing the atrocious seafoam green dress Madison—yes, Addison's mom made sure their names rhymed—forced me to wear. It was too short, too itchy, too frilly, and overall, too much. Sort of like insisting the wedding happen on my birthday.

I remembered today so clearly. For a minute, I thought I was dreaming. Or, more accurately, that I was caught in a nightmare. This was a bad day—the first of many to follow.

I had pouted the entire ceremony the first time around and got drunk on stolen rosé during the reception. I made a loud, obnoxious scene and cried until I threw up all over one of the exotic flower beds. Back then, I had no idea today would mark the start of my downfall, or that it would start the timer on the days I had left with my father in my life. The wedding was the beginning of the end for both of us.

I was mentally scrambling, trying to figure out how one second I'd been in the middle of an inferno that felt like the gates of hell had opened to standing in a posh garden in an ugly dress watching my father about to make the worst mistake of his life. For the second time. It made little sense. It couldn't be real. Except those nails digging into my shoulder really hurt, and I could feel the curious looks from the wedding guests boring into me. It seemed like I could've skipped the public humiliation if I was dreaming or having a nightmare.

I shook free of the talons holding me in place and dropped the bright bouquet I was holding. I gave my head a hard shake and lifted my hands to slap my cheeks, trying to get my thoughts in order.

I was blown up. That happened. Didn't it?

I clearly remembered the heat and flames. I could still smell the stink of gasoline and natural gas. My skin prickled uncomfortably, and my head continued to throb painfully. I saw Addison's manicured hand moving toward me once again, so I wildly sidestepped out of her reach.

I had begged for a redo in those last moments before everything went dark and got too hot to handle, a chance to go back and fix everything that went wrong in my past. Was it possible someone or something larger than my simple life had heard me? Did I really earn some cosmic brownie points by making sure nothing happened to Tobi and Jordan before the motel was blown to hell?

Or maybe I was in an alternate reality.

None of it made any sense, but I wasn't about to miss the opportunity to save my dad from the vile woman he was about to marry. I was going to stop the wedding this time, even if it was all only happening within my fractured mind.

I smacked Addison's hand away and moved forward to give her a little shove. The rest of the bridesmaids gasped in shock, and I heard an uneasy rumble move through the gathered crowd.

"I object!" I spun around and frantically searched for my father. He was standing under an elegant arch waiting for Madison, who was standing at the end of the aisle. Addison reached for my arm, her flawless face frozen in a look of annoyance as she tried to pull me back in line with the other attendants.

"What in the hell are you doing? Are you fucking crazy? Vesper, pull yourself together right now!" My former best friend whisper-yelled the angry words while trying to keep a smile on her face.

I couldn't believe my dad was alive and well. I wanted to run to him. I wanted to wrap my arms around him and hold on as tightly as I could. My reaction was visceral and raw. I almost fell to my knees, weak with relief at the sight of him. My heart felt like it was beating double-time, and my fingers were shaking uncontrollably. The void that was left inside of me after he died filled back up with a rush of too many tumultuous emotions to name. I wanted to scream for him at the top of my lungs, but the fact that I was standing in front of a crowd of well-dressed people jerked me back to reality.

I would have been mortified by causing such a scene like this at the original wedding. Even though I felt slighted, I would have been sick over ruining my father's big day. I was spoiled rotten, but I always behaved almost too well, because my dad was all I had, and I never wanted to disappoint him.

I grabbed my aching temples and stumbled toward my father. I kicked off the stupid, nude high heels I was wearing, and once again yelled at the top of my lungs, "I object to this union! You can't marry that woman!"

I didn't know if objecting really worked, but it stopped plenty of weddings on TV shows and in the movies. It was all I could think of on such short notice and through the pain making my ears ring and my head throb.

The broke, pitiful twenty-five-year-old version of me would be aghast at the eighteen-year-old version kicking away shoes that cost enough to feed more than one person for well over a month. She would be appalled at the long nails and heavy makeup my teenage self was currently sporting. Once I ended up in the Point, I did everything in my power to blend in and go unnoticed. Attention was the last thing you wanted in a place where everyone was either predator or prey. Before today's utterly bizarre reawakening, I couldn't recall the last time I'd worn anything flashy or bright. I couldn't remember a single moment when I tried to make myself look *more* attractive after ending up in the Point. I usually spent my time making sure I looked as unremarkable as possible. It was no easy feat considering my unusual eyes, pale skin, and dark hair, and long, lean build. I was the epitome of the goth dream girl without even trying, so I always attracted unwanted attention by merely existing.

My dad caught me just as I stumbled over the lacy fabric that made up the aisle when I started to run toward him. His hands were warm where they wrapped around my arms, and his eyes were full of concern as they moved over me from head to toe. Considering our relationship until this point, he was probably worried that I was reacting to the wedding upstaging my eighteenth birthday. Originally, I'd asked for a gigantic party with all my friends at an exotic location full of fun and sun. He would've given me anything I wanted, until Madison Martin, his new fiancée, insisted on having their nuptials on my birthday. She swore their venue at the botanical garden only had one opening this time of year. It was the same weekend I was planning on having my party. My dad was in a tough spot. He never wanted to disappoint me, but he also didn't want to let down his bride-to-be. If I hadn't relented and agreed to be in the wedding and have a massive graduation party instead, the poor man might've perished from a heart attack before Addison and her mother got the chance to go all black widow on him.

"Honey, what's wrong with you? Are you sick?" My dad's concern was palpable while the bride's fury at having her ceremony interrupted pulsed with life.

I gasped and continued to clutch my head. The minister who was officiating the ceremony cleared his throat and tried to salvage the situation with a joke.

"Young lady, we are nowhere near that portion of the ceremony yet. You jumped the gun."

Uneasy laughter drifted through the crowd. My dad asked someone to get a bottle of water as Madison started to make her way angrily down the aisle to see what the hold-up was.

Knowing I only had a few seconds, I grabbed the lapels of my father's elegant white linen suit and warned him, "She's going to kill you. She's only marrying you for your money. It's what they do. You're not the first victim, Dad. Addison and her mom are terrible people."

I knew I sounded crazy. Until this very moment, Addison and I were the very best of friends. We already acted like sisters, and from the outside, her mother had very much embraced me as her own. There were no signs of the evil that lurked within or hints of how ruthless mother and daughter could be.

"Did one of your friends put you up to this, Vesper? You never act out in such an unruly way. I don't know what's going on with you, but this isn't funny or appropriate." My dad pulled one of the curly black twists that was hanging near the side of my face. He gave me a gentle smile and tried to guide me toward one of the folding seats that currently filled the fragrant garden setting. "Have a seat, and we'll talk later."

I held onto him even tighter and tried to get my panic across through my eyes. "Dad, I can't explain it, but if you marry this woman today, you're going to die. And I'm going to get blamed for it."

"Honey..." His voice trailed off as he looked at me helplessly. He looked confused as hell and very concerned about me. Before he got the chance to ask about his impending demise, familiar hands once again grabbed my shoulders, those sharp-ass nails digging into my skin. By now, Madison had made her way to us, and even through her ornate veil, her twisted, ugly expression was visible. It was the first time she let her mask slip while my father was still alive to witness it. Mother and daughter were both experts at putting up a front.

"You rotten brat. I can't believe you're ruining our special day. What is wrong with you?" The bride's words were cutting and shaky with rage. I noticed my father finally stopped looking at me like I was out of my mind and looked at the woman he was about to marry with new clarity.

"Madison, clearly, something is wrong. I don't think calling Vesper names is appropriate. Why don't we all take a minute to collect ourselves and try this again when everyone calms down? It will be all right if we pause for a moment, right, Father Cohen?"

The minister nodded and smiled kindly. "Of course, Mr. Bell. Everyone gathered today is here to witness a joyous event. I'm sure they'll be understanding." He cleared his throat and lowered his voice slightly. "I suggest opening the bar up early and maybe having hors d'oeuvres passed around."

My dad waved a hand and nodded his agreement. He tried to pull me away from the grip Addison had on my shoulder, but those claws of hers were not moving. My head was still a hazy mess, and my vision was still a bit wonky. But I would say what I had to say even if I passed out right at his feet.

"If you won't stop the wedding, make her sign a prenup, Dad." I was begging with everything I had in me. My pleas were filled with all the agony and despair that I'd lived with after he died, and I ended up at the lowest point imaginable.

"Prenups come *before* the wedding, you moron. What are you even talking about? Mom and Nelson have been together for over a year. If they felt a prenup was necessary, they would've already addressed it. You're out of line right now, Vesper." Addison barked the words and looked at me like she was ready to burn me alive.

I reached up and forcibly removed my former friend's hold on me. Of course, my dad wasn't the kind of guy who would ever consider a prenup because he believed in true love and the idea of happily ever after. My mom had been the love of his life, and it devastated him when she left us all alone. A lot of the money I grew up with came from her estate, but my dad was a very accomplished man in his own right. He was a very successful author—one who wrote tragic love stories set in small towns. If you asked him, they weren't *romance novels*, they were love stories. However, the rest of the world knew he was writing romance. I'd honestly lost count of how many of his novels had been adapted into film and television shows. My mother's wealth was a bonus, but it wasn't needed to maintain our lifestyle.

I was a moron, because I told Addison all about how loyal and romantic my dad was as we became friends. I loved the idea when she suggested setting him and her mom up on a blind date. I wanted him to have someone in his life since it was always just me and him against the world. I was going off to college soon, or so I thought, and I wanted to make sure he was happy and had someone to take care of him. Madison Martin seemed perfect. She was down-to-earth and kind. She didn't seem obsessed with money and status like so many of our classmates' parents. And she was good to me, which I honestly ate up. I missed having a mom around, regardless of how amazing my dad was. The whole thing felt very reminiscent of *The Parent Trap* movies.

"Fine. If a prenup is out of the question, promise me you'll revise your will. Make sure Madison and Addison can't touch any of the money or property Mom left behind. You need to include a clause that prevents them from touching any of your assets if you die for at least the first ten years of your marriage. And you need to make sure they can't touch any of your books, past or present. Everything you've worked for will be destroyed if you don't listen to me. I know it seems extreme, and I sound like a crazy person right now, but I'm begging you to trust me, Dad." My voice broke and my knees wobbled.

One of the biggest 'fuck yous' the mother-daughter duo pulled off after my father died was to let a shady publisher put out books under his name written by a ghostwriter, claiming they were unfinished projects he was working on before his death. The books were trash. Mostly just reworked versions of the stories he'd already written, and because my father's work was beloved around the world, people bought them. They tarnished his legacy beyond belief.

I yelped in surprise as my hair was suddenly grabbed and yanked hard. My entire body jerked backward from the force of the pull.

"What are you talking about, you troublemaker?" Madison screeched the words at the top of her lungs. I felt less bad about causing a scene because the one she was creating would go down in history. My dad swore under his breath and struggled to pry his almost-bride's hand out of my hair as she demanded, "Where is all this coming from? You know I just want us all to be a family. I don't care about your dad's money."

I struggled free and swatted at her hand. I glared at both mother and daughter, using my dad's shoulder to hold myself up and to brace against the hatred I could feel wafting in my direction.

"If you just want us to be one big, happy family, then you won't object to signing away your right to any and all of my dad's assets.

You also won't object to him running a thorough background check on you. I'm pretty sure you never mentioned that you've been married before, or that your previous husband passed away under suspicious circumstances. And that's not even Addison's father, who also disappeared without a trace. They have a shady past, Dad."

Madison gasped in shock and fell back a step. Addison swore loud enough that guests in the front few rows overheard her. Everyone's attention was definitely on the drama happening under the arch, but I didn't care. I was too late to save my dad in my last life. I would not be merciful in this one.

"She's gone crazy, Nelson. You need to have her committed as soon as this ceremony is over. I have no idea what she's talking about. Vesper, you're embarrassing your father and making me very uncomfortable. You need to stop what you're doing right this instant. Do you have any idea how expensive this wedding is?"

My father held up his hands placatingly and gave a soft smile. "I think maybe we need to put the brakes on everything today and revisit the situation once we all sit down and have a serious discussion as a family." He looked directly into Madison's eyes as he spoke.

The beautiful woman in the equally beautiful wedding gown balked and shoved back the veil covering her face with flailing hands.

My father reached to pat the hand I had on his shoulder. "It's obvious we need some more time to get to know each other and integrate our families. If Vesper is this upset and what she is saying about your past is true, I'm afraid I'm not comfortable moving forward with the ceremony today. I was under the impression you knew just how important my daughter is to me. She always comes first."

God. I would've given anything to hear him say that to me before everything went to hell. It was the reassurance I needed the most when our relationship started to fracture due to outside influence.

Madison sniffed and shot a look at her daughter. Addison was glaring at me with the fire of a thousand suns in her sharp gaze. It was hard to tell who was more aggravated by my sudden outburst and my dad's decision to switch gears.

"If that was the case, why did you agree to have our wedding on her birthday? Does that seem to you like you're putting her first, Nelson?" The bride stamped her foot furiously. Out of the corner of my eye, I noticed every single person was watching the drama play out with captivated eyes and dropped jaws. My dad was going to be horrified when he realized he would be the center of gossip in the swanky neighborhood for months, if not years. The videos people were recording on their phones were bound to go viral as soon as they were uploaded.

He tilted his head questioningly, and his shoulder tightened under my palm. "You told me this was the only weekend available this season. I asked you to look at other venues with open dates, but you insisted on this one. I only agreed after Vesper compromised. Are you telling me you planned the wedding on this date to force me to choose between you and my daughter?"

All the color leached out of Madison's face, and Addison swore loudly again. Both women suddenly looked around, almost like they were looking for an escape. My father didn't get angry very often, but it was quietly terrifying when he did.

"I'm not admitting to anything. I'm supposed to be getting married right now, not put on trial." She sounded shrill and afraid.

"No one is getting married today." My dad's voice held a thread of finality that couldn't be ignored. "I apologize. I want to thank everyone for coming today, but there are obviously some personal issues we need to address privately. Enjoy the bar and stay for dinner since everything is already paid for."

Finally, I felt like I could breathe again. I squeezed my dad's shoulder and tried to smile, but everything in front of my eyes swirled together into a kaleidoscope of color. I started to breathe heavily, and I could hear my heart racing between my ears. I knew I was going to pass out. I felt myself pitch toward the ground and vaguely heard my dad call my name.

I didn't know if I was finally dying now since I got to go back and undo all the damage those two women had done to my life and to my

16

father. Or, maybe I would eventually wake up and really be back in the past when I was still eighteen and it was just me and my dad, like it used to be before Madison and Addison. Hell, there was always a chance I was going to end up in the middle of that damn explosion again.

Before I fully fell into the darkness forcefully pulling at me, I wondered if that boy with the colorful hair—and the kids I saved— were somewhere here in this world that appeared to rewind to the exact point where my life started to nosedive. Or was I the only one who got a second chance to right all the wrongs that haunted me?

TWO

NO GOOD DEED

When I woke up, I was disoriented. But my head didn't hurt as bad, and my vision was clearer. I could tell right away that I was in the hospital. The strong antiseptic smell assaulted my nose as soft beeping from the monitors above my head filled my ears. I squinted, trying to gauge my surroundings. Was I in the hospital after the explosion, or was I in the hospital after passing out at the wedding? It was hard to keep things straight. I was alone in the room, so I had no immediate way to tell if I'd managed to halt the wedding from hell regardless of what timeline I was in. Everything in my mind was hazy, and I still felt like I was dreaming. I knew there was no logical explanation for all the impossible things that had happened after the explosion. Nothing made any sense, so I wasn't about to jump to conclusions or make assumptions until I had more to go on.

I could see the patient info board on the wall across from my bed. It had my name and vitals written in dry erase marker. The date indicated that I'd been unconscious for at least a full day. I was in the reality where I'd just turned eighteen, and none of the horrible, tragic events that followed that cursed birthday had occurred. I was in a place where I didn't yet know what it was like to live without.

Without love.

Without means.

Without options.

Without hope.

Without trust.

Right now, I was the girl who rarely heard the word *no*, the one who rarely did anything to rock the boat. I was spoiled rotten, but I tried my best to behave in such a way that my father questioned none of my choices. In hindsight, I knew his generosity and indulgence had more to do with him trying to make sure I never once felt the loss of my mother than anything else. He wanted to make sure he gave me everything so I didn't feel like anything was lacking.

But right now, on the inside, in my mind and in my heart, I was still very much my older self. Every hard lesson I learned was embedded within me, and the tarnish that came with both loss and betrayal was still fresh. My outsides might fit right into this previous life, but everything that made me the bitter, angry person I now was felt much closer than this ideal life that was a mere memory.

Right now, I knew the only thing I couldn't live without, when it was all said and done, was my dad. The way he was taken away from me, the injustice of it all, ate away at me every single day. My resentment was the only thing I held onto from my former life. Well, that, and the sluggish heat that warmed my blood the longer I thought about how different things would be if I managed to save him from Madison and Addison. It was the only thing that felt familiar, even though I was currently reliving days I'd already lived through.

I reached for the call button for a nurse when the door opened and revealed the man I was just thinking about instead.

My dad was very handsome in an eccentric, creative type of way. If I was Wednesday Addams, he was Gomez. He even rocked the slicked-back hair and the artfully trimmed facial hair. He was still young and wildly successful. It was no surprise he was considered quite the catch among the single moms and husband hunters among the parents of my classmates. However, my dad was a tried and true romantic. He wasn't the type to take dating lightly. He'd had a couple of long-term girlfriends come and go when I was younger, but it wasn't until I introduced him to my former bestie's mother that he fell hard. Looking back on everything with a more mature and cynical understanding of the world and how relationships worked, I wondered if he liked Madison so much only because *I* liked her so much. She was the first woman in his life I ever welcomed with open arms and truly made an effort to help integrate into our small family. I even told her and Addison exactly what it was about my mom that made my dad fall in love so fast. They had a cheat code to win long before I realized our lives were nothing more than a part of the game they were playing.

"Oh, you're finally awake. Thank goodness. I was starting to get worried. The doctor assured me you were only seriously dehydrated, which caused your blood pressure to fluctuate wildly. I need to let your nurse know so she can call the attending physician." My dad walked toward the bed and paused when he was close enough to look down at me with eyes full of concern. I waved away his worry and flashed a weak 'ok' sign with my fingers to let him know I looked worse than I was. "They tested you for all kinds of things, Vesper. I was worried about drugs because you were acting so strange, and the doctor even mentioned the possibility of poison or other toxins since your behavior was bizarre before you passed out. I know you were upset about the wedding, but all that talk of murder really took me by surprise. It wasn't like you to blurt out something like that. Thankfully, all the tests came back clear. I was very relieved with that news until you refused to wake up." He reached out and grabbed my hand. One of my hands had an IV line tapped in the back of it; the other looked very pale and fragile in his grasp. "You gave me quite a scare, honey. Sorry I wasn't here when you woke up. I've been by your side the entire time, but there was a situation today I needed to take care of."

I blinked and chewed on my lower lip as I struggled to pull my fuzzy thoughts together. I frowned when he mentioned thinking I might be on drugs. I was a good girl, even when I was living in the worst place. I never gave in to the lure of oblivion drugs offered. The lack of control they brought with them scared me to death, especially in a place like the Point. Even though I didn't have the widest knowledge of narcotics, there was no denying the odd rewind of my entire young adult life felt like a wild hallucination brought on by something cooked up in an illegal garage lab somewhere. I couldn't tell if I was more relieved or freaked out that there was nothing concerning in my system to explain what was happening to me.

"Can you get me a glass of water?" My voice sounded like my throat was covered with sandpaper. It hurt a bit to get the words out, but I sounded much calmer and far more rational than I had at the wedding. After taking a sip of lukewarm water, I made a face and asked, "Did the situation you had to handle have anything to do with the Martins?"

My father sighed again and nodded. "Madison is having a hard time adjusting to the sudden shift in our relationship. She's understandably upset that the wedding was canceled at the last minute. But her behavior about everything else is unreasonable and over the top. I don't like the way she's handled herself, and I won't tolerate her attitude toward you. I feel like I don't even know the woman I almost married. I've been imagining what might've happened if you hadn't stopped the wedding when you did. If you knew Addison and her mom had such a questionable history, why did you wait so long to tell me? Did you think I wouldn't believe you?"

He sounded devastated at the thought. We'd always been super close. I rarely kept anything from him. I trusted him with all the dirty details that came and went with being a teenager. My tirade at the wedding must've come as quite a shock to him.

I curled my fingers around his and gave his wide hand a reassuring squeeze. Even if this was all a dream or some kind of mental breakdown from being severely injured in a massive explosion, I was still grateful that my father found out the truth before he married that woman. He could protect himself and his work now, even if I wasn't part of the picture when the world—at least mine—went back to normal.

"I didn't find out how awful they were until right before the wedding. I would've tried to find a way to tell you, but things were just so hectic. Addison kept me so busy with bridesmaid stuff..." I trailed off and shrugged helplessly. It was true. Back in this timeline, my former best friend *had* kept me so busy I could barely think before the wedding. Originally, it was to keep me from bitching about my birthday being ruined, but now I knew it was more to keep me distracted as the date drew closer so I wouldn't suspect anything was amiss. They needed that wedding to happen no matter what. "I should've found a better way to discuss things with you. I didn't handle it well because I've been under a lot of stress lately."

Also, not a lie. Every single day trying to stay alive and keep some sense of propriety and principle when you lived in a place like the Point was ridiculously stressful.

"I could tell you haven't been acting like yourself lately. I thought it was nothing more than college admissions and worrying about finals. You've always been so unproblematic. I should've been more careful with what I was doing when I realized something was off with you. I won't be so reckless again. That being said," he blew out a breath and gave a lopsided grin. "You caused quite a stir. They aren't going to let the situation go lightly. It seems we're both going to have an enemy moving forward."

I coughed and shifted uncomfortably in the bed. My body was stiff, and my toes were starting to tingle. I needed to use the bathroom. And I was dying to look into a mirror. The last time I saw my face, it was gaunt and hollowed out. It was far from ugly, but it wasn't exactly pretty either. Which was an accurate depiction of my life in the Point. When I was older, I often recalled my teenage face and form and longed for the days when self-confidence was effortless. Once I entered my twenties, the thing I needed most to survive was self-awareness.

I was looking forward to being someone who finally had both of those things in abundance.

"Did you end things with Madison?" I asked the question cautiously. Was he safe from the mother and daughter's machinations from here on out? Had this inexplicable time slip served its primary purpose? I knew the first rule of time travel was to never change the past because it would impact the future, but my future was fucked. So, I had no intention of following any stupid rule that would keep me from keeping my father safe.

My father nodded and lifted a hand to rub his neatly trimmed goatee. "I was willing to sit down and talk things out with Madison if she agreed to explain why she never told me about her previous relationships, and if she agreed to sign off on some of the legal protections you mentioned when you interrupted the ceremony. I told her I needed to make sure you felt a sense of security if we were going to make things work. I'm not sure why you think she might kill me, but I could tell you were very worried about me. I knew you weren't simply acting out and being spiteful. Madison wasn't willing to compromise. I witnessed a whole new side to her and her daughter. Addison trashed our living room when I informed them they were no longer welcome in our home. I gave them until the end of the week to move out and find other accommodations."

I snorted, which turned into a fit of coughing. I waved a hand and told my dad to call a nurse or someone to help me out of bed before I had an accident. I still needed to use the restroom, which was probably the most normal thing that had happened to me since the explosion.

While we were waiting, I muttered, "You're probably headed home to a pilfered house. They want your money. They're going to take everything that has any value."

He snorted. "They can help themselves to whatever. The most valuable thing to me is right here in this room. And everything I hold dear from your mother, everything I kept for you to pass down to you as you get older, is in a safe-deposit box at my bank. If they clean me out while I'm at the hospital waiting for my daughter to wake up, then that's a small price to pay to get them out of our hair."

I silently agreed and almost shouted with relief when the nurse finally showed up and went through the routine of taking me to the bathroom. She looked frazzled and apologized profusely for not being in the room when I woke up. She assured my dad several times she would page a doctor to the room as quickly as possible as she rushed through taking all my vitals. She was pleasantly surprised everything registered back in the normal range. If I hadn't been unconscious for an extended period of time, no one would be able to tell there was anything wrong with me.

After she situated me in the bathroom, she told me she had to either wait in the room with me to make sure I didn't fall because of my previously unsteady blood pressure or wait near the door if I felt like I could sit and stand on my own. It was already a touch embarrassing to do one's business in front of a total stranger, but there was no way I wanted to explain why I was examining my face like I'd never seen it before.

While I was leaning on the sink and looking into the reflection of my eyes, I overheard the nurse tell my dad, "We had a difficult situation. It started almost the exact same time as your daughter. We're short-staffed at the moment, so it was a struggle to get it under control." I heard her making a *tsking* sound as she continued to lament. "Every single time we get a case that comes in from the other side of town, it seems to be problematic." She chuckled slightly. "You should've heard the crazy story we just listened to. Something about an explosion in the future and time going backward. It sounded like something from a fantasy novel." I could hear the excitement in her voice when she told my father, "Hey, you could write something like that, and I bet it would be a bestseller."

Those eyes that appeared so much older than eighteen blinked in shock, and the face that was the same but so different paled further.

My dad made polite small talk while I jerked myself back to reality in the bathroom. I threw open the door, startling both of them, and looked at the nurse with wide eyes.

She started to admonish me for not calling her when I was ready to get up and move from the bathroom, but I cut her off before she could start.

"The patient talking about the explosion, how old are they? What do they look like? Can you tell me what room they're in?" The questions were rapid-fire; each one sounded raspier than the first.

The nurse made a face and reached out to help me back to the bed, pulling my IV pole along next to her.

"I can't tell you any of that. I shouldn't have said anything. I was just flustered because I was late to your room check, and I was nervous trying to make conversation with Mr. Bell. I'm a huge fan of your dad's work."

I gritted my teeth and crawled back into the hospital bed with my dad's help. I flopped onto my back and asked, "When can I go home?"

I wasn't sure if *home* meant back with my dad, or back to the Point, but either was preferable to being in the hospital, trying to figure out if I'd lost my mind. The longer I was in here, the more likely it was that someone would figure out I wasn't quite right in the head.

The nurse looked up from her tablet and lifted an eyebrow. "That's up to the attending physician. However, now that you're awake, you're doing great. We might even be able to get you something small to eat." She gave me a cheerful grin while she reached out to pat my leg. "Everything will be fine. Use your call button if you need anything else." She cast a look at my dad on her way out of my room, muttering under her breath, "If it wouldn't cost me my job, I'd run home on my break and grab all my books for you to sign."

Being the congenial kind of guy that he was, my dad offered to send her a signed book if she left her address. The nurse looked like she had died and gone to heaven. Once she opened the door to the hallway, it was easy to hear a commotion happening outside. Voices were raised, and I could hear someone scream,

"Give that crazy son of a bitch a sedative!"

If my legs didn't feel like Jell-O and I was more convinced of my sanity, I would've rushed to the door to see if I could catch a glimpse of the problem patient. There were too many similarities between their outlandish tale and my own epic redo. I was torn between hope that the patient was the quiet car guy from my old life and dread that it was him. On the one hand, it would be nice to know I wasn't the only one going through such an unlikely situation. On the other, that guy had a direct hand in landing me here. If he hadn't carelessly tossed the cigarette, who knows where I would be right now?

"This is one of the best hospitals in the country. I bet they didn't plan on it being so dramatic over the last few days." My dad's voice was laced with humor. I tried to smile at him, but it was hard to get my face to follow my commands. I was one hundred percent preoccupied with the mystery patient. "Madison was very loud when she showed up." He reached out a hand and ruffled the top of my head. It was a familiar gesture full of fondness and affection. It made my eyes tear up and my throat scratchy. "You're such a good girl, Vesper. I hope you always remember that."

I did.

I remembered it when I was accused of pushing him down the stairs and ending his life.

I remembered it when I was arrested and every moment I sat in jail awaiting my trial.

I remembered it when I sat in front of a courtroom and was belittled and harassed by a community that obviously didn't believe a word I was said when I declared my innocence.

I remembered it when I was finally acquitted but still viewed as guilty by everyone in my old life.

I remembered it as I sank deeper and deeper into despair.

I remembered it when I took my first job cleaning toilets so I could afford to eat and have a place to sleep that was somewhat hospitable.

I remembered it when I finally accepted who I was and my place in the world once I hit rock bottom.

I tried to be good my entire life, and it got me nowhere and did me no favors other than keeping me the apple of my daddy's eye.

This time around, for however long I had, I was going to do my best to focus on embracing the bad things and spend less time trying so hard to be good. Maybe being bad was going to be better for me, because it was painfully obvious that being good got me absolutely nowhere.

THREE

WHO ARE YOU?

After the attending physician thoroughly checked me out, they decided I should stay one more night for further observation. I got a distinct feeling they made the call more to cater to my father's notoriety and wealth than my actual health. No one wanted to end up on his bad side, so they were keeping an eye on me out of an abundance of caution, even though I felt much better. I was going stir crazy now that I was awake and alert and had nothing to do but lay in a hospital bed. Once my head stopped hurting, I decided to embrace the absurdity of my situation for however long I had to relive my life.

Not only did I plan to protect my father and return every awful thing they'd done to him tenfold, but I also had an unquenchable thirst for revenge on a personal level. Before the mother and daughter duo successfully orchestrated the highly suspicious death of my dad, Addison bulldozed through my entire life. She upended my reputation. She killed any shot I had of going to college. She destroyed my faith in the people I thought were my closest friends. She put a bright light on just how foolish my teenage heart was. And she had convinced me to empty my personal savings that were given to me after my mother left, making sure I had zero means to support myself once the rug was pulled out from under me.

All of those events fell on me like tumbling dominoes as soon as our parents said, 'I do.' So, if the current timeline stayed the way it was, there was plenty of time for me to ensure my former best friend never got the chance to manipulate my downfall.

I nagged my dad for an hour until he agreed to go home. He needed a real meal and some sleep. I assured him I would be fine on my own since I was in a private room. He stayed until I was served a bland, mushy, hospital-approved dinner and made me promise to text him if I started to feel off. I promised profusely, and as soon as I was alone, I spent several hours scrolling through the cell phone my teenage self had permanently attached to her hand. From what I could gather, the world seemed identical to what it was like when I was originally eighteen.

All my old social media profiles were the same. My family's history and the way I'd lost my mom when I was only five were still the same, as was the way her side of the family had little to do with me and my father because they never approved of how he made his living. Writing romance novels wasn't art, according to them. It wasn't a skill or a talent. Their rejection of my father and the marriage was ridiculous. My dad made more money than any of the offspring born into that family, including my mom when she was still part of our lives. They might have been one of the founding families of the Hill's portion of our city, but it was guys like my dad who kept the exclusive suburb relevant. No one was moving here because of the old money and private clubs. They moved here and frequented as tourists because my dad often used the town and the occupants in subtle ways in his stories.

All the kids I had considered my friends until they turned their backs on me after my father died were also the same, according to my social media. There was nothing on the internet concerning the events that occurred after my dad's wedding, and there wasn't a peep about an explosion in the neighboring bad part of town. With drugs ruled out and no apparent wormhole sucking me through space and time, I had no logical way to explain how I ended up going all *Groundhog Day*. I decided I wasn't going to waste any more time worrying about the *how* of it. Instead, I would put my energy into the *why* of it all. There had to be a reason bigger than my grievances for why I was getting a second chance on such an epic level. I needed to talk to the other patient in this hospital. I needed to understand why they talked about an explosion and time travel that sounded eerily similar to my own story.

If it was the car guy from the motel parking lot, it meant both of us had come back at the same time. Maybe my starting point of the wedding was just a coincidence, and the real reason everything was topsy-turvy was because of him. It was entirely possible that this was his reboot, and I just got caught in the cosmic whirlwind.

If we were both blown back at least seven years in time, did that mean the mother next door was also in this timeline? And what about Tobi and Jordan? Were they here as younger versions of themselves? I knew the kids had lived with their father at some point. The way Tobi had explained it in her young, fanciful style led me to think the kids also started out somewhere nicer than the Point. There were a lot of unanswered questions, but I felt I could find answers to these, which was a good diversion from focusing on how this happened.

I couldn't sleep once my mind started whirling. Plus, I'd been out like a light for plenty of hours after I passed out at the wedding. It felt like a giant waste of this opportunity to sleep any more than was absolutely necessary. I had too much to do and too many bridges to burn the fuck down.

Once the activity on the floor quieted down, and the nurses started spacing out their trips to my room from every hour to every couple of hours, I decided to see if I could covertly find the room of the mysterious patient. If they were sedated, it was a failed mission before it even started. But I knew I couldn't let the opportunity pass. If it was the car guy, I had no other way to find him in this timeline. I didn't know his name. I didn't know how old he was. I had no clue if he was in the Point by choice or if he ended up there while trying to disappear. I didn't think he'd still be at the motel. Earlier, the nurse seemed pretty certain the patient didn't belong on this side of town, but I didn't know what she was using to make that judgment call. It made me even more anxious to see if she was talking about the car guy.

In my original life, the car guy gave off an aura that let anyone know he wasn't someone to take lightly. However, I was keenly aware my aura also changed when I started living in a place that challenged my humanity every hour of every day. It was impossible to tell if he'd always been a badass or if the Point turned him into one. Regardless, it would be far easier to talk to him *if* he happened to be the problematic patient than it would be once I was discharged from the hospital and attempted to track him down. Nothing was easy in the Point.

I was no longer on an IV line, and I kept taking off the little fingertip monitor so I could use my phone. The nurses stopped checking on me after the fifth or sixth time the warning beeped. I promised the night shift nurse that I would put it on before I went to bed, which appeased her. I may have also thrown my father's name around when she seemed reluctant. After all, this was the biggest hospital in the Hill, and here, money and influence mattered the most.

I opened the door and was greeted with a quiet, darkened hallway. I could hear voices coming from somewhere, and something that sounded like a television, but no one was visible. There were doors along the corridor. Some were shut, others were cracked open. There were so many I couldn't decide how to start my search. It didn't occur to me until after I tiptoed to the first door that if the patient was someone other than the car guy, I would have no idea who they were. I didn't even know if the mystery patient was male or female. I wanted to smack myself in the forehead over my impulsiveness, but I was afraid of the sound it would make. I figured I already had access to the address of the original nurse who mentioned the unruly patient, since she'd given it to my father. I could track her down outside of the hospital and harass her for information if I had to.

Deciding I would just look for the colorful boy and cut my losses if the patient turned out to be someone else, I peeked into the window of the room next to mine and quickly noticed it was empty. So were the next two. The two closest across the hall both had older patients in them who appeared to be asleep. The next room had the door cracked open a sliver, and inside was a girl around my age. She seemed to be watching something on her phone, which was probably where the TV sounds were coming from. She must've sensed someone at her door because she called out a questioning, "Hello?" before turning back to her screen.

I got more frustrated as my search went on. Not only were there no faces I recognized, few were the right gender or age. There were only a handful of rooms left on this floor, but suddenly I heard the sound of a cart being rolled at the other end of the hall. A woman's voice carried through the empty space as she spoke into a cell phone. I knew that she would come around the corner any minute, and I was going to get busted for acting like a creepy stalker.

I couldn't make it back to my room by the time she reached the hallway. I was going to brazenly lie through an excuse for my weird behavior when I suddenly caught sight of a public bathroom at the very end of the hallway. The lights were dimmed like the rest of the hospital at this time of night, so the entrance was hard to notice at first. I breathed a sigh of relief and made my way to the convenient hiding spot when the door to the very last room on the corridor opened, and a strong, heavily tattooed arm shot out.

I would've yelped and given myself away if a rough hand hadn't smacked across my mouth as I was roughly yanked into the room. I nearly fell on top of my abductor. I pulled at the fingers clamped over my mouth and whipped my head around to glare at the person who had put a halt to my escape plan.

I locked eyes with the guy from the parking lot of the motel.

In my gut, I knew the patient had to be him. It couldn't be anyone else.

We stared at each other, both of us breathing hard as we took one another in.

He looked the same as he did on the night everything went BOOM. Only, his hair wasn't that faded violet. Now it was more of a rosy pink that looked far too soft and sweet for a guy who looked like he could break any number of laws, and bones, at any given moment. He was too tall, fit, and rough-looking to pull off cotton candy-colored hair. His face was all kinds of sharp angles and harsh definition. He wasn't a pretty boy, or even what one would consider a handsome young man.

He was something that was all his own.

Compelling. Interesting. Memorable.

Those were the words that I would use to describe him now that I had the opportunity to get up close and personal with him in this way. Despite his hard edges, I desperately wanted to get closer to him.

"It's you." His voice was deep and growly. My guess was he had been a smoker even back in this lifetime. "What are you doing here?"

He let go of me, and we both glanced away from one another since we were clad in very unflattering hospital gowns. His barely reached his mid-thigh and looked like it had been tied hastily when he jumped out of bed. Even in the high-end hospital, the attire was still far from fashionable.

I cleared my throat nervously and made sure I kept my thin garment closed with a hand. "Why am I here in this hospital? Or why am I here, in the past?"

The guy had very dark eyes. So deep and rich that the brown looked almost black. The only things that kept them from being vast pools of inky darkness were the faint flecks of gold scattered throughout.

"Both. Why are you here in both those places?" He practically growled the question as he continued to glare at me.

I lifted a shoulder and let it fall with a carelessness I wasn't feeling. "I'm in the hospital because I fainted after I stopped my dad from marrying the Wicked Witch of the Hill. I was unconscious until a couple of hours ago. As for the other," I gave him a pointed look. "I was hoping you could tell me. After all, you're the one who caused the explosion." I wanted to make sure he remembered he was the catalyst for all this insanity.

The guy frowned at me, lifting a hand to push through his pink hair.

"The explosion. That's the last thing I remember. I thought I would be in hell or the burn ward when I opened my eyes. Instead, I was back at my older brother's funeral. I had to bury him all over again. At first, I thought I was being forced to relieve my worst day repeatedly, and *that's* what hell is. But I passed out, and when I woke up, I was here. How can it be the past? What kind of fucked-up shit is happening to us?" He shook his head and finally met my gaze. "This hospital is too nice. They freaked out when I started asking questions and raised my voice. They wanted to sedate me and threatened to strap me to the bed. They only backed off when I quieted down and promised to behave. I think one of the nurses has a crush on me. He got them to back off on the sedative."

I nodded. "Yeah. I heard a couple of nurses talking about an out-of-control patient. They mentioned they were ranting about an explosion and talking crazy about time travel. Once I could think straight, my guess was they were talking about you. What's your name, by the way? We never introduced ourselves back when we originally knew each other." I saw him every single day, but he was still a stranger. One I felt I knew surprisingly well.

He still seemed to be struggling to put things together in his mind. Absently, he muttered, "I'm Oscar. Oscar Osborn."

I ducked out of the line of sight as I heard that cart rattle outside his door in the hallway. I was looking toward the bathroom in case I needed a quick place to hide.

"I'm Vesper. Vesper Bell." We both had old-fashioned names, which seemed like such an odd connection. I didn't want to read too much into anything, so I told him, "The night of the explosion was my birthday. I just turned twenty-five. My dad's wedding was on my eighteenth birthday. This is my eighteen-year-old self." I waved a hand over my hospital gown-clad body.

When Oscar responded, his dark eyes were unreadable, and his expression remained harsh. "The night the motel exploded was my birthday too. I was about to turn twenty-eight. My brother's funeral was on my twenty-first birthday. Do you think our birthdays had something to do with this time slip?"

I sighed and shrugged, recognizing there were connections I couldn't dismiss. "Sharing a birthday is as good a reason as any for both of us to have survived the explosion and end up back at a pivotal point in our lives. I'm honestly open to suggestions that might explain whatever the hell is going on. I'm just glad I'm not the only one who remembers where I was before I ended up back here. I thought I was hallucinating or dreaming. We can't be having the same dream at the same time, can we?"

It was Oscar's turn to shrug. I watched his broad shoulders move and realized how intimidating he was even with that pink hair, dressed in a cartoon-covered hospital gown. "I don't dream. You lived in the Point long enough to know what a big waste of time that is. I don't think we're asleep. We had to die. The explosion was massive. I bet it leveled the entire motel." He swore and then shook his head. "Good riddance."

Before I could stop myself, my hand shot out and thumped him heavily on one solid shoulder. "Stop smoking. Do it now, so if we end up reliving our lives and we reach that moment again, you won't accidentally kill us all."

He narrowed his dark eyes at me but eventually nodded. "You might have a point." He looked around the room and then down at himself. "I need to get out of here. It doesn't matter what phase of my life I'm in; I can't afford to be in this hospital."

"How did you end up on this side of town in the first place?" I asked the question, not knowing his answer would make my heart hurt for him.

"When I buried my brother, I did everything in my power to make sure he wasn't going to spend eternity in the Point. He gave enough of himself to that damn place. The cemetery where he's buried is close to the Hill. They must've brought me to the closest ER when I passed out. I try to avoid this side of town if I can help it. I prefer to know exactly who my enemies are versus having to guess."

I blinked and put a hand out to stop him when he looked like he was going to move toward a pile of clothes stacked on a chair. He wasn't wrong about how things worked in this neighborhood. I couldn't see the knife coming for my back until it was already buried to the hilt. Still, the Point was far more dangerous. I couldn't believe he was in such a hurry to get back to such an awful place.

"What's your plan? Are you just going to go back to your normal life? Are you going to pretend like you aren't relieving your younger days all over again? Shouldn't we figure out if anyone else from the motel is going through this? Don't you think there has to be some divine reason for this to happen to us?" I sounded a bit hysterical as I fired the questions at him.

Oscar looked at the place where my hand landed on his arm and slowly shook it off. "I don't have a plan. And the only reason I can think that I was brought back to this particular moment in my life is so that I can avenge my brother's death. I don't know why I wasn't brought back to stop him from dying, but I can make sure the person who put him in the ground pays the price this time around."

I was taken aback and couldn't stop the surprised words from tumbling out. "You couldn't make them pay before? You were pretty scary back then." He may have saved me more than once, but that didn't mean I was dumb enough to believe he was one of the good guys. Nothing about him screamed *righteous man*.

"Scary? I guess I would seem that way to someone like you." He practically growled his entire statement. "It's better to be the person who makes others afraid than it is to be the person who is afraid in the Point."

I couldn't argue with anything he was saying. Things in the Point operated differently than the rest of the world, and only the strong survived. If he was going after someone he couldn't get to in his previous life, I wanted nothing to do with it. There was no way two predators could clash without bloodshed, and I had no intention of being a casualty in his war. However, this pink-haired hoodlum was the only other person on the planet who sort of knew me before I went back in time. He could relate to what I was going through. I had no plans to end up back in the Point, but I wasn't willing to let him disappear completely.

"I'm so sorry you lost your brother, and that whatever is going on didn't bring you back in time to save him." I really was. But ultimately, I needed him, so my sympathy could only go so far. "I'm not going to try and stop you from doing whatever it is you have to do. I have things that I need to straighten out as well. Right now, you're the only one who knows I'm not an eighteen-year-old girl getting ready to go to college. I can be my normal self around you. I can be the girl who lived in that motel when I am with you. She's very different from the *me* I am right now. I think I might like her better. You can also be your grown, grumpy self with me. I need that. I think we'll both need each other for that as time goes by. You can walk away from the Hill, Oscar. But you can't walk away from me. I won't let you."

He turned his back to me and dropped his hospital gown. I gasped and lifted a hand to cover my eyes as he stood there in nothing but a pair of black boxer briefs. Before I blocked out the view, I noticed he had a large tattoo of a crow that spanned his back between his shoulder blades. He also had a strong back and long, muscular legs. He didn't need a pretty face to be super-hot and ridiculously compelling. He was way better than any of the teenage heartthrobs my current self was so determined to chase. He was also head and shoulders above the boy my teenage self adored enough to give all my major firsts. That douchebag was sleeping with Addison behind my back the whole time and couldn't turn on me fast enough when my shine started to dull. Thank goodness this time I could avoid giving that loser anything that mattered.

"I'm not going to walk away from anyone. I'm just going home." He was blunt and didn't say much, just like I remembered. "I don't remember the older you being this pushy or needy."

"She wasn't. Sadly, she had every single emotion drained out of her by the time you met her. I forgot how to feel anything." I frowned as I turned his words over in my mind. "By going home, do you mean back to the motel in the Point? You lived there even before I knew you?" I couldn't fathom how anyone would willingly consider that crumbling building home.

"I've always lived there. My family owns the motel. My dad ran it until he vanished, then my brother took over. I took over from him after he passed. If you need me, you know where to find me." He said it so nonchalantly. Like it was every day that he lost a loved one and inherited a dilapidated building that would eventually kill us both. I liked him better and felt more comfortable around him when we didn't speak to each other. He was far more intense than I anticipated.

As we looked at each other for a long moment without saying a word, it felt like an uneasy understanding started to fill the space between us.

We would need each other in the future—I mean, the past, our present—which meant we would have to trust one another. However, it was clear that trust didn't come easy to either of us.

Not now and not then.

FOUR

A VIEW FROM THE TOP

Oscar made it clear he wasn't hanging around to wait for a regular discharge. It took some serious pleading, and even the threat of calling the nurse who was still wandering the halls, to get him to agree to exchange phone numbers with me. The model of cell phone he fished out from one of his pockets was old and had a cracked screen. When he flicked it on, it displayed a fractured photo of two young men. The similarity in their looks made it easy to guess they were brothers. Oscar looked a bit shell-shocked when his gaze landed on the image. It had to be impossibly hard to go through the emotions of losing a loved one, not once but twice. I realized I was super lucky that I had the opportunity to stop my father's demise in this current timeline. After Oscar was dressed in the ill-fitting suit he must've been wearing at the funeral, he slipped out of the room into the dark hallway and crept along quietly until he reached the emergency stairwell. I watched him go with curious eyes. I made a mental note to ask my dad to pick up the tab for Oscar's short hospital stay, but the longer I thought about it, I realized he probably hadn't left any trace of his real identity behind. If he was born and raised in the Point, making sure you weren't easy to find was one of the first survival instincts one had to learn.

Once the coast was clear, I tiptoed back to my room and slipped into the hospital bed. I put the finger monitor thing back on and waited for someone to poke their head in to check on me. I didn't think I would fall asleep considering how busy my mind was, but the next thing I knew, the night shift was switching to the day shift. The nurse informed me I would be going home as soon as someone processed my paperwork. Since I was eighteen, there was no need to wait for my father to look over the discharge papers. But the nurse was the same one who declared herself a fan, so she prolonged the process until my dad showed up to take me home. I bit my tongue to stop from asking her if anyone even noticed the patient down the hall was missing, or if the entire hospital staff had written off Oscar's disappearance as a good thing since he wasn't from this part of town.

It was pretty surreal once I was out of the hospital and in the car with my dad on the way to a place that stopped feeling like home long ago. Once Addison convinced me to introduce my dad to her mom, it felt like there was no time for him and me to be alone. The two inter-lopers wormed their way into every single facet of our lives without me being aware of it at the time. Now, it was apparent they wanted our father-daughter relationship to appear strained and hostile. It helped the narrative they built after the death of my father that I was a jealous, angry young woman who felt like she was replaced by her new stepmother in her father's heart. When they raised the suspicion that the fall that killed my father wasn't an accident, and none too subtly pointed the finger in my direction, people had no problem believing I pushed him in a fit of anger after an argument. In the public's opinion, I was a demon daughter who couldn't handle hearing the word 'no' or stand seeing my father happy with a wom-an who wasn't my mother. They also bought into Addison's big fat crocodile tears when she claimed I treated her horribly and had bul-lied her out of extreme jealousy once our families merged. I was the perfect tabloid fodder—the heiress in distress. I learned very quickly that everyone loves a fall-from-grace story, and it was even better when the object of said story was a pretty young girl who lived a life

THE BEST BAD THINGS

of privilege. The more I lost in the fall, the more people reveled on my way down.

"How was the house when you got home? Did Madison clean you out?" I asked the question to fill the silence.

My dad looked distracted as he wound through the roads of the wealthy and exclusive subdivision. Most homes here were on gated lots and had security personnel. Some backed up to the golf course; others overlooked the water. The waterfront wasn't exactly beautiful and pristine. You had to drive through the rough part of the city and wind your way through shipping docks and rundown warehouses to reach the shore. The houses surrounding me now cost a fortune and felt like they were a galaxy away from where I was used to living. It all seemed so excessive and wasteful now that I understood the difference between necessity and indulgence.

"No. They both packed up their basic belongings and left. I told both of them they were welcome to anything they bought for the house and were welcome to keep anything I gifted to them. Surprisingly, they left rather quietly." He sounded relieved, but I was suspicious. Nothing about the Martins was quiet. "How do you feel about heading back to school after everything that went down? I know you have finals on the horizon, but you're bound to be at the center of gossip after what happened at the wedding. You're going to bump into Addison even if you try to avoid her. That could be very awkward for both of you."

If he was asking the normal eighteen-year-old Vesper, she absolutely would've begged and pleaded to stay home to avoid facing Addison's wrath and the curious looks from her classmates. She would've avoided confrontation at all costs. When I was a teenager, I wanted everyone to like me and to be included in everything. Now that I was a world-weary young woman who knew exactly how it felt to have everyone turn their back on you when you needed them the most, I didn't give a single shit what would be waiting for me at high school this time around.

I wanted to go back to school for various reasons. All of them centered around making sure Addison got her just desserts. Every opportunity she ruined for me, every road she blocked, I was going to open back up. I had no interest in playing the hero in this lifetime. I planned to take a page out of Oscar's book and embrace being a bad guy. All I knew was I refused to be a victim now or ever again.

"I don't mind going to school. I'm not scared of Addison or what anyone else might think of the situation. If they want to focus on the fact I stopped the wedding rather than Addison and her mom's questionable past, that's up to them. Graduation is right around the corner anyway. Who cares about the dumb things that happen in high school? They're all so pointless in the grand scheme of things."

My dad looked at me out of the corner of his eye as we got closer to our house. We lived in one of the houses higher up on the hill, so we could see all the way to the water and through the slums that stretched out before it. The reality was that a person was always close to having it all or losing everything—literally one wrong step away—depending on the direction you moved.

"Are you sure you're my daughter? When has Vesper Bell ever been so mature and level-headed?" The hint of surprise in his voice made me smile.

I shrugged and looked down at the phone I held in my lap. I doubted I would hear from Oscar first. I would have to reach out to him when I could better grasp what was going on with us. For now, just knowing there was someone else out there who knew the girl I'd grown up to be made me feel centered and self-assured.

"Being on the verge of something terrible happening was very eye-opening. When I imagine what might've happened if you had married Addison's mom, it makes me realize what's important. I feel like I grew up a little bit over the last few days." I'd grown by leaps and bounds after he was gone, but he would never understand if I tried to explain the reality behind my sudden personality improvement.

"A little growth is always beneficial. But don't get to the point where you don't need your old man anymore. I'm not quite ready to let you go just yet." He reached out and patted my knee fondly as we finally reached the house.

I smiled as I put my hand over his. "I'm not going anywhere."

Originally, I'd planned on attending a college in a different state. In hindsight, I understood that I was just blindly following Addison when she said we should move across the country after graduation. She had a whole spiel about spreading our wings and finding our most authentic selves if we left the security of the Hill behind. I bought it hook, line, and sinker. I even paid for everything; the moving expenses, the swanky apartment in the most expensive part of the city, even a whole new college-in-the-big-city-appropri-ate wardrobe. Pretty much every penny I had left over from the trust my mother left me was gone before we even stepped foot across state lines. I was so foolish and eager to bankroll someone else's happi-ness. Looking back, I wanted to shake some sense into my teenage self and sit her down and explain how the world worked. I couldn't believe I'd ever been so naïve.

"Dad, I have a feeling my original college application got messed up. I wasn't very careful when I filled them out, and I didn't take the essay portion seriously." The truth was I trusted Addison when she told me she wanted to work on the applications together because she was stuck on what to write for the essay. Like an idiot, I filled out all my information and attached my essay but left everything for her to send after she looked mine over for inspiration. She never clicked send on my portion after straight-up plagiarizing the essay I wrote. Not only did I not get into a single school in my past life, when I tried to reapply with my original essay, I got busted for trying to copy what Addison had already submitted. I was pretty much barred from ev-ery elite school, and my private high school even refused to give me the honor of being valedictorian because I was accused of plagiarism and cheating. Every good grade I earned while attending was called into question. In this timeline, teenage me had yet to figure out that

Addison hadn't sent my applications, so I had a chance to undo the damage. There was also an opportunity to make her pay for putting me through all of that when I thought she was my best friend.

"Maybe it was a blessing in disguise. I think I'll apply to schools closer to home, so you aren't alone in this huge house by yourself." I was thinking out loud, but the idea appealed to the new me much more than it had to the old me.

My dad chuckled as we walked into the house. "I want you to do whatever makes you happy, Vesper. I support your decision no matter what. Even if you decide college isn't for you. There are many ways to find what you're meant to do in life, and I don't think higher education is always the answer. You have all the time in the world to figure it out."

That's right. My dad was so successful, it was easy to forget that he only had a couple of semesters of college under his belt. His education, or lack thereof, was a huge sticking point with my mother's family when the two of them started dating. They were appalled he had attended public school and scorned the traditional path of most who were ridiculously wealthy. They never understood the passion behind every move he ever made. Every word he ever wrote.

I paused at the entryway of our house and looked out at the horizon where the sea met the dark, caustic air of the Point. It was such an ugly place sandwiched between two stunning vistas. I couldn't believe how often I'd simply overlooked it before. We all pretended to ignore the Point like it wasn't there. We acted like the people who lived there didn't exist and pretended it was miles and miles away, when in reality, it was at the base of the Hill. The two places were far closer in location and corruption than anyone gave them credit for.

"What about them?" I pointed a finger toward the hazy city-scape. "Do they have all the time in the world to make decisions about their lives, or are they just stuck accepting whatever happens to them? It doesn't seem very fair, does it?"

My dad followed where I was gesturing, and his face shifted to a look of surprise. "When did you become so socially conscious? I wasn't aware you even recognized there was a different type of life out there. One without much choice. One without much hope. It's good you recognize you have certain privileges. You're reminding me more and more of your mother when she was your age. I was always worried I gave you too much with too little expectation."

Was I really so bad, so out of touch, that he couldn't see her best qualities within me before? Man, I thought I was miserable and at my worst when I landed in the Point. Could it be possible that the real worst version of myself was the girl who had it all and was blind to the suffering of those who barely had enough to survive? It sure seemed like it. Maybe I had to suffer to build character. I had to lose everything to get the sense of what I should hold onto with all my might.

"I'm glad you can see parts of her in me. That means we won't ever forget about the good times with her." I said the words softly because I was lost in memories of how short-sighted I'd always been before now.

He leaned over and dropped a very fatherly kiss on the top of my head. I had to fight back the sudden rush of tears at the gesture. Those were the little things I missed when he was gone. Those were the moments I felt robbed of and that had kept me awake, seething with rage, when I finally found my feet in my new life. I hated myself for ever taking the easy affection for granted when I was a teenager. "Not a chance. I'm sure you're hungry. Let's go in and get something to eat. We can talk more about your choices for college and why you think you bombed the first round after you get settled."

I nodded in agreement as my stomach started to rumble. All I'd had to eat was that bland hospital food, and I felt like my anxiety and excitement after searching for and finding Oscar had burned all those calories last night.

My dad went in first, but I couldn't pull my eyes away from the sight of the city sitting below us. I lifted my phone and tapped out a quick text message.

~ I just wanted to see if this was really your number.

45

It still didn't make sense that Oscar was so eager to get back to the place that could eat anyone alive. It freaked me out when he told me there were people even scarier than him in the Point. It made me realize just how close to the edge of absolute ruin I had been living all along. I considered him the pinnacle of being a bad boy. Anyone willing to live at the motel their entire life by choice had to be hardened. Someone who had zero expectations. It never occurred to me he might be one of the not-so-bad guys, all things considered. Maybe he was even a good guy depending on the day.

~ It's my number. I already told you where to find me. Why would I lie about something like that? Don't tell me you're regressing into the mindset of a teenage girl just because you look like one now?

I scowled at the message. His words made me blush because he wasn't far off base. I was acting like an unsure teenager where he was concerned. I'd attached a lot of importance to him, both then and now, without him asking for it.

~ I have to go back for the last part of my senior year. So, I need to get into the mindset of a teenage girl. Otherwise, someone might figure out something is wrong with me.

There was no response for a moment, then my phone pinged when I was about to walk back into the house.

~ Reliving high school for a couple of months sucks, but it's better than working the late shift at that damn diner down here. Keep things in perspective so you don't end up back at this motel. It seems like you have a chance to change your fate. Don't blow it.

He made some very good points, but he seemed to have forgotten he also had this rare opportunity to change his destiny.

I decided to remind him we were in this mess together.

~ Get that motel updated. If you can't afford it, I'll talk to my dad and see if he can use a big donation for a tax write-off. Get the gas lines looked at. Work on the electrical system. Make it safe for the people who live there because they have no other choice.

And just in case he forgot how deadly his bad habit was...

~ I was serious last night. You should quit smoking.

Oscar didn't respond. I hoped he would consider my suggestion about the motel. Fixing it up wasn't the answer to the major class disparity between the Hill and the Point, but it was a tiny footpath I could walk between my two worlds.

I don't know how Oscar's brother was able to manage the motel when he was so young, because the picture I glimpsed showed two young men close in age. I couldn't figure out how Oscar kept it up and running after his brother was gone. Rent for the rooms was dirt cheap, and obviously, the accommodations were far from luxurious. He was more interested in his car than the maintenance of the hotel, but the roof didn't leak, and before the explosion, everything worked the way it was supposed to for the most part. He wasn't a great landlord, but he kept the creeps at bay, so I knew he could be much worse. I wondered if he cared more about the property and his legacy when his brother was still alive. It sounded like the older Osborne was invested in the motel in a way Oscar never had been.

My stomach growled again. I put a hand over it and walked inside. My battles were waiting. I couldn't worry about Oscar's war. Once my nemesis was no longer a threat, and she got a taste of her own medicine, I would put some serious effort into seeing what I could do to help him from my elevated position. I knew exactly where I came from, before and after the explosion. I might be at the top of the mountain right now, but I would never, ever forget just how painful the fall to the bottom had been.

FIVE

FALLOUT

If there was anything that was going to drive home the fact that I was truly reliving my past, it was putting on the school uniform I'd worn all four years of high school. On the outside, I looked like any other teenage girl wearing a blue and yellow plaid skirt, white button-up, and a tailored blazer. On the inside, I felt like I was wearing a costume for Halloween and couldn't help but cringe when I completed the outfit with knee-high socks and designer flats. I changed the shoes to a pair of low-heeled boots before walking out of my room. They were a far cry from my usual thrifted combat boots the older me preferred, but they made me feel less like an imposter than Chanel flats.

I grabbed a laptop that cost more than I would make in several months waitressing at the diner and headed to the kitchen to grab something for breakfast. My dad usually made sure he had time to start the day off with me, but after the disaster of the wedding and all the fallout, he told me I would have to fend for myself today. He had meetings with lawyers and his financial advisor. I guess almost marrying a possible black widow opened his eyes to just how vulnerable his legacy and my future might be. He swore he was locking that shit down as tight as possible, so no matter what happened to him in the future, and no matter who entered our lives, both his work and I would be protected. It was a step that was long overdue. I could tell he was mad at himself that he hadn't taken legal precautions before now.

We had a very nice lady named Carlotta who usually took care of the stuff he was too busy to get to around the house. She often cooked for me and looked after my basic needs when he was out of town or when he locked himself in his office when he was on a deadline. Today she left some toast and fresh fruit on the counter, which I assumed was for me. Back in my original youth, I rarely interacted with her or acknowledged how well she kept our household running. I didn't appreciate how much she did for me or how well she took care of me. I accepted her actions as something she had to do because it was her job. It never occurred to me she might genuinely care about me and my father. I never bothered to think of her as family, even when she made it obvious that's what she thought of me and my dad. When things went south, she was the one who kept me from going to prison for murder. Her testimony at the last minute offered reasonable doubt to the jury. She was the only one who knew I would never be capable of killing my father. She refused to believe all the bad things being said about me. She was the one who verified I wasn't even home when my father was pushed down the stairs. She wasn't just my only character witness, she was my rock-solid alibi. No question, she saved me. And I never got to thank her for it. She vanished as soon as the trial was over. I always thought Madison was somehow responsible for the woman's unexplained disappearance.

Just because I was good in the sense that I never got into trouble or created chaos, it didn't mean I was a good person at my core. Honestly, my eyes had been opened to just how crappy of a human being I used to be. There was so much room for improvement, and I was very fortunate I got the chance to take those steps forward this time around.

Now, my previous behavior turned my stomach. After eating the breakfast that she'd set out, I tracked down Carlotta where she was working on a hefty pile of laundry and thanked her. I got choked up trying to figure out a way to convey my gratitude for her selfless actions in the future without freaking her out. It was really hard to balance the *then* and the *now*.

She blinked at me like I'd suddenly grown a second head and nodded like she was in shock. She frowned at me and reached a hand up like she was going to touch my forehead to see if it was warm.

"Are you sure you're feeling well enough to go back to school so soon? You aren't acting like yourself, Vesper." Her slightly accented voice soothed my soul in a way I was not prepared for.

I caught her hand in mine and gave it a little squeeze. "I'm fine, Carlotta."

"Are you sure? In all the years I've worked for your family, I don't think you've ever once used my first name or said thank you. It's a little strange you sought me out today. Maybe you should stay home and wait for your father to get back. I'm worried about you."

I patted the strong fingers in my grasp and offered the kind woman a soft smile. "I should've said thank you for everything, every day. I should've appreciated all you do for us before now. Let's just say I had a wake-up call recently, and I hope you'll notice some changes for the better from here on out. Tell my dad I might be back a bit later than normal. I have a meeting with my academic advisor after class today."

The woman watched me go with a confused look on her face. I figured she would probably call my father to mention my odd behavior. It was a good thing. They could discuss all the changes, big and small, together. It would make it easier for both to adjust to the new and improved me.

I got behind the wheel of the expensive sports car I'd gotten for my sixteenth birthday. It took me a couple of minutes to remember how all the bells and whistles worked. The last time I drove this car was when I took myself to my father's funeral because Madison wouldn't allow me to be part of the funeral procession. After that, there was no need for one. Not when I was in and out of the legal system after the first time I was arrested on suspicion of murder, and it definitely wasn't needed in the Point. It was nearly impossible to afford a vehicle then, and even harder to hold onto one. I often wondered if Oscar kept his car in a state of disrepair in front of the motel all the time just to avoid having it get stolen.

I parked the sporty black car in the gated lot of the exclusive and expensive private school. I took a deep breath and braced myself to reenter the jungle that was high school. I was better prepared for it this time around. I knew how insignificant the superficial relationships forged here would be to the rest of my life. I realized my accomplishments as a teenager were only worth so much. And I was deeply aware there was so much to learn that would never be found in books or show up on a test, especially in a place with outrageous tuition that placed as much emphasis on status as it did on education. This school would never be able to teach real-life lessons. The outrageous tuition hadn't done jack to protect me or propel me forward in the past. All it did was paint a giant bull's eye on my back.

I was painfully aware all eyes were on me as I made my way into the school. The stares and whispers were obvious, but I didn't let the speculation faze me. I kept my head held high and my gaze straight ahead, pretending like everyone surrounding me was invisible. I used to try so hard to win the approval of these snobby, elitist people. It was sickening. I wanted to knock some sense into my previous self.

"Vee. Hey, Vee. Stop for a second. I want to talk to you." The loud, male voice made my steps falter. I didn't want to slow down or stop and talk. But I knew the owner of the deep, cultured tone wouldn't let me go.

Rex Wallace wasn't the kind of guy who allowed others to ignore him. He was tall. He had an extraordinary face. He was an all-star athlete. He was a top student. He came from old money. His family had been around the Hill almost as long as my mother's. His dad was a judge and his mother worked for the governor, but she had her own lofty political ambitions beyond that office. His ego was huge, and so was his sway with both the student body and administration.

He also made one hell of a compelling witness when I was on trial. I couldn't forget how he got on the stand and tearfully told the entire courtroom how I confessed to him that I wanted my dad gone. He did everything he could to back up Addison's claims about me being a bully and told the jury under oath that I was constantly fighting with my father after the wedding.

I remember how betrayed and heartbroken I'd felt watching the boy I convinced myself I could love turn on me. I had no idea he and Addison had cooked up his testimony against me long before I was on trial. Rex played me just as much as she did; only he got the added bonus of taking my innocence and toying with my heart on top of screwing me out of everything that was rightfully mine. Fortunately, I waited until graduation to sleep with him. The experience must've been bad enough that I couldn't recall the exact details of the intimate moments. It was all a blur, something I wanted to block out. This go around, I was going to avoid handing anything of value over to the golden idiot.

I stopped and turned to look at Rex as he pushed off a row of lockers and made his way toward me. His smile was blinding, and I swore his hair was spun gold. He looked like the perfect example of what a future Ivy-League graduate should be.

"Hey. I tried to call you all weekend and the days you missed school. I heard some crazy stuff went down at your old man's wedding, and you passed out. I wanted to visit you in the hospital, but your dad said you weren't up for visitors. I've been super worried about you."

He moved in for a hug. My hands flew up and landed on his strong chest, pushing his considerable bulk back. It was instinct. One I acquired—out of a sense of survival—in my future life. Never let anyone get close enough to touch you. If they did, you never knew if they were hiding a weapon or going to try and drag you somewhere away from prying eyes. Keeping a safe distance from those who might cause harm was second nature to me now.

Rex's bright blue eyes widened as he was forced back a step by my shove. For a brief second, he couldn't hide a flash of hot anger

THE BEST BAD THINGS

in his gaze. His smile dimmed, and a frown tugged at his perfectly sculpted eyebrows.

I moved out of grabbing distance and sniffed slightly. I schooled my features into a confused expression and looked at my former crush like I had no clue who he was.

"Do I know you? How do you know my name?" I wasn't sure how long he would buy that I might have amnesia, but for the moment, it was a good ploy to get him to back off. "I'm sorry. I don't remember much." I batted my eyelashes and started to walk backward, putting more distance between us. "The doctor told me the brain fog is probably temporary. He mentioned it's common to forget anyone who isn't very important to me."

Rex's expression shifted to one he wouldn't normally show in public. He was very good at keeping his perfect mask in place. Clearly, my words riled him up and touched a nerve.

"What do you mean someone not important to you? You're my goddamn girlfriend. How could you forget that? Of course I'm important to you. I'm the most important person in your whole world."

I wanted to snort. He never asked me to be his girlfriend. He dangled the promise of being in an exclusive relationship in front of me the entirety of my senior year. It was the tool he used to get me to go along with pretty much every single one of his whims. I couldn't believe I was ever that clingy and pathetic. What did I ever see in him? I liked the quiet guy who was always covered in grease so much more, who was there whenever I needed him.

"No. I'm sure I don't have a boyfriend. I would remember that. And if I did, my dad definitely would have encouraged him to come to see me when I was in the hospital." I turned around and called over my shoulder as I hurried away, "I have to get to class. I'll ask around, and if someone I trust confirms you're my boyfriend, I'll try and make it up to you."

Rex swore loudly behind me. I couldn't stop a smile from tugging at my lips. He knew no one would tell me he was my boyfriend because he made it a point to let our entire school know he was single and available, even if we spent a lot of time together. It was fun to finally pull one over on him. It was nice to finally see a guy like Rex for who he really was—and to realize that he wasn't the kind of person I wanted in my orbit.

I coasted through my first few classes without incident. My classmates tossed a ton of questioning looks my way, but I refused to acknowledge them. I managed to avoid a run-in with with Rex, which took some work. A few of the girls I considered my friends from before tried to talk to me. I claimed to be too busy making up schoolwork and brushed past them. They weren't there when I needed them, so now, I had no time to pretend for them. I ate lunch in the library while pulling together everything I needed for my meeting with the advisor after school.

I shared my last two classes with my former best friend. I was nervous about running into her after the wedding. I knew she couldn't do anything to me in the middle of a classroom, but it would be stupid to underestimate her. She was not the type to take having all her plans ripped to shreds lying down.

Fortunately, she was a no-show for both classes. I overheard one of our formerly shared friends mention Addison hadn't felt well since the wedding. I felt the accusatory glares pointed in my direction from across the room. I should've told them the real reason she was absent was that she was worried her sordid past was making its rounds through the campus. It was always big news when a student's wealth and status came into question. There were plenty of kids at our school who were only enrolled through family connections or favors. Normally, the daughter of a parent who kept marrying up wouldn't ping on anyone's radar. But if all those partners had met their ends under suspicious circumstances, that was the kind of drama and gossip that would explode and spread like wildfire. It would be better than anything streaming on Netflix. And if the scandal happened to knock the most popular girl in class down a peg or two, even better.

I knew my luck would eventually run out, and I would have to face Addison sooner or later. I wanted her to know I was no longer a pushover. I wanted her to see that I wasn't going down without a fight. I made my ruin entirely too easy for her in my previous life.

This time, if she wanted to destroy me, she needed to work for it.

After class, I dodged Rex again and avoided the few persistent girls gathered around my locker waiting to demand answers from me. I briefly toyed with the idea of pretending I didn't remember any of them, but that would lessen the sting to the boy who double-crossed me.

I practically snuck into the academic advisor's office. She appeared startled by my stealthy appearance. The woman was young to be working in a school like this. Her academic background had to be stellar. Either that, or she knew someone. Most of the teachers here were older than my father, and they were overwhelmingly male. There wasn't a lot of progression in these hallowed halls.

"Vesper. You startled me. I heard you fainted this weekend. Are you sure you're up to talking about your college admittance results?"

Was the old me so fragile that everyone thought I was going to wilt away after blacking out for a minute? I didn't recall feeling very breakable, but that must've been the impression I gave others. No wonder Oscar could tell I wasn't from the Point right from the start.

"I'm fine. I want to address this situation and get it straightened out as quickly as possible." I took a seat across from her and pulled my laptop out of my backpack.

She frowned at me and tapped a finger to her chin. "I already told you, there isn't anything the school can do about your applications not being sent. That is the student's responsibility. You can always reapply. I encourage you to do just that." She narrowed her eyes slightly and told me, "I would suggest revising your personal essay. There have been some complaints of plagiarism floating around as of late. Most first-choice schools are aware of the situation. I would hate to see you caught up in something like that."

I looked at her over the top of my computer. "Funny you should mention plagiarism. I want to file a complaint about that subject. I know for a fact Addison Martin copied my college application essay. She's the reason none of my applications got sent. As soon as I reapply to all those schools you mentioned, she's going to claim I copied her when the reverse is true. I let her use my application for a guide, thinking she would send it in when she was done. Instead, she copied my essay and never sent in my stuff."

The advisor sucked in a breath and leaned back in her leather chair. "That's a serious accusation, Vesper. You can't say something like that about a fellow student without proof. I know something happened between you and Addison and within your joint family over the weekend, but that's no reason to drag her name through the mud. We don't do revenge at this school. We're better than that."

I scoffed and rolled my eyes at the woman. "Of course we do revenge at this school. It should be an extracurricular activity we spend so much time on it. But this has nothing to do with what happened between our parents. I have proof she stole the essay. Look at this email." I turned the laptop around and showed her the email chain between me, my dad, and his editor. I sent the email over the summer before school started and asked for feedback on my rough draft of the essay. "Read through my essay and the changes my dad and his editor suggested. This was all before the semester started. Unless Addison can show you a file that predates this email for her essay, it proves I wrote the original."

The advisor sighed, but she reached out to take my computer so she could scroll through the emails. Her brows furrowed, and she bit her lip. Without saying a word to me, she pulled up something on her office computer and started reading through it. The longer she stared at the monitor, the deeper the frown on her forehead became.

In the original scenario, all of this came to light *after* I resubmitted all my applications. Addison and her mother had made themselves at home in my dad's big house by then. Addison had plenty of time to fiddle with my laptop and make the email chain with my dad disappear. I wasn't sure who deleted it on my father's end, but my guess would be Madison. No one was allowed in my father's office, but I caught her coming in and out of the sacred space more than once when we lived together. As for my dad's editor, Madison was the reason no one ever questioned the validity of the email. My new stepmother convinced my dad that we should handle the issue within the family, that it would be poor form to drag his professional acquaintances into the mess. She lamented that there was a good chance the editor would lie to cover for me, thus making it impossible for me to even realize I'd done something wrong. My dad was hesitant at first because I'd never done anything that warranted punishment or required me to learn a hard lesson, but he let himself be swayed by his new bride.

It was all so infuriating looking back. If I'd pushed harder, if I'd advocated for myself just a little more, Addison never would've gotten away with sinking my college plans. And I never would've let the argument over who was in the wrong be the start of the dissent between me and my father.

"There are obvious similarities between the two. I will have to dig a bit deeper. Addison came to see me a couple of weeks ago and said she was worried you might do something drastic since you didn't send your applications in on time. This evidence is compelling, but I have to tell you, we all know your father is very capable and has a lot of connections. I don't know how easy it would be to forge this kind of communication, but I'm sure your father has the means. And his editor isn't the greatest witness since your dad makes that publishing house a fortune. It would be no big deal to have his editor lie for him—and for you."

She looked up at me, and I could tell she was conflicted. She probably wanted to believe Addison because it would be a much bigger deal if Nelson Bell's daughter could prove that the school he paid hundreds of thousands of dollars to send her to had screwed up her academic future.

The corner of my mouth hitched up, and I pulled my laptop back toward myself. I scrolled through a few more emails and clicked on the one that was my smoking gun.

"Okay. If you don't think the emails between me and my father are good enough, how about the one I sent you over the summer asking you to take a look at my essay?"

I knew I sounded smug, but I couldn't help it. I flipped the screen around again and tapped on her name in the address bar. "You never responded. I can't blame you. After all, what administrator wants to work during the summer? In my defense, you did tell all incoming seniors you would be available twenty-four-seven to prep us for college admissions and graduation. I very easily could've asked my dad to talk to someone above you for not responding, but I didn't."

I wanted her to know that more than just the plagiarized essay was on the line here. If I wanted to, I could go after her job for her all-around incompetence. However, this woman wasn't my target. She was simply trying to get by in a hostile environment. I didn't blame her for ignoring the email. Old me had no respect for boundaries when they were inconvenient for her. But I was glad she was an overachiever because it would be the nail I needed to seal Addison into a coffin.

The advisor gulped and once again turned back to her computer. After several minutes of scrolling, she audibly gasped. The email was there on her side somewhere, long forgotten about.

"Oh my. I... I honestly don't know what to say about this, Vesper. I can't believe I missed it." Her voice shook, and she suddenly looked very pale. She knew she didn't respond purposely. When I originally spoke to her about the essay, she claimed to never have received anything. It was better for me to lose everything, and all credibility, than for her to admit her mistake.

I waved a hand dismissively between us and leaned closer to the edge of the desk. "I don't care that you didn't reply to the email. I care about Addison stealing it and then accusing me of copying her. I know there is no way to prove she didn't send in my applications, but

I can prove she stole my work and tried to pass it off as her own. I'm going to apply to different schools and maybe do a late admission at this point. I'm going to write an entirely new essay so there will be no doubt that the words are my own. But I will not let her get away with this, and if you help her, just know that I won't let you off either."

In the past, my dad was on his honeymoon when the whole plagiarism scandal broke loose. I was trained to do the right thing; I didn't want to bother him on his first real vacation in a very long time. I tried to navigate it on my own and ended up steamrolled by both the school and my former friend. I remembered feeling like no one was on my side. It foreshadowed all the terrible things to come. This woman was the one who had smirked at me when she told me I was no longer allowed to be the valedictorian and informed me I wasn't allowed to walk with my class at graduation. The school had a zero-tolerance policy for cheating, and the only reason they allowed me to receive my diploma was because my dad had threatened to storm the castle if they didn't.

The advisor stood up and started to pace behind her desk. "Of course, I'll launch an investigation. I'll ask Addison to provide proof of when she first wrote her essay. I'll have to get the headmaster involved and take your accusation to the disciplinary committee so they can decide a proper punishment for whomever is at fault."

I shrugged and picked up my computer so that I could throw it back in my bag. "That's fine. But if you're so quick to accuse me of giving you fraudulent evidence, you better make sure to vet whatever Addison provides as well. If I find out you and the rest of the administration take whatever she says at face value after knowing you were ready to believe the worst about me, you'll regret it. You said it yourself; my dad has a lot of money and connections. I won't use either to cheat, but I have no qualms about utilizing them for justice."

Another anxious gulp filled the silence. "Of course. I'll make sure the investigation is handled thoroughly. I'm so sorry this is happening to you. If you need any guidance going forward with the new applications, please let me know."

I snorted as I slung the strap of the bag over my shoulder before getting one last dig in. "I think I'm good, especially since I didn't get any help from you the first go-round."

That was another thing living in the Point taught me and the reason that I wasn't backing down on this. No one did anything without a hidden motive. If they offered to help, they wanted something in return, and you were shit out of luck if you had nothing to give.

SIX

FRENEMIES

I walked out of the school feeling empowered and triumphant. Speaking up for myself wasn't something I felt entirely comfortable doing in either lifetime. However, I now knew you had no control over the plot if you let someone else write your story. You didn't get the option to choose if you were the main character or cannon fodder destined for a miserable existence when someone else controlled the story line. This time, I was in charge of my narrative. I was no longer a bit player in a tragedy created by someone else. I didn't even mind being the bad guy, as long as events unfolded the way I wanted. I was looking forward to moving through the surreal fantasy, which had taken over my life the night of the explosion. And because I'd been surrounded by romance and romance novels my entire life, I would be remiss if I didn't at least look for a little bit of love between the other lines on the pages.

While I was thinking about romance, my mind wandered to Oscar. I was upset with myself for treating him like a threat instead of an ally when I lived at the motel. I was so focused on my misery and grief, so caught up in my anger at the world, it never occurred to me I might find a kindred spirit in sorrow in the slums. If I had befriended him before, maybe my days in the Point wouldn't have felt so long and burdensome. I kind of wanted to ask him why he always stepped in to save me when I got into trouble. I wondered if it was part of his character or if I was somehow special.

Plus, there was no denying he was hot. Not in the perfect, Prince Charming way that Rex was. In a more real, in-your-face way. His hotness was a bit threatening because it felt impossible to ignore. I still didn't understand the candy-colored hair, but it in no way took away from his rough appeal. When he stripped to get dressed in the hospital, I may have peeked through my fingers, and the sight of his strong, tattooed back was something I had no intention of forgetting anytime soon.

I wondered if he looked for other people who might have gotten caught in the time slip the same night we did. He would know best if any motel residents lived there in the past and present. It would be a huge clue if we could figure out if only the two of us, born the same day but worlds apart from one another, were affected, or if it was everyone in the blast radius.

My hungry curiosity meant I was going to make a trip back to the Point much sooner than I expected. While I was living there every day, if anyone had asked what I would do if I got my life on the Hill back, my reply would've been, "Never look back." I wanted to leave that place so far behind. I wanted it to be nothing more than a painful memory. I would put some space between myself and the inherent danger of being stuck in the rough part of the city. But having been given that opportunity now, I could see how much I'd gained and grown by being forced to make do with the bare minimum. I wasn't scared of the Point the way I used to be. I respected it a whole lot more and had to give credit to years of living hard for my newfound fortitude. I could do bad all by myself, but only because the Point taught me how.

Still thinking about Oscar and wondering how he would feel if I showed up at the motel with no warning, I completely missed that someone was standing next to my car until I was almost directly on top of them.

Like Rex, Addison wasn't someone easily ignored. She was a bit too much in every single way. She was too blonde. Too tall. Too curvy. Too pretty. Too smart. Too savvy. Too funny and coy. She was too well-dressed and poised. Everything about her was precise and pointed. She knew she was the best and wasn't shy about flaunting her superiority. Before she showed up at this school, I held my own in terms of popularity and confidence. I wasn't the center of the world outside my home, but I wasn't drifting off in the void of social outer space either. I had a few friends I considered close, but my uptight, Mary Sue personality tended to alienate me from most of the kids in my class. We all came from families that never met any rule that money and influence couldn't bend or break. It was only after Addison befriended me and started including me in everything she did that my classmates decided to look beyond my boring façade to see the shy girl underneath.

I stopped myself before I bumped into the stunning blonde. She was dressed down. Well, as down as someone like Addison Martin ever dressed. She had on tight black pants, shiny black heels, and a cropped Balenciaga sweater. She looked like a famous influencer or YouTuber. She looked expensive. She looked flawless as always. She looked annoyed, like she'd been waiting on me for a while.

I shifted my bag on my shoulder and lifted my eyebrows as we stared each other down. Old me would've backed down immediately. New me wanted to grab a fistful of perfectly shiny hair and wrestle her to the ground. I would never get over what she did to my dad or the things she said when she was testifying against me.

"If you're here because you think I got your homework for you since you missed class, you're going to be disappointed. You need to find someone else to run your errands. And find someone else to worship the ground you walk on. I'm not doing either anymore." I lifted my chin and narrowed my eyes. I'd never been in a fight in my life, minus fighting off unwanted advances from drunk customers at the diner and the creepy lowlifes who prowled the streets of the Point. I was ready to throw a punch right now. All I needed was for

Addison to make the first move. I didn't want to get suspended for starting a fight when I was so close to straightening out my last few months as a high school senior.

"I don't know what's gotten into you, Vesper, but if you think I'm going to let any of your recent insanity slide, you're out of your mind. I think your dad needs to consider having you committed for your own safety. It's like you're an entirely different person. It's concerning." She smirked at me when I stiffened because of her none-too-subtle threat.

"If you and your mom don't leave my father alone, I'm going to convince him to take out a restraining order against the two of you. Your reputation is already in the trash. Do you want to keep digging this hole? I'm happy to help shovel. If you get any deeper, your mom won't be able to scam any other eligible bachelor on the Hill into marrying her. What will the two of you do then?"

Addison glared at me and pushed off my car's black fender. She crossed her arms over her chest. Her blue eyes were frigid, and I swore I could hear her teeth grinding together.

"I don't know what you think you know about my mom and the men she married, but you have no right to judge either of us. You have no idea how hard it is to come from nothing. You will never understand what it's like to worry about where your next meal is coming from, or if you're going to have a warm place to sleep. You don't get to question what someone else is willing to do to pull themselves up from the bottom, to make an opportunity when none is given. You never had to get your hands dirty, and it shows. The poor-little-rich-girl act you pull is pathetic, Vee. No one likes you. They just feel sorry for you. I'm the only friend you ever had, and I only approached you because my mom wanted an easy way to meet your dad. No one will remember you."

She was good. Everything she said was spot on and zeroed in on all my old fears and insecurities. My previous self would've crumbled at her brutal onslaught. But Addison had no idea that I had experienced all the struggles she mentioned and more thanks to her.

The things I feared now were far bigger than being disliked and forgotten by a bunch of kids who had found me annoying when I was a teenager.

"You're right, Addy. I don't know your story. I don't have the right to judge what you and your mom had to do to move up in the world. I was born with a lot, and never bothered to give much back. I can't say that I don't deserve most of your anger. Maybe I owed you some of the things you took from me." The shot at my top pick for colleges. My inheritance. The boy I thought I liked. My reputation and my freedom. All of those things I could consider a debt paid for being shortsighted and ignorant. But my dad's life? That price was too steep for any debt I owed. "You changed things when you brought my dad into the picture. He never deserved what you and your mother had planned for him."

Addison made a face and took a step back. She cocked her head slightly and looked at me like she was trying to figure out a complicated math problem. "What are you even talking about? What did I take from you? What do you think we have planned for your dad? You aren't making any sense."

I swore under my breath and shifted anxiously. I forgot that she didn't know that I knew about everything she was plotting. To her, I was still the quiet girl who followed her around like a lost puppy. In her eyes, I was clueless and couldn't possibly know anything about the evil that lived under her polished surface. If I wasn't careful, I would give her even more reason to question my current behavior. If she started paying too much attention to me, she might even find something that would convince my dad to really have me committed.

I cleared my throat and looked over her shoulder to hide my nervousness. "Never mind. Just leave me and my dad alone. If you mess with me, I'm going to retaliate. You're super smart. Don't waste your energy on me. Focus on yourself, Addy. Put all your focus and attention on your future. You can be unstoppable if you quit trying to find the easiest way to get what you want." I truly hated her, but I still admired her. It took an evil genius to manipulate and maneuver everything the way she and her mom had from the beginning.

She glared at me even harder and pointed a finger right at the end of my nose. "I can't figure out what game you're playing, but I will."

I smacked her hand away from my face and reached for my keys in the pocket of my blazer. "It's the game you started. I'm just finishing it since I never asked to play in the first place. As for the guy who is very forgettable, I know you've been fucking him since the start of the semester." I sniffed a little as I nudged her to the side with my hip so I could pull open the door to the sports car. "You two are kind of a perfect match now that I think about it."

They suited each other, not only because their golden looks and auras meshed. Because they were both ruthless and selfish and would do anything to get ahead. I bet they competed to see who could come first when they were together. Neither could stand being second place in anything.

I put a hand on the roof of the car and turned my head to look at my former friend. She looked stunned, and for the first time since we met, she appeared to be speechless.

"I also know you copied my college essay and used it as your own when you applied. You didn't send in my applications on purpose so I would get busted for plagiarism when I sent my original essay when I reapplied. I already talked to our academic advisor about it. I filed a formal complaint. I have undeniable proof of when I first wrote the essay. If you can't show when you wrote yours, you're looking at possible expulsion. I understand how you took me for an easy target throughout our entire friendship. I let you believe I would never stand up to you or fight for myself. I'm not that girl anymore. This is the only time I will warn you to watch yourself around me. School is almost over. Let's stay clear of each other until we can go our own ways."

My former friend looked a little like she was going to throw up. Her face was pale, and I noticed her hands clenched into fists.

Those gel-coated nails of hers were probably drawing blood from her palms. She didn't seem to notice. Instead, she watched me with wary eyes.

"Who the fuck are you? You aren't the Vesper you always were." She sounded certain, and I could practically see the wheels turning in her head as she took in everything I just left at her feet.

I blew out a breath, sending my short, straight bangs fluttering across my forehead. "You're right. I'm the Vesper you created."

I closed the door and started the car. When I pulled out of the parking spot, Addison barely moved out of the way. She kept her troubled gaze on me until I passed through the gates and drove out of view.

I let out a breath and flexed my shaking hands once I had a moment to gather myself. I still wasn't a fan of confrontation, but it felt good to go toe-to-toe with my archnemesis. It was a little unfair. I was fighting with her over things that hadn't happened yet, but I carried a lot of resentment and grief from the past that still needed an outlet.

I didn't know if anything I said or anything I did could change the trajectory that Addison was already on. I didn't know if she'd been born devious and duplicitous or if she decided to behave that way because she had no choice. Part of me wanted to give her the opportunity to find a different path, but a bigger chunk was still damaged and broken from finding my father at the base of the stairs with his head split open. I couldn't forget all the blood. I couldn't forget how heavy my heart felt, and how instantly alone I was once the coroner took him away. I thought it couldn't get worse than that moment until a detective showed up to arrest me. Addison had only smiled at me and gave me a jaunty little wave when they put me in cuffs.

Redemption was for those who deserved forgiveness. Revenge was for those I could never forget.

SEVEN

OLD HANDS

I felt both proud and a tad petty after my confrontation with Addison. I was glad I finally got the chance to lay all my resentments on the line, even if she hadn't done half of what I knew she was capable of yet. I had a tingle of alarm ringing down each vertebra of my spine as I drove away. Now that I'd drawn the battle lines, I didn't know what kind of retaliation she might have in mind, but I knew it wasn't going to be pretty. This was merely the eye of the storm because I had forced it to shift trajectory. I knew the real wrath was still bound to make landfall somewhere else in my life. I was still looking at the potential for massive destruction.

I got home and found my dad was still out handling the aftermath of the canceled wedding. The house was dark and lonely. Carlotta had made dinner and left it in the oven for me, so I shoveled some food in my face and decided to work on rewriting that college essay and reapplying for schools closer to home. Originally when I planned on going across the country for school, I looked at art schools and design schools. I don't know why I thought that's what I wanted to pursue for my future, other than that's what Addison was applying for. I'd never really had an interest in either art or fashion. And I couldn't care less about interior decorating. I didn't even have a portfolio of work to submit. I always figured I could throw something together at the last minute. Back then, I would be hard-pressed to pinpoint any real passion. All I cared about was being the best.

The best daughter.

The best friend.

The best student.

The best potential girlfriend.

The best collegiate candidate.

Now I knew I wanted to help kids like Tobi and Jordan. I wanted to put myself in a position to make sure the kids in the Point didn't have to go hungry, that they didn't have to stay with a parent who did more harm to them than good. I wanted to make sure that they had the same resources as kids on this side of town. I didn't know if that meant going into public service, or aspiring for something greater, but I finally had a firm goal in mind and a solid starting point. I decided that was what I would base my new essay around. The disparity between the available services for kids from the Hill and the Point was monumental. After all, kids were ultimately inno- cent and had no choice but to be born on one side of the class line or the other. My previous essay was centered mostly on the challenges of growing up without my mom and being in the public eye because of my father's career. It really was a poor-little-rich-girl sob story. Addison wasn't off base when she asked if I was tired of playing that role because others were tired of the act.

When she stole my essay, she tweaked the deceased parent to be her father, and she struggled to grow up with a mother who want- ed her to be a carbon copy of her. Both aspects were true, and she could've written the strong sentiment on her own. Plus, she already had an excellent design portfolio. The plagiarism wasn't about that. The entire act of copying my essay was the first step in the multi-step plan to drive a wedge between my father and me and get me out of the picture. Of course, someone who wrote books that were often pi- rated was going to be furious at his child for doing the unthinkable. But since I didn't do it, I pushed back vehemently in denial. It would be the first real rift we'd ever had in our relationship, but that tiny crack opened the door for all kinds of other doubts to build. Their plan worked perfectly.

Just as I was wrapping up what I was working on, my dad sent a text saying he was meeting his lawyer for a drink and wouldn't be back until late. I let him know I ate dinner and was working on homework, all very typical exchanges from back when I was really eighteen. It felt nostalgic and made my heart warm. However, once I was alone in the big, empty house, I started to get antsy and anxious. I sent a few messages to Oscar asking about any progress he'd made talking to the other residents from the motel, but they all remained unanswered. I decided I couldn't sit around and wait to see if Oscar had searched out others to see if they experienced a time slip as well. I didn't acknowledge it made me twitchy that I hadn't heard from him all day. I didn't have any claim on the pink-haired boy, but for some reason, it made me very uneasy when I couldn't speak to him or see him.

I knew I couldn't drive my flashy car to the Point, and it was unlikely a ride-share or cab would drop me off anywhere past the train tracks. I had to get as close to the dividing line of the two parts of the city as possible, then risk walking to the motel or catching a bus to where I needed to go. I knew I couldn't wear anything in my closet if I was going back into the dark part of the city. Those designer labels were just asking for someone to rob me and literally take the shirt from my back. I raided my dad's closet and finally dug up an old flannel shirt he used to wear when he was in college. I remembered him telling me it was the shirt he wore on his first date with my mom, so I knew he would keep it somewhere despite his taste and style evolving over the years.

It was long enough that I could wrap a belt around the middle and call the whole thing a dress, which saved me from having to find an appropriate pair of pants to wear. I put on some black tights and the same boots I wore to school today, making a mental note to buy some low-key basics before my next trip down the hill. After all, a

girl needed a good pair of sneakers and some worn-in boots no matter on what side of the tracks she lived.

I got as close to the outskirts of the Point as I could. Just like
I figured, the cab driver refused to cross the train tracks and go
into the city. Even after I offered him a huge tip, he still declined.
I thanked him anyway and made my way to the nearest bus stop.
When I lived at the motel, the only way I could get around was on
my own two feet and public transportation. I had to learn how to use
both the bus line and the subway system. Now, I was a pro. I knew
not to make eye contact or talk with any other passengers. I knew to
sit on the outside seats so no one could pin me next to the window. I
knew to get as close to an exit as possible in case I needed to escape.
Neither bus nor train were particularly safe in the Point, which was
one of the main reasons I stuck with the job at the diner because of
its proximity to the motel. I could walk to and from.

Since it was already dark, the bus was mostly empty and dropped
me off in front of the gas station across the street from the motel
without incident. I looked around and noticed how little seemed to
have changed from the past to the present in this neighborhood. The
motel still looked as battered as it did when I moved in. The gas
station was still covered in graffiti and had bars over all the windows. The street signs were still littered with bullet holes, and there
were still cars without their wheels and with broken windows dotted
around the parking lot.

This felt like stepping back in time all over again. Like I was
back at the beginning of all the weirdness that had overtaken my
life. Walking toward the motel, which now had an old, broken-down
truck in the place where Oscar always had parked his car felt more
like my life than being back in that big house up on the hill.

I looked at the truck and realized it was probably Oscar's original project. I thought he was always tinkering with that stupid car
because he couldn't afford a better one. It seemed like he picked
project vehicles on purpose, maybe so he could fix them up and flip
them for a profit. Now that I thought about it, I'd never seen him

drive anywhere. He also took the bus or walked wherever he was going. I thought he took public transportation because he sucked at working on his car; now I realized it was a choice. Yet another I didn't understand, just like his recent choice to come back and run this motel when he had the option to start over and do something else with his life.

I walked into the motel's office to ask where I could find him. I was surprised to find a girl who appeared to be around my age behind the counter. She was leaning on her elbows, watching something on her phone, and barely looked up at me as the brass bell over the door rang. She was pretty. Prettier than Addison. Her hair was long and very curly. It was caught somewhere between red and brown, and there was a bright white streak that framed her face. She had small features with huge green eyes, making her look almost doll-like. However, the hard edge in her gaze was something I'd only ever seen in people who called the Point home. She hadn't been around when I first moved to the motel. An elderly Asian woman originally rented me the room. She was always in the front office whenever I walked by, so I had always assumed she was the owner. I was still baffled that Oscar owned the whole place.

"We only have rooms available for the hour tonight. Everything else is booked." She looked me up and down as if she was trying to determine just how long I'd have to work to make a profit if I worked on my back for an hourly wage. She must've decided I didn't have much potential as a sex worker because she sighed and pointed in the direction of the road in front of the building. "There's another motel about two blocks over. It's bigger than ours, so you can probably find a room for the night. But this isn't a nice part of town. You should probably just head back to wherever you came from."

I shook my head and tried not to blush at her assumption. "I'm looking for Oscar. I don't need a room."

The girl's phone hit the counter with a thud as her head jerked up so she could stare at me. Her eyes narrowed to jade slits as she glared.

"What do you need Oscar for?" Her tone was biting, and I swore if looks could kill, I'd be dead on the spot.

Before, I would've balked and probably walked away under the intense scrutiny of this girl. I avoided confrontation at all costs. Today, I was going to confront people who got in my way and kept me from achieving my goal, no matter how big or small.

"I don't think I need to explain why I'm looking for him to you. If he's not here, I'll just text him and ask him to meet me." I acted like I had all the time in the world, but the reality was, the buses were going to stop running soon, and there was no way I was walking back to the edge of the city in the middle of the night. I might end up stranded here if I couldn't find Oscar.

"I know everyone who has a reason, be it good or bad, to look for Oscar. I don't know you. But I can tell by looking at you that you don't belong here." She sniffed a little and picked up her phone. "Go ahead and text him if you have his number."

I shrugged and started to type out a message, but never got to finish it because a hand wrapped around my arm from behind and squeezed my bicep painfully.

"What are you doing here? I thought you planned to avoid this place like the plague once you got out." The raspy voice in my ear made the hair on the back of my neck stand on end.

I didn't hear the bell over the door ding. I looked over my shoulder at Oscar in surprise. How could he move so quietly? Was that another survival instinct he picked up living in this godforsaken place?

"Where's Ms. Nam? Why are you behind the counter, Devon? I told you not to fuck around if you're going to insist on hanging around here every single day." His voice was low and clearly showed his irritation.

The pretty girl behind the counter seemed unfazed as she rolled her eyes at him. "Ms. Nam had to run a few errands. I told her I would watch the front for a few hours until she returned. I tried to text you to let you know, but you didn't respond... like always." The girl he called Devon sounded seriously put out by his lack of response.

Oscar's fingers tightened on my arm, forcing me to bite back a whimper of discomfort. "I'm back now. You can take off. I'll make sure Ms. Nam pays you for the hours you covered for her."

The girl practically pouted as she slid around the counter and walked toward us. "I was helping you, not her. I don't need you to pay me, Oscar. You know I'm here for you. I want you to know you can count on me." She gave me another pointed look. "I've known you since we were kids. I know how hard losing Elliot has been on you. You can't trust anyone who isn't from around here. You know that."

Oscar sighed and dragged a hand down his face. His dark eyes were hard to read, but his expression was one I'd be scared of if I was on the receiving end of it. I tried to subtly pry his fingers off my arm before he cut off the blood supply. He let go as soon as he realized his hold on me was painful.

"I told you I don't have time to play around, and I don't have time to entertain you. I asked you not to hang around the motel unless you want a legit job. I'll pay you fairly for your time, but that's the extent of my willingness to be involved with you, Devon."

He stepped toward the door and pulled it open. This time the bell jangled noisily as the girl slipped out, muttering furiously under her breath.

"She seems nice." Sarcasm dripped from every syllable of my words once I was alone with him in the dingy office space.

"She's not." Oscar's tone was flat as he moved to stand behind the counter. "Don't make her mad, and stay away from her."

I absently rubbed my arm and lifted my eyebrows at his warning. "I think it's a little late for that. She was mad as soon as I mentioned your name. I don't remember her from before. She wasn't around when I moved here."

"In my original timeline, I got hammered right after my brother's funeral and slept with her because I was too fucked up to say no. It messed up our whole dynamic. She read more into it than there was. She wanted more from me than I could ever give. Our friendship imploded, and she moved to another state before you showed up. In this timeline, I ended up in the hospital after the funeral, so I managed to not screw things up."

I sighed. His life was relentlessly complicated. The more I learned about him, the more I started to think my issues were ridiculously common. "She's really pretty. If she's known you forever and she's into you, maybe you should give her a chance." I saw that he was watching me rub my arm where he grabbed me, so I dropped my hand and propped myself against the opposite side of the counter from him. "Given the opportunity to do things differently this time around, we should capitalize on fixing all the relationships in our lives."

He grunted and looked at me with narrowed eyes. "Devon was my brother's girlfriend, well, ex-girlfriend. They broke up a month before he was murdered. She didn't take his death well. She started to cling to me because my brother and I looked and sounded alike. But our personalities are the opposite of each other. Elliot was kind. Tolerant. He believed there was always good, even in the worst places and people. He adored Devon and treated her like a queen. I have no patience for pandering. I'm not interested in extending any effort to make another person a priority in my life."

I blinked at his harsh view of relationships. "Ouch. That's a pretty bleak way to view having someone you care about in your life."

He gave me a blank stare and switched topics. "Why are you here? I won't believe you if you tell me you missed this shithole."

I cleared my throat and nervously looked away. I didn't miss the motel, but I missed him. It was odd. I definitely had more memories and attachments to the place, but it was the person who was foremost in my mind. Before, he was just part of the Point. Now, he was something else. Something I felt like I couldn't live without.

"I wanted to know if you had looked into the other people who might've been in the explosion that night." He didn't need to know I was bored and lonely in a huge mansion up on the Hill. Even I thought I seemed pathetic when my real reason for searching him out crept under my skin. "I can't stop thinking about why the two of us are experiencing all this and why no one in the past seems to be affected. I can't sit around and do nothing while we're in this situation. I need answers."

"You wasted a trip. I went through everyone who lives here now and compared them by memory to who was there the night of the explosion. Only a few people fit the bill: me and you, Ms. Nam, and the agoraphobic woman who lives in the last unit on the top level. She was here before either of us, and since she never leaves the unit, we can assume she was there the night of the explosion. Ms. Nam doesn't live at the motel, so she wasn't here that night. I can't get the recluse to open the door. I'm not sure she would even notice if she suddenly woke up seven years in the past. For her, every day is the same. I don't think it's related to the motel. You didn't live here seven years ago, but I did. You just happened to be here the night of the explosion."

I nodded absently as he talked. Everything he said made sense but... "I still want to try and talk to the shut-in. I don't think we just overlook her because she won't answer the door."

He sighed. "You're stubborn."

I shrugged my shoulders and looked down at the counter. I used the tip of my finger to trace a long crack in the plastic. "I didn't used to be. It seems to be a new personality trait."

"You can try and talk to her, but not tonight. You can't force your way inside the apartment. I have to run this place like my brother would've wanted. I'm not going to let it crumble around me like I did last time. He would've been so pissed at everything I did back then. He hated my indifference. He hated that I didn't have any ties to anything or anyone. He wanted me to value my life, even if it never felt like much of one."

I nodded and tried not to reach for him. His words made me want to hug him. But Oscar Osborn did not seem like the hugging type. "I won't force the issue with the recluse. And again, I am truly sorry about what happened to your brother."

When I looked up at him, he lifted his dark eyebrows in a questioning manner. "You have to know the buses are about to stop running. You're going to get stuck here again. Don't forget it took a literal act of God to get you out of the Point last time."

I curled my fingers into a fist on the countertop. "Is it strange that I feel like I belong here more than I do at my dad's house? It's strange to be parented again. It's not like I'm a kid anymore. I was on my own for a long time after he died. I survived things he can't even imagine and things that I can't talk to him about. I'm not who he thinks I am anymore. So, it's weird being back up on the Hill." I leaned my elbows on the chipped surface of the counter and rested my chin in my hands. "I hated every part of my life when I lived here. But I can admit now that the time spent here made me a better person. I'm more aware of what I have and what I can do with those advantages."

Oscar tapped his fingers on one of his tattoos where his hand rested after he crossed his arms. He continued to watch me carefully like I was a bug he wasn't sure he should squash or take outside and set free. "What did you survive? Sure, you were down on your luck when you showed up here, begging Ms. Nam to take you in. I don't remember you being any worse off than anyone else who ends up in this place. You were just another lost little lamb waiting for someone to show you the way home."

I snorted at the description. "I almost went to prison for murdering my father." The shocked look on his face was very satisfying. "The case was solid; the jury was ready to convict me. I was in jail for a year, waiting while lawyers and the media discussed my fate. I wasn't even a person—just an easy headline. I couldn't get anyone to believe that I would never, ever hurt my father. He's all I've got. It has always been me and him against the world until he got married. The only reason I ultimately escaped a conviction was because our housekeeper testified that I wasn't home when my father fell down the stairs. His neck was broken, and his head was split open. It was a terrible way to die. I'm convinced the woman he married orchestrated everything that happened: me and my dad falling out with each other, the fall that killed him, and the murder accusations that followed. And even getting our housekeeper tangled up with her own legal issues. The new wife and my stepsister accused her of stealing once my dad was gone. She was basically lost in the system for most of the trial and out of the way just like they wanted. Fortunately, my family on my mother's side had enough of having their good name dragged through the mud and attached to the circus that was my trial. They found the right people to get Carlotta released, and she testified in the nick of time. It was a hung jury when the verdict came back, but the DA declined to retry me because the evidence was so sparse, and I was only close to being convicted because of hearsay and accusations from others. When I was finally free, I didn't have a friend in the world. My inheritance, everything my father had built in his lifetime, was all stolen out from under me. The other side of my family wanted nothing to do with me because of the trial. They didn't think I had any value, and I was expendable since I don't have their last name. I had no one and nowhere to go. So, I ended up here. Granted, I didn't have to serve hard time or anything like that, but I still lost a year of my life and was blamed for my father's death." I scowled as the memories swirled around my mind. "I wasn't a lamb when I showed up here. I was more like Bo Peep. I lost my sheep and had no idea where to find them."

Oscar's look switched to one of consideration. "I got arrested for stealing cars. The only way I wasn't getting sent away for a minimum of five years was if I agreed to rat out the people who used this motel for all the illegal shit that goes on behind closed doors. They wanted me to be a rat, knowing it would put my life in danger and put the rest of my family in the line of fire. I was ready to do the time." He shook his head, and a wry grin broke across his face. "I was stubborn. I figured I could do five years easily, and maybe even learn a little something behind bars, but my brother wouldn't stand for it. He jumped in before I was sent away and made a deal in my place. He agreed to be an informant instead. I think the cops and the people pulling their strings kept me out of the way just long enough for Elliot to have no other option if he wanted to save me. They played him, and I couldn't save him. He was kind of like you. Too soft for this place. Too kind and considerate. He never should've put me first."

I pulled back a bit and frowned while I tried to work through that information. Nervously, I asked, "The people responsible for your brother's death are the police?"

In the Point, the law enforcement officers were a different breed. In a place where the bad guys called most of the shots, the police had to play by a whole different set of rules. No one wanted to be a good guy when the bad guys were already winning the war on the streets. It took some real outside-the-box thinking to be an effective authority figure in this palace.

Oscar slowly shook his head, and a few strands of mint-green hair drifted over his forehead. "No. The cops here generally suck, and I think it's bullshit they let him take my place in a shady-ass deal, but they did their best to protect him. I don't think anyone who was ever busted through the motel knew my brother was behind the info that took them down. He knew it was dangerous and tried to be careful. He was killed in a random robbery. He was in the office just like he was most nights. A couple of teenagers busted in, waved a gun around, and demanded money. The motel had been robbed more than once. Before my old man vanished, he was up to his eyebrows in gambling debt. People came in all the time trying to get paid what he owed them. Both Elliot and I knew to hand over the money. Nothing in this shithole was worth losing our lives over. This time something went wrong. The kids who busted in that night shot Elliot point-blank as he pulled the money from the safe under the counter. The robbers didn't know how to use a gun. It was pretty clear they weren't familiar with what they were doing. There's no surveillance in a place like this. And none of the residents want to talk to the cops. But Ms. Nam just happened to be in the parking lot when they fled. So, we know they were kids and she could see it all going down." He paused, seeming like he was trying to decide whether to share more with me or not. "And I know that the car they used to get away is expensive and rare. Not a vehicle anyone would willingly bring to this part of town. This all tells me they weren't from the Point. The police don't have much to go on, and if all roads point to the kids being from the Hill, they'll turn a blind eye anyway. I don't know what a bunch of rich kids were doing robbing a motel in the slums, but that's what happened. Maybe it was a dare. Maybe it was some type of fucked-up initiation. Maybe they were just bored and looking to add some excitement to their pathetic lives. Whatever it was, those kids got away the last time this all went down, and everyone forgot my brother died. It's not going to happen again."

He sounded truly heartbroken when he spoke about the loss of his brother. It was the first time I noticed any expression in his eyes. The dark depths were full of sorrow.

"I was supposed to be watching the desk for him that night," Oscar grunted in disgust. It was directed at himself. "I didn't show up because I was mad at him for making that deal with the cops. I was acting like an idiot. It was supposed to be me behind the counter, not Elliot. You went to jail for a crime you didn't commit, and I didn't go even though I should've." His tone sounded wry, and his expression was solemn. "Our destinies got switched somewhere along the line. Maybe that's why we were brought back here together. Fate wants a chance to unfuck the future."

"Oh, Oscar. That's terrible. But you know it's not your fault, right? The only people to blame are the kids who came in to rob the place. I understand why you're so determined to punish someone for your brother's death now." I wanted to cry for him. I could practically feel the guilt and regret weighing down on him. I understood why he was focused on payback instead of finding out why we were sent back in time. If our cosmic rewind had sent us back a few more days, he might've been able to save his brother.

Maybe he felt like he *had* to do something to those kids responsible. Obviously, he felt that was his only reason for returning to this point in time. He didn't seem to be a half-measures kind of guy.

"I know nothing will bring him back, but I don't think he deserves to die in vain either." He looked past me to the fast-approaching night outside the office windows. I could tell he was done with the baring-our-souls portion of the visit. "You should grab the last bus. Come back during the day if you want to talk to the hermit. You know it's not safe to be out at night around here."

It didn't slip past me that he never said who his targets of revenge might be or what his plans for them were. He clearly didn't want to share that information with me. It wasn't like we were close or that he trusted me. We just happened to be stuck in this weird alternate reality together. He obviously didn't need me the same way I decided that I needed him.

I didn't miss that he stepped outside of the office with the excuse of needing a smoke so he could watch until I was on the last bus and headed back to the Hill. I decided not to remind him he should quit smoking since he was once again looking out for me despite himself. It seemed to be a habit he couldn't break, which led me to believe I really was special to him in some way.

EIGHT

ONE OF THESE THINGS

B ack at school and settling into my previous life with my new attitude and awareness, it only took a matter of days for me to go from being an *it* girl to being *that* girl.

As in, *that* girl is the one who ruined her father's wedding.

That's the girl who got Addison Martin expelled right before graduation. She accused her of copying. Like she didn't try and do everything the way Addison did in the first place. She's always been so pathetic.

Did you hear the rumors *that* girl tried to spread about Addison and her mother? She's terrible. Who would do *that* to their best friend?

That girl is crazy. She pretended not to know who Rex Wallace is. How embarrassing for her.

Stay away from *that* girl unless you want everyone to start talking about you too.

It was annoying being stared at everywhere I went, but since this was my second time fighting my way to graduation, I didn't let anything get under my skin or bother me too much. I missed my chance to enjoy finishing school last time. I had my future stolen. This time, I would make sure my foundation was strong enough to withstand any external force. If I had focused more on myself and invested more time into forming my own plans and personality, Addison would never have been able to kick over and break apart my entire life like it was a cheap toy.

A couple of Addison's most loyal followers went out of their way to make my days as difficult as possible, but I'd spent a year locked up in my previous life. Their petty pranks and snarky attitudes barely blipped on my radar. However, it was nearly impossible to avoid Rex and his very evident rage directed at me. He was pissed that I got his little girlfriend kicked out of school. He was furious that I was still acting like I had no idea who he was. But more than that, he was practically rabid over the fact I convinced my father to stop his donation to his mother's upcoming campaign. When I had a crush on him and thought we would eventually be a couple, I begged my dad to make a sizable donation to the Wallace camp. My dad liked to keep out of politics publicly, but in private, Rex's mom was on the other side of the aisle than he was. However, he rarely denied me when I asked him for a favor. Even though I knew he hated every minute of it, he publicly promised to make a huge donation to Rex's mother right before the wedding. Back then, I was trying for brownie points and hoped to use them to get Rex to come with me to my big graduation party.

In this timeline, the first real dinner I sat down to enjoy with my dad when we both weren't busy, I apologized for being immature and for putting him on the spot with my request. I explained that I was no longer interested in Rex and wanted nothing to do with that family. I told him I hoped he could withdraw the donation, even if it meant he might get some bad press over it.

To say my father was elated over my change of heart was an understatement. I couldn't tell if he was happier about the money or the fact I'd finally woken up to what kind of guy Rex was. He'd never been a fan of my obsessive crushing on the guy and had even tried to dissuade me from spending time with him. Chasing after Rex was the only time I ignored my dad or defied his wishes, which should've told me exactly what kind of guy he was in the first place. If my dad didn't approve, what was I doing when I planned on giving the guy everything?

Avoiding him, and especially avoiding any situation where he could catch me alone, became like a giant game of hide and seek we played every day. It sucked. I was very much outnumbered once he started having his minions report on my whereabouts. I even managed a full week of steering clear of him and his bros, but my luck ran out on Friday.

I was distracted. I kept scrolling through my messages on my phone, understanding why that Devon girl was so cocky when she dared me to text Oscar to find out where he was the day I dropped by the motel. I had sent him at least one message a day, just checking in and asking if he'd seen the recluse yet. I wanted to know how he was feeling and if he felt unsettled all the time like I did. I was concerned about his mental state now that I knew all the details of his brother's death. Mostly, I wanted to make sure he didn't do anything stupid and end up in jail because his thirst for revenge was so deep. Oscar didn't seem like he was scared of much, which left me to be scared for him. I mean, the guy talked about spending five years in prison like it was no big deal. There was no telling what his bottom line might be.

But he barely responded to my messages. When he did reply, it was usually just a one-word answer like, *yes* and *no*. It was impossible to get a read on him, and it frustrated me to no end that I was the only one who felt a bigger-than-both-of-us connection to him. Once again, I walked up to my car without realizing someone was leaning against the side of it. As soon as I caught sight of my unwelcome visitor, I swore at myself and tapped my forehead with the corner of my phone. I was an idiot. And once again, I walked into a bad situation because I wasn't using my head. Proving my theory true that bad things were bound to happen when you were being dumb.

I'd made a habit of leaving school early or waiting until the last possible minute to walk to the parking lot. When I left early, there was a crowd of people rushing to go home so I could lose myself in the crowd. When I left late, I always had a security guard escort me, so I was never alone and easily ambushed. Security was a perk of going to private school, and I planned to take full advantage of it until Rex backed off.

Because I was forced to deal with a locker that had apparently been super-glued shut courtesy of Addison's friends, I got the timing wrong and wound up in the parking lot when it was mostly empty. There were still enough students scattered about that no one would think it was odd that someone was waiting by my car.

I took a deep breath and braced for whatever the prince of this private school was going to throw at me.

"Are you still going to pretend that you don't know who I am, Vee? If you really have no clue, then you might want to explain why you've spent all week avoiding me." He crossed his arms over his chest, and the smile on his face sent shivers racing down my spine.

"I don't have anything to say to you. That's why I've been avoiding you." I tried to move around him to grab the door of the car, but he blocked me. He grabbed hold of my wrist and squeezed hard enough I knew I was going to have a bruise.

I scowled. I'd had just about enough of guys who were bigger and stronger than me grabbing my arms and yanking me around. I tried to pull free, but Rex only pulled me closer. When he spoke, his breath was hot against my ear.

"I don't know how you found out about me and Addison, but it doesn't change anything. She's not my girlfriend either. You need to talk to your dad and get him to give my mom the money he promised. Because of you, both our families look bad." He squeezed my arm even tighter, and I swore I heard something pop as pain shot through my hand. "My parents are demanding that I bring you home like some sort of runaway bride. Do you have any idea how badly you've fucked everything up?"

I used my other hand to try and pry him off me. Seriously, that side was going to be black and blue for a month after the way I'd been manhandled lately. Being grabby was a bad habit that bossy boys who were rich and poor seemed to share. How annoying.

"I don't care how things look. I never should've asked my dad to donate money to try and impress you. I can't remember what I ever saw in you, but my eyes are wide open now. You and Addison are a much better fit."

He pulled me closer, and the jerk made my teeth snap together. I kicked him in the shins and tilted my head as far away from him as possible, but he had a solid hold on me, and there wasn't a lot of wiggle room. I debated screaming for help at the top of my lungs, but I doubted anyone would run to my rescue. Rex was a good guy in everyone else's eyes, and I was the weirdo.

"My parents will never let me be with a girl like Addison. They think her mom is trash. She doesn't come from the Hill. She has no beneficial connections. Her father isn't in the picture. She's not the kind of girl who can withstand the intense media scrutiny that comes with my name. They'll pick her apart, and she'll drag me down with her. My parents want you, and I wasn't given a choice in the matter."

I kicked him again and tried to push him away with a hand on the center of his chest. We were full-on struggling now. My backpack even dropped to the ground, and I lost the grip I had on my phone. It felt very similar to my run-ins with the creeps who loitered in the dark corners of the Point. It was slightly jarring to realize it didn't matter what side of the tracks you called home; if you were a woman caught unaware and alone, you were seen as vulnerable and easy pickins'. I couldn't believe I was being manhandled all over again. I guess some things were universally shitty, whether it was the past, present, or future.

"Addison is smart. She's pretty. She's conniving. She's the perfect candidate to be a politician's wife. Maybe grow a backbone and stand up to your parents if you want to be with her. There's no way in hell I'm letting you use me as some kind of pawn, and I'm not going to ask my dad to change his mind about the money. Get away from me right now."

I yelped in alarm when one of his hands suddenly grabbed my face and squeezed my jaw. The way he pinched my cheeks together hurt, and I knew I would have red marks once he let go. Rex spun us around, pressing my back against the side of the car, and he leaned into me. I had nowhere to look but at his hostile gaze. His breath felt like it scorched my skin as he put his lips right on my ear and growled, "I'm not asking you to play nice, Vesper. I'm telling you what you're going to do. You're going to get that money from your old man, and you're going to play the adoring girlfriend until I say otherwise. You don't have an option."

I tried to wiggle free enough to lift my knee, aiming for the sensitive juncture between his legs. He pressed so close to me I couldn't get any leverage and was left clawing helplessly at the hand he was using to hold my face. The situation escalated so quickly, and I was starting to fear just how far he was willing to go to get his way.

As I started to fight back, the weight pressing down on me suddenly lifted, and the vise-like grip on my face vanished. I sucked in a relieved breath and slid down the side of my car until my ass was on asphalt. I hacked a cough out and immediately lifted a hand to rub my stinging cheeks.

I squinted against the afternoon sun to see who intervened on my behalf. Just like old times, Oscar was standing between the assailant and me. Rex was on the ground, looking bewildered as the skin around his eyes reddened and swelled. I'd missed what happened when Oscar pulled him away from me, but I'd guess he took a fist to the face.

I gathered my wits and climbed to my feet, swearing when I grabbed my phone because the screen was shattered. I could see several missed calls and text messages through all the spiderweb cracks. It looked like Oscar finally decided to acknowledge my existence, and when I didn't respond, he came looking for me.

"How did you know I went to school here? And how did you get past the gate and security?" My voice was raspy as I shook my head and tried to gather my composure. "This school is locked down like a maximum-security prison." I said that as someone who knew just how heavily guarded a prison was.

"I Googled you." He kicked Rex in the thigh when the big, blond jerk tried to get to his feet. Oscar pointed a finger at him and barked, "Stay down." He shifted his gaze back to me and quirked an eyebrow upward. "Are you honestly asking me how I got around a gate and a sleepy security guard? I think I'm offended. I was going to chew you out for not answering your phone, but I see you have a good reason." He hooked a thumb over his shoulder in the direction where Rex was still sprawled on the ground. "What's the deal with this charmer?"

I swore again as our little trio drew an audience. Sure, no one wanted to pay attention when I was getting tossed around like a rag doll, but now that there was a cute boy who did not belong on this campus giving a beating to the current king of the school, everyone wanted to see what was going on. It made my blood boil.

From the ground, Rex found his voice. "She's my girlfriend. We were having a bit of a disagreement. Who the fuck are you? You don't belong here."

I snorted and moved closer to Oscar's side. His minty hair faded from the last time I saw him, and he looked tired. I reached out to put a hand on his arm. I stumbled a little and would've smashed my face on the asphalt if he hadn't caught me.

"He's not my boyfriend. He's no one." I looked up at Oscar, a million questions in my eyes. "What are you doing here?"

He stood out like a sore thumb. Not because he had on ripped jeans, scuffed boots, and a plain t-shirt instead of a preppy school uniform. And not because he was tattooed and had candy-colored hair. It was more about how he carried himself, and the absolute disdain he had for the obvious wealth and privilege that surrounded him. Status meant nothing to him, and neither did gilded gates and the dividing class line he crossed over when he stepped up to rescue me.

One of these things was definitely not like the other.

"She's not your girlfriend. And if you ever put your hands on her again, I'm going to break your teeth out of your face one by one. I thought rich kids like you had better manners than this. Don't you guys have to take classes for this stuff? Shouldn't you know what fork to use, as well as the general rule that it's wrong to push women around?" If the sarcasm in Oscar's tone was any heavier, Rex would've been crushed under the weight of it. As it was, the blond guy struggled to his feet, aggressively knocking dirt off his red and black plaid uniform pants. He looked like an overgrown toddler on the brink of a breakdown.

"You're just going to believe her? She's not acting like herself lately. If you really know Vesper, you would know that." Rex smoothed his tie and glared at Oscar. He took a threatening step forward, but immediately backed down when Oscar matched him step for step. The boys were about the same height, and Rex was bigger in terms of bulk, but I doubted he had ever used any of those gym-created muscles for self-defense. Anyone looking at Oscar could tell he wouldn't back down from a fight. Rex didn't stand a chance.

Oscar snorted. "I bet I know her better than you. She's acting the same way she always does when she's around me." He gave me a smirk. "She's a bit mouthier now, and a lot more stubborn, but I don't hate either of those on her." Rex looked flustered and made like he was going to grab me again. Oscar caught the hand I was using to keep my balance by holding on to him and maneuvered me closer to him. His palm slid up my arm, and his other hand landed on my waist. He grinned at Rex and muttered, "I don't ever just believe anything anyone says to me. People lie about everything, but their actions are rarely as dishonest. I can prove she's not your girlfriend easily enough."

I froze when his head lowered, and his lips covered mine. I gasped in surprise as the kiss shook my whole world.

In my previous life, my experience with guys was limited to Rex and a random guy I met a few weeks after my trial was over. I was just looking for some contact, a bit of affection, and connection. It turned out the guy was a reporter looking for an exclusive. I'd never been kissed by someone who saw me as something more than a way for them to advance their agenda. I knew Oscar was only kissing me to prove a point, but it still felt different.

It was warm. It was soft, which was strange because he had such a hard exterior. I could tell in the few moments his lips moved against mine that he had more skill in this area than Rex ever would. I was a little mad the timeline didn't go back far enough that *this* could be my first kiss. I liked the way it made me feel so much. I enjoyed the hint of danger I felt swirling under the surface of the seemingly innocent gesture. Kissing Oscar felt like it was the start of something bigger and better.

My hand held onto him without me being aware I was clinging to him. I felt my skin heat up and my heart start to pound. If I hadn't been in the parking lot of my school, and if I wasn't yet again the center of unwanted attention, I would've wrapped myself around him and kissed him back like my life depended on it. After he playfully flicked the tip of his tongue against the seam of my lips, he pulled back and gave me a wink. He lowered his colorful head and whispered into my ear, "I always wanted to make out with a girl in a school uniform."

He looked back at Rex and lifted a taunting eyebrow. "Don't think she'd let me kiss her without complaint if she was your girl, Richie Rich. Back off."

Rex looked like he wanted to retaliate. Fortunately, some of his friends finally got brave enough to pull him away. I'd yet to figure out a way to retaliate against him in the same way I'd hit back at Addison. Today was a good reminder that Rex also deserved a taste of his own medicine. I needed to figure out a way to take him down beyond embarrassing him in front of his family.

Once Oscar and I were mostly alone by my car, I rubbed the back of my hand against my tingling lips and looked at him from underneath my lashes.

"I tried to message you all week, and you basically ignored me. Why did you suddenly come looking for me today?"

He picked up my backpack and made a *gimme* motion with his hand when I pulled my keys out of the pocket of my blazer. When I hesitated a second before tossing them to him, he scowled at me and grumbled, "I'm not going to steal it. If I was, I wouldn't need the keys."

I stuck my tongue out at his back before I went to the passenger side and climbed in. Oscar threw my bag in the back and turned to look at me before pulling out of the empty parking lot.

"I was busy all week. I had the city check that everything was up to code with the motel, so contractors were everywhere. Getting anything done through the right channels in the Point takes the patience of a damn saint. I also tried to dig up more information on the kids who killed my brother. The cop who busted me boosting cars is actually a pretty good guy. He kept telling me I reminded him a lot of his younger brother. He agreed to look into the murder for me, even though it's not his case. I kept an eye on the woman who never leaves her apartment all week as well." He swore and gave me a sharp look out of the corner of his eye. "And I had to avoid Devon. I don't remember her being so aggressive. Since I didn't have anything new to tell you, I figured I wouldn't bother you. You've got to be about ready to graduate in this timeline, so that should be your main focus. But I do need a favor, and you're the only one who can help me. I knew you would answer if you could. It bothered me when you didn't respond, so I Googled you to figure out where you went to school. Since your dad is hella famous, your whole life is on the internet."

The security guard gave us a hard look when we reached the gate. I reached across Oscar to flash my student ID before he could ask for Oscar's nonexistent visitor's pass. I offered a wan smile as he waved us through.

"I'm glad you're getting the motel up to code. That makes me feel better about you always being there. What kind of favor can I possibly do for you?" I couldn't imagine a scenario where I could help him out. Unless he was looking for a glowing reference on his ability to show up exactly when I needed him.

I put a hand on the dash as he scrolled through his phone with one hand and raced my car through the manicured streets of my posh neighborhood with the other. I don't think anyone had ever driven my car this fast. Oscar handled it like an everyday driver and didn't seem to register the excessive speed.

He shoved his phone in my direction and told me to look at the notice on the screen.

"I want you to get me into that fundraiser." He gritted his teeth, and a muscle in his jaw twitched as he briefly glanced in my direction. "Consider it payback for saving you from that jackass just now."

According to the website he had open, the fundraiser was being held at the country club. It was members only and black tie. There was also a thousand-dollar-a-head entry fee. None of that was unusual for an event like that. I was miffed he assumed I could just waltz into that kind of gathering with no effort.

"It says here that you have to be a member of the country club to go. And we're not. My dad hates golf and rubbing elbows with the rich and famous. He only moved here because my mom's family is here. He stayed after she passed away because he didn't want me to have to change schools, and he always hoped my mom's side of the family would accept me more than they accepted him." I wasn't sure why I wanted to share my whole life story with him, but I gave him a little bit more of my history every time we talked. I was acutely aware that I wanted him to view me as more than a girl who couldn't save herself.

"Can you get in if someone on your mom's side of the family vouches for you?" He sounded so determined that a sliver of unease slid under my skin.

"Maybe. I have an uncle I can ask. But there is no way you're getting in looking the way you do now." I had a very bad feeling about his reasons for wanting to get into such a formal event.

The dress code was strict, and they wouldn't let him anywhere near the front door with his visible tattoos and purple hair, let alone inside the clubhouse. He might be able to find his way into my school with no problem, but a black-tie fundraiser with all the big wigs from the Hill was a different animal. It was a very vicious, protective animal that didn't want any outsiders near its secrets and misdeeds.

"Whatever it takes. Get me into that club, Vesper." He made it sound like I didn't have a choice. Since he'd never asked me for anything and always rescued me without asking for anything in return, I guess I didn't have any other option. I owed him more than one at this point.

NINE

MAKEOVER MADNESS

The only person I kept in contact with from my mother's side of the family was her youngest brother. My Uncle Doyle wasn't considered as much of a disgrace as my mom had been, but when he started openly living his life as a gay man, complete with a partner he planned to marry in a lavish ceremony, the family didn't take it well. But since my mother was gone and they had no intention of welcoming me and my father into the fold, they pretended to be accepting of his relationship whenever the world was watching. In private, Uncle Doyle was as much of an outcast as my mother had been. I figured that was why he made an effort to keep in touch with me over the years up until the trial. He was still a touch snobby and tended to look down on anyone outside his social sphere, but so had I, until that circle narrowed into a noose. The man he married came from a family on the other coast that was as well-off as his own, so he maintained his membership at the country club through his husband rather than his own family connections. That degree of separation made asking him for an invite less intimidating.

When my uncle asked why I was suddenly interested in attending a fundraiser at the clubhouse, I made some excuse about needing experience mingling at formal events before I went to college. He praised me for knowing that success was all about having the right connections early on and agreed to get me and my plus one into the event. He even sounded excited to finally see me in an element that both my parents tried their best to keep me away from. My father always told me that just because I was born with a silver spoon in my mouth, no rule said I had to eat from it forever. While he spoiled me rotten after my mom passed away, my father still wanted me to know the value of things I earned for myself. I think that's why he always pushed me to keep my grades up and was so open about my plans for the future. He didn't care if I went to college, a trade school, or learned on the job. He just wanted to make sure I found a way to support myself and found purpose in life. He wanted me to have my own worth and find what made me valuable as a human beyond my last name or lineage.

After the invite was secured, I worked to ensure Oscar wouldn't get turned away at the door since the fundraiser seemed so important to him. The first thing he had to change was the pink hair. I was honestly sad to see it go. The soft, cheery color made him seem more approachable and less like a looming threat. I could pretend he wasn't dangerous and continue to act like we were becoming friends when he kept his soft side. Once the pink hair was gone, everything about him was dark. Hair, eyes, demeanor, the ink that covered so much of his skin, everything gave off an air of menace. I found myself nervous again when I was around him.

Over the weekend, I alternated between running Oscar to the salon and a tailor to get him fitted for a tux, all while watching the room of the recluse whenever I was back by the motel. I was waiting for any sign of life so I could talk to the lady behind the door, but so far, no luck. I couldn't say why I felt she was so damn important, but I knew I wouldn't be able to find a moment of peace until I spoke to the shut-in. The only person I ran into repeatedly was Devon. She had some choice words for me about the change in Oscar's appearance once she saw his newly buzzed head. Apparently, I wasn't the only one who missed the cotton candy-colored hair.

As soon as Devon laid eyes on the new style, which left Oscar with very short black hair, she went ballistic. She called him a bunch of names and threw a stapler at him. When he told me she wasn't nice, he meant it. She was yelling at both of us, ready to fight. He caught her around the waist when she tried to come across the counter at me. Her hands were outstretched like she wanted to wrap them around my throat. If Oscar hadn't intervened, I'm sure I would have added even more bumps and bruises to my growing collection. He carried her, kicking and screaming, out of the motel office, and then proceeded to argue with her in the parking lot. I had a feeling it was more than grief that was causing her to act so possessively when it came to him. I didn't say anything to Oscar, but it was pretty clear she had feelings for the younger brother that had nothing to do with the older brother being gone. What a complicated mess.

Oscar purposely avoided talking about Devon and his brother and avoided answering my questions about his need to attend the fundraiser. He kept telling me that once he was inside the gates, I could leave. He said it would be better if I ditched him once we arrived. He never talked much as it was, but when he was trying to dodge a subject, he got even more tight-lipped. I spent a lot of the weekend talking to myself, frustrated by Oscar's distant behavior. If he wasn't going to talk about his past or plans for the future, there was no shot of getting him to talk about that surprise kiss in the parking lot.

My brain knew he kissed me to prove a point to Rex. He did it to wound the other boy's pride and kick him while he was down. But it resonated in my heart and throughout my body differently. When I went to bed at night, I still felt his lips against mine. I felt the heat from where he held me thread through my veins. When I was alone in the dark, there was no stopping the dirty direction of my thoughts. They spun into what it would feel like if he kissed me for real, or what he would do if I made the first move and kissed him. These feelings, the curiosity, the heady, heavy longing, were all very different from the childish crush I had on Rex when I was eighteen.

After all, I was a world-weary young woman on the inside. It made sense the attraction I felt toward Oscar seemed more mature and intense than anything I felt when I was younger.

Unfortunately, my teenage hormones in this body had no common sense and were out of control.

When Oscar was finally situated in the modern tuxedo he would need to get into the fundraiser, I almost jumped him. Even with the buzzcut, he looked elegant and gorgeous in formal wear. It was the equivalent of taking a predator out of the wild and putting him behind glass so the prey could observe him unafraid. Once he was all dressed up and groomed within an inch of his life, he looked closer to civilized than I'd ever seen him. He was beautiful and lethal regardless of what he was wearing. The clothes didn't make the man, in Oscar's case. But they definitely didn't hurt. He looked better than I imagined, which kept him on my mind for an uncomfortable length of time. I felt like I was obsessed with him, and it had little to do with the time slip. I wondered how I had missed how magnetic and alluring he was when I walked past him every night on the way to my unit. I was baffled how I managed to treat him as nothing more than part of the scenery when I lived in the Point.

Now, it seemed like all I could see was him. Oscar was smack dab in the center of everything, which made the fact he didn't want to open up to me or interact with me beyond what he deemed necessary slightly soul crushing.

Sighing over my dramatic thoughts, I stared out the grimy window of the motel office and watched as Oscar and Devon continued to fight in the parking lot. Things escalated enough that she was pushing him with both her hands on his chest while Oscar was doing his best to restrain her. I could hear they were both yelling, but not what they were saying. Things had been going on like this for at least twenty minutes with no end in sight. I thought I would get time to coax more information out of Oscar about his motivation behind wanting to get into the country club, but it appeared he was going to have his hands full for a while. Silently, I admitted I was jealous of how close he and Devon seemed to be. Even though they were mad at each other, he said more to her in those heated moments than he had to me the entire time I'd known him. She showed absolutely no fear when she faced off with him, and it was clear they had a long, convoluted history between them. I was a tad ashamed that I wanted him to focus on me the way he focused on her, even though I could tell how irritated he was while talking to her. I felt like he would never let me get close to him because I wasn't from his world. There was always going to be an insurmountable distance between us, no matter what I did to get him to share anything with me.

Sighing heavily and feeling like a dumb, lovelorn girl, I was just about to pull away from the dirty window when a slight movement at the top level of the motel complex caught my eye. The door to the hermit's room crept open just a crack. It was enough to send me bolting out the door of the office, the bell jangling loudly in my wake. I ran past a startled Oscar and ignored the ugly name Devon called me. I didn't pay either of them any mind as I ran up the rusted metal stairs to the upper levels of the motel.

By the time I was in front of the door, the recluse shut it firmly once again. I used the side of my fist to pound on the wood. I bent over to catch my breath from the wild sprint. There was no answer when I straightened up and called, "I just want to ask you a question real quick. I promise to stop bothering you if you'll talk to me. Five minutes tops. You don't even have to open the door all the way." I knew I sounded a touch hysterical, but I was desperate.

There was no response. Not even a rustle on the other side of the door. I swore loudly and dropped my forehead so it hit the door with a *thump*. I wasn't certain why I was so sure the woman secreted away from the rest of the world might have the answers to what was happening with me and Oscar and our trip back to this point in our lives, but I couldn't shake the feeling she was a key piece of the puzzle. I felt like I was going to die if I never got the chance to speak to her.

"Come on! Will you open the door for a hundred bucks? How about a thousand? At this point, I'll give you whatever you want if you agree to talk to me." I was yelling at the door to no avail.

I knocked again, but the other side was eerily silent. I finally kicked the door out of frustration. All I got in return was a sore big toe. I grumbled under my breath as I limped down the steps. When I reached the bottom, I practically fell on top of Oscar when he suddenly appeared and startled me. I missed a step and gasped as I pitched forward. If Oscar wasn't there, my face would've hit the cement, something that was becoming an all-too-common occurrence. Was I always this disaster prone?

"I don't remember you being this clumsy before." His words echoed my thoughts. This time when he held me, he kept his grip light. I guess he noted all the black and blue marks decorating my arms.

I held onto his arm and limped down the last few steps. "I don't think you paid close enough attention to me back then. If you did, you wouldn't be so surprised by all my faults now."

Oscar snorted and looked up at the room. "I paid attention. You were the one who had tunnel vision. You looked at everything the same way until those kids finally got through to you. You were like a zombie. Half the time, I wondered if you were sleepwalking. That's why I always watched you walk back when you got off work. Anyone else would've seen the threats you walked into from a mile away. It was almost like you were looking for trouble by not seeing the world around you."

Startled, I turned my head to look at him with wide eyes. "All those times you stopped me from being harassed were because you were watching me? It wasn't because you just happened to be outside and saw what was going on?"

Didn't that mean I mattered to him? Wasn't that a sign he wasn't as indifferent to me as he seemed?

"When you first showed up at the motel, I thought you would only be here for a little bit. Obviously, you were from a different part of town, and you had a different lifestyle. Folks hit hard times regardless of where they start out in life. Some have it rougher than others, but you always seemed like a girl who would bounce back. You never tried to fit in here or adapt. I figured that meant you always planned on going somewhere else as soon as you got the chance. I can't tell you when I started to keep an eye on you, but it became a habit. I'm not sure why, but I felt like it would be a real shame if something happened to you. This place is full of wolves. I wanted you to stay a lamb for as long as possible."

I pulled him to a stop and stared at him without blinking. I was a girl who once had everything, but hearing that Oscar wanted me to remain untouched by my harsh surroundings was probably the nicest gift I'd ever received. Who went out of their way to help someone keep their innocence and sense of security? Instead of bringing me into his world, he tried to protect me from it. My heart turned soft and gooey inside of my chest. The butterflies he brought to life in my belly started to do the tango, and I felt a flutter throughout my body.

I liked him.

Really liked him.

I liked his face.

I liked his brooding intensity.

I liked his gruff voice and the few words he graced me with.

I liked his drive and determination.

I liked his edge and all the jagged points of his abrasive personality.

I liked everything about him that was so different than everyone else I'd ever known.

I didn't care that he was quiet and liked to keep secrets. Even if I didn't know his intentions, I still sensed his heart was in the right place. It was all too easy to convince myself I made the hard, brittle parts of him shift and soften when no one else had. I was so mad that I missed everything good about him the first time we collided.

"I like you." The words spilled out before I could stop them.

I blushed as soon as I said them, and I bit the tip of my tongue to stop myself from embarrassing myself further. I was never that forward. It was like I couldn't keep the feelings bottled up. They were too big to keep quiet.

Oscar looked surprised. Whatever he might've expected me to say after his admission, it wasn't that.

I took full advantage of his shock and threw myself at him like I'd been dreaming about the last few days. My heart felt like it was going to explode when our chests touched. I wrapped my arms around his neck and held on for dear life. I clutched him like he was a buoy in the middle of a vast and raging sea. I felt his hands reach for me. It was unclear if he was going to pull me closer or push me away, so I kissed him while I had the chance.

This kiss wasn't a performance. It wasn't for anyone other than me. I wanted to show him how much I liked him. I wanted to kiss him for the pure pleasure of it. I knew I had to get my fill while the opportunity presented itself. Good things didn't last very long in the Point, so if you missed your chance, you were pretty much shit out of luck. I wasn't ever going to let the things I wanted slip through my fingers again. It took a trip back in time to teach me just how important it was to have a solid grip on the things that mattered to me. And right now, that meant keeping a hold on Oscar Osborn because he was important to me.

This kiss was softer than the one that was for show.

I felt his breath brush against my lips and felt his fingertips rest on my waist underneath the hem of my short black t-shirt. The heat from his rough hands was scalding, and the taste of his lips against mine was addicting. I could taste the lingering hint of a cigarette, and the bitterness of black coffee when he let his tongue tangle with mine. The kiss was immediately deeper than I had prepared for, and my mind went a little cloudy with lust.

I felt his teeth tug on my bottom lip and his fingers dig into my sides. Everywhere we touched was hot, and almost instantly I knew I was in over my head. On the inside, I could fool myself into thinking I was wise and experienced, but my body would betray me. I lit up like a firecracker from a simple kiss and a small caress. Oscar thought I was an innocent little lamb, and I wanted to prove him wrong, but he took control of the kiss, and I surrendered embarrassingly easily.

I scraped my fingers over the short hair at the back of his head and pressed even closer to him. I knew he was strong and had a nice build, but it was a different feeling having him rub up against my own body. He felt hard and unbreakable against all the soft and vulnerable places on me. I was more excited, more stimulated than I'd ever been. It was as if every time I kissed him, a piece of the memories that weighed on me so heavily was chipped away. He hammered all my regret with an ease that I should find alarming, but instead was overwhelmingly grateful for.

The kiss went from soft and sweet to punishing and messy in a matter of moments. It felt like he was invading all my senses, and the noises I was making and the way he was sliding his palms across my skin under my clothing was not appropriate for a parking lot. Even a parking lot in the Point had standards. I was enamored with the skilled way he twisted and tangled his tongue with mine. This wasn't a sloppy, rushed make-out session. It was a seduction. Every second he was luring me closer with the flick of his tongue and the nip of his teeth. If his hands climbed any higher up my ribcage, the entire motel was going to get a view of the fancy undergarments teenage me liked to indulge in. He wreaked havoc on my sanity and made all my sensitive places throb. Everything was moving so fast, but I felt like time stood still. I wanted him almost as much as I wanted the chance to make everything in my life right. If I had to pick one over the other, I don't think I could.

I wanted to pull back and catch my breath, and maybe remind him this wasn't the right time or place to push these kinds of limits, but he broke away first.

Oscar was breathing hard, and his eyes looked darker than usual. His face was flushed, making the tattoos on the side of his neck and on his collarbone stand out. He frowned at me and took a step backward, his hands falling to his sides.

His dark eyebrows furrowed over his eyes as he cleared his throat. He lifted a hand to rub the back of his neck where my fingernails no doubt left marks. His reaction was sheepish and almost shy, but his voice was firm and resolute when he spoke.

"Don't like me, Vesper. I'm not a good guy. I wasn't back then, and I'm not now. Don't forget it's my fault we're in this situation. I didn't take care of the motel like I should've. If I did, there wouldn't have been a gas leak. I not only got you and me blown back in time, I'm responsible for everyone else who may have died or gotten injured in that explosion. I got you killed once already. You need to remember that no matter what. I don't want you any more involved in what I have going on this time around than I did in the original time frame. You're a good girl. I want you to be able to stay that way."

I was working my way through his words, vacillating between being hurt and offended, and feeling like I won a prize because he never said he didn't like me back, just that he didn't want *me* to like *him*. Some serious mental gymnastics took place as I thought about his words. I knew he was deeply affected by his brother's death, but I didn't realize he was carrying around so much guilt over what happened the night of the explosion. He didn't seem like he was feeling the weight of possible lives lost because of his carelessness, but maybe it was because he was too used to bearing a heavy load. I was stuck on the certainty of knowing that if bad things could keep happening to good people, wasn't it possible for the reverse to be true? Couldn't good things happen to bad people every once in a while? Wasn't that the kind of balance the universe demanded?

"You made a lot of mistakes back then. I get it. But you're doing the right thing now. You can't save your brother, but you can save this motel, the people who live here, and me. If you didn't care and killed everyone on purpose, you wouldn't be fixing all the things you did wrong the first time around. And you're wrong about me, Oscar.

I'm not just a good girl. I'm a girl who's going to do whatever it takes to protect the people I care about. That includes you."

I was fully prepared to be bad, if need be, whether he liked it or not. After all, it was always Bo Peep's job to protect her flock.

TEN

BLACK TIES AND BLOOD RED SHOES

After the kiss, Oscar went back to treating me like I was a nuisance he had to tolerate, rather than someone he wanted to be around. I spent the next week barely functioning at school because he went from answering me occasionally when I messaged him to completely ignoring me. He only texted back a couple of times, and that was to make sure we were still on for the fundraiser. It was as if getting into the swanky event was the only thing on his mind. He wouldn't even tell me if the shut-in had appeared again. All he said was, "Don't forget about Friday," and, "Make sure you're ready for the fundraiser on Friday." As if I could forget.

Not only did I have to make up an excuse to convince my Uncle Doyle to get me an invite, but I also had to lie to my father about where I was going. Easier said than done when I left the house in a sparkly white cocktail dress and spiked white high heels. I no longer had any friends whose houses I could go to and get ready. Homecoming and prom were already long gone. The only reason I could think to explain why I was so dressed up was for a friend's party. It was a hard sell because my dad was well aware I'd cut most of my previous ties. I was also conditioned to dress nicely and look cute in my previous existence, but to never overshadow the main character... Addison.

After a week spent seething and trying to avoid everyone who was out for my blood, I decided I was going to go all out for this not-really-a-date with Oscar. After all, I saw how amazing he looked in his tux, even if it wasn't his usual style. I wanted to look like I belonged next to him, regardless if it was all pretend. I wanted to show him I could be as much of a chameleon as he was. I could dress up and look like I stepped out of the pages of a fashion magazine, and I could dress down to blend in with the people in the Point. If he wanted someone adaptable, there was no better option than me. I was a girl who lived in both privilege and poverty. I had the skills to survive both. Maybe I could adapt and be a wolf in sheep's clothing, not as far removed from him and his lifestyle as he made it seem.

My dad asked some very confused questions about where I was going when he caught sight of my dressy ensemble, and he wanted to know exactly when I would be home. I wasn't going anywhere looking for trouble, which was mostly true. I was accompanying the boy who was bound to create chaos once he got inside the lavish event. I didn't want my dad to know I called my uncle for the invite. He was particularly sensitive where my mom's family was concerned. If he could, I knew he would keep me from them entirely. I think he was worried they would welcome me into the fold and chip away at all the values and morals he helped me build over the years. His worst fear was that I would end up a worthless trust-fund kid. I couldn't blame him. If things kept going the way they were in my original youth, I would've ended up living frivolously with no direction. I would've gone from being spoiled by a loving father to being spoiled by a wealthy husband. I would have been nothing but a trophy wife with no agency of my own. I shuddered at the thought.

To keep him calm and to cover myself, I assured him I was done with both Rex and Addison. I might run into Rex's family at the fundraiser, but I doubted the golden boy was willing to give up his Friday night to rub elbows with the country club set. His weekends were usually spent with teammates competing and celebrating wins.

And Addison and her mom were still lying low, trying to let the accusations I hurled at them so publicly die down.

It took some time to convince my dad to let me out the door. I didn't remember him being so protective and cautious. I guess he was worried about payback from scorned women. If Madison lost more than one husband through suspicious circumstances, there was no telling what she might do to a teenage girl. It was no secret she blamed me that her relationship with my dad fell apart. So, it was more likely I would end up the target of her wrath than my father would. I promised him I would watch my back and call him if anything odd cropped up. It was super weird to ask for permission and not go my own way like I was used to.

There were pros and cons to returning to my teenage self. The inability to be completely independent was one of the downsides. It grated on my nerves that I needed to be accountable for my whereabouts and actions. I knew he was only acting out of fatherly concern, but even in this timeline, I was technically an adult, and even more than that, I'd never once given him a reason to doubt me. All those years of being a goody-two-shoes should've earned me unlimited trust.

Once I finally finagled my way out the door, I called Oscar and told him I was on the way to our agreed meeting place. He told me he would come to me so I didn't have to take my car into the Point. He knew as well as I did it wouldn't last ten minutes once I drove across the train tracks. I wasn't sure how he planned on getting to the small coffee shop where we agreed to meet. But he managed to get through my school's security measures; he didn't need my help figuring his way around the hard-to-reach places in the Hill. And if he wanted to walk around in a tux, he wouldn't be out of place. There was always some sort of black-tie affair taking place on the Hill. Evening gowns and tuxedos in this neighborhood were as common as bikinis at the beach. The people who lived here were always looking for a way to flaunt their wealth. A ten-carat diamond needed a ten-thousand-dollar gown to go with it and numerous well-trained eyes to appreciate the value of both.

In the process of pulling my car to a stop in front of the coffee shop, the passenger door was pulled open. The sports car was still moving, so I gasped and pressed the pointed toe of my shoe on the brake. Oscar waved a hand in my direction like I was being dramatic, and kept his gaze focused straight in front of him.

"Even the coffee in this neighborhood is stupidly expensive." He grunted the complaint and started to tap his long fingers against the velvety black fabric encasing his thigh. His tux was black on black. It looked very modern and sharp. With the neatly trimmed hair and his penetrating gaze, he looked like a young celebrity on his way to collect some major award. He was going to stick out at the country club, even though he did his best to tone down everything that made him unique. There was no changing the sharpness of his gaze, the alert way he carried himself, or the hints of black ink from his tattoos that peeked over his collar and past his sleeves. It was evident that you could take the boy out of the Point, but there was no taking the Point out of the boy. Where he came from was buried deeply into who Oscar was as a person. The city was buried in his bones and honed his entire being.

We didn't say a word the whole way to the country club, but just as I pulled into the driveway through the actual golden gates and approached the small army of valets and door attendants, I glanced down and noticed Oscar wasn't wearing the shiny wingtips we got to go with his formal attire. On his feet were the black boots he always wore. They had obviously been cleaned and polished, and the laces were new. The ties were even velvet to match his tux.

"I don't know if they'll let us in if you're wearing those boots. They're pretty strict when it comes to black-tie attire." My voice was low, but it sounded disturbingly loud in the silence between us. It also sounded accusatory, which wasn't my intention. I was simply surprised since he'd made such a big deal about getting into the event.

This wasn't a real date. I knew that. But all the reason and rationale in the world couldn't stop my stupid heart from pounding at the sight of him. The rest of my body wanted to pretend we were going somewhere together, and I was disappointed that Oscar was risking it all because he couldn't leave his ties to the Point behind. I knew I was the silly one in the scenario, but that didn't stop my feelings from being hurt. I needed to get my head in the game. Nothing about the two of us made any sense. There wasn't even a way to explain how we were both back here to begin with.

"You're going in alone. I just needed a way past the gate. This one is the real deal. Not like the one at your school. If I need to find my way inside the clubhouse and around security, I will." Oscar turned his head and sent his gaze skimming over my outfit. "You look good. Did you dress like a virgin sacrifice on purpose?"

I cast a look down at my all-white outfit and fought back a pout. I thought the all-white looked sophisticated and more in line with my actual age. The color made my dark hair and pale eyes pop, and the shoes made my long legs look dramatic and eye catching. I wanted to put my best foot forward because I knew we were walking into a lion's den. But I also wanted Oscar to see me at my best, and maybe move his appreciation needle from totally emotionless to budding attraction.

"You told me I was a good girl. Figured I should play the part while it has its benefits." I sniffed and did my best to stuff my irritation down into a deep pit inside my stomach. I already felt like I was suffering from heartburn. Might as well add some unrequited love-related indigestion.

Oscar snorted. We reached the top of the circular drive that was in front of the country club and Oscar tensed up when valets came to both sides of the car. I saw him take a deep breath as he forced his features into a bland, neutral expression. I went to hand the keys to the valet, and I was shocked when Oscar intercepted them. He reached across the car to hand a sizable tip to the valet and quipped, "She never lets me drive this baby. Do you mind if I park it?" He gave the kid a look that only guys must understand because the valet relented shockingly easily.

He stepped out of the car and came around to open my door. When I frowned up at him, he winked at me and muttered, "Just play along."

I grabbed his hand when he helped me out of the car. He looked down at the touch with surprise, but quickly adjusted his features when he noticed I was watching him closely. I heard him take a deep breath and was alarmed when I felt just how tense his muscles were under the lux fabric of his tux. I didn't know what he was playing at, but this moment was clearly important.

"For the record, you don't need to dress in all white to look innocent and pure, Vesper. Your untouched soul and spirit shine out of you. It's in your eyes. It's in your smile. It's in the way you talk about the people close to you. You could walk around in nothing but leather and lace, and your inherent goodness would still show through. We can't hide who we are from people who are paying attention, even if we want to." His gaze drifted down to his boots, and a wry grin tugged at his mouth. "Case in point."

I didn't respond. What he said was kind but annoying. I was tired of everyone having some type of perceived image of the type of person I was. Oscar and my dad were obsessed with me being good. Tobi and Jordan thought I was a hero. Addison and Rex thought I was a pushover. Carlotta thought I was selfish and immature. Devon was annoyed by my mere existence. I was always going to be the specific fragment of Vesper they wanted me to be to make dealing with me easier for them, and I had to prove them all wrong in different ways. That was a lot of damn boxes to be separated into.

I wanted to dump them all out and put myself together how I saw myself. Those bits and pieces made one entire girl who was both good and bad. She was easy and hard. She was strong and weak. She was a hero to some but very much a villain in the making to others. I was frustrated that it seemed like I was only accepted on an all-or-nothing basis.

Shoving down my growing resentment, I walked up the stairs to the ornate doors of the club and watched Oscar pull away in my car. A bitter piece of my heart wondered if I would ever see either again after tonight. A uniformed man scanned my ticket at the door and gave me a quick once over. He tipped the bill of his bowler hat down and quietly said, "All non-members have to go through extra security. Club policy."

I was escorted to a side room where I was lightly patted down and had a security wand waved half-heartedly around me. It seemed like Oscar was already aware of the extra precautions in place for the event, which made his hasty retreat a little more palatable.

A sliver of suspicion slid under my skin, and unease tickled the back of my brain. I felt like there was something I was missing. The reason Oscar wanted to come to this party should be right in front of me, but I was having a hard time seeing it through the haze of everything else I'd been through lately. I shouldn't have agreed to bring him without forcing him to tell me why. I trusted him with no reservations because he saved me in the past, and because he was reliving his youth with me. I thought we had more big, cosmic things in common than little differences from coming from two different economic backgrounds.

I suddenly felt like a fool. I felt like I was being used... big time.

I did not know Oscar. Then or now. And just like how he wanted me to be something I wasn't to fit into his narrative, I wanted Oscar to be someone I imagined he was. I wanted a kindred spirit, one who didn't exist. All the things I liked about him were still there, but his unwillingness to share anything with me made him feel unreachable. I didn't care if he was the bad guy he kept insisting he was. I cared that he wouldn't let me get to know him, good or bad, regardless of how vulnerable and honest I was with him. I was irritated he refused to let me make up my own mind about him.

Wanting to kick myself for being so dumb about boys in both timelines, I sighed and pushed through the doorway of the massive ballroom, eyes scanning the beautifully decorated room in search of my uncle. The tall man with a flair for fashion should stand out among the crowd, but all the black suits and tuxedos made it hard to differentiate one rich man from the next.

I gritted my teeth in aggravation and stepped around a waiter holding a silver tray of champagne flutes. Finally, I saw my uncle and his husband across the room. It'd been so long since I'd seen him, I forgot how much he resembled my mother. The revelation took the wind out of me for a second, so I stood in the entryway, frozen in place. I pretended not to notice when he waved me over while I pulled myself together. I snagged one of the glasses of bubbly and downed it in one gulp before anyone could question my age—another annoying part of being eighteen again. I couldn't drink away my sorrows without breaking the law.

Eventually, I bobbed and weaved through groups of mingling, expensively dressed people. The crowd was older, and it occurred to me that I had no idea what they were even raising money for. Even with the demographic, I still recognized a couple of kids from my school and a few familiar faces who were at my dad's ill-fated wedding. They were all looking at me like I had lost my mind as I slipped through the crowd. My dad would find out I lied sooner than I planned if any of them ratted me out, which sucked.

When I thought I was doing something to help Oscar, like we were teammates, I wasn't concerned about my father's feelings. Now that I'd been left behind like dead weight, I regretted both the effort I put into my appearance and the lies I told to get me in the door. I didn't think I would be walking this road alone. Now that I was, I wanted to go back.

I was almost to the side of the room where my uncle and his husband were standing. I slowed my pace when another couple approached them. I wanted to thank him for securing me the hard-to-come-by invite, but my deeply ingrained manners kept me from interrupting adults when they were talking. I grabbed another glass of champagne and waited for a turn to speak to my uncle. Before the glass touched my lips, the sound of several glasses shattering filled the big ballroom. Many of the conversations faded out, and several snickers and quiet laughter followed the commotion.

I stepped around the waiter and watched as a young server, a girl who looked younger than me, burst into tears as a man next to her let out a belly laugh. He clapped his hands loudly and encouraged his friends who were gathered around to chuckle at the girl's misfortune along with him. I glanced around and quickly realized no one would help the humiliated girl. She stayed on the ground, shoulders shaking as she knelt among the broken glass. No one offered her a hand up. No one stopped to ask if she was okay. And no one seemed like they were going to question why she had the accident in the first place. But I took one look at the leering man standing over her and had no doubt he did something to the poor girl that caused her to drop the entire tray of drinks.

Silently fuming, I angrily slammed down the champagne flute in my hand and started toward the girl. I ignored my uncle when he called my name and refused to stop when another server subtly tried to block my path. By the time I was on the edge of where the carpet was soaked through with liquid that cost as much as a nice car, the man behind the mess had crouched down and was taunting the young girl.

"Not very steady, are you? How did you get this job? Let me guess, you had to prove your worth in other ways. I've been a member here for over fifteen years. I can make sure you get all kinds of benefits that they didn't tell you about when you applied."

I couldn't tell if the man was drunk or always a disgusting human being. Either way, I had enough of his harassment. It reminded me too much of those creeps who picked on the weak in the Point. But this was worse. Anyone using their position of power to coerce someone in a less advantageous position was just evil. It wasn't fair to force someone who literally had no other choice but to go along with whatever malicious thing you might have planned for them.

I bent over as much as my short, sparkly dress would allow and offered a hand to the girl. I glared at the lurking, laughing man as I helped the server to her feet. The glass from the flutes had cut her hands and her knees. She smelled like a bar floor, and I could tell she was fighting back tears. I didn't recognize her, which made me think she probably wasn't a local.

"Are you okay? You're bleeding. Let's find a first-aid kit and take care of those cuts." I gave her fingers a gentle squeeze and tried to pull her closer.

I bit back a swear word when the boisterous creep reached to pull her back. "Are you a member here? I don't think I've seen you around before, young lady. It's best not to interfere with staff. Who did you come with? I'll have to have a word with the member who sponsored you for the evening. We have standards at this club."

I chomped down on the tip of my tongue and forcibly yanked the girl away from the lecher. I didn't want to drag my uncle into a mess I created, so I didn't respond. I wrapped an arm around the shaking server and started to guide her out of harm's way. I wanted to tell her everything would be okay, but that would be a lie. There was no telling what would happen after offending any of the people in this room. Their reach was far, and their need to seem superior was all-encompassing.

"He touched me." The girl sounded like she was going to be sick. "I'm only a temp. I just showed up for this job because I need the money. Why is this worse than working on the other side of town?"

I was getting ready to reply when a meaty hand grabbed my arm and pulled me off balance. I swore I was never wearing high heels again, and any etiquette and desire to keep my cool fled as I was once again yanked around like a doll. I spun around and used both my hands to push the groper away from me. He stumbled back in surprise; eyes wide as he looked at me.

"Don't touch me. And don't touch her. Keep your fucking hands to yourself." I sniffed. "Creep."

The man caught himself and advanced once again. His neck was red above the collar of his shirt, and his face was flushed. "Who do you think you are, you little...."

"She's my niece. And Nelson Bell's only child. Think really hard about what you're going to say next, Alfred." My uncle appeared at my side. He took one look at the shivering girl next to me and silently offered her his tuxedo jacket. He was far more chivalrous than I expected him to be. "Are you all right, Vesper?"

I nodded and continued to glare at the man who grabbed me. "I'm fine. If I hadn't lied to my dad about where I was going tonight, I would be pressing charges against this jerk right about now."

The man with the grabby hands balked and looked apologetically at my uncle. "Sorry, Doyle. I had no idea you even had a niece."

My uncle snorted and looked at his husband, who appeared silently behind me as he helped the injured girl through the crowd toward an exit. By now, security was starting to investigate what was going on, and once again, I was the center of attention because I caused a commotion I would've never dreamed of starting in my previous life.

"Apologize to Vesper and to the young woman you harassed. She was just trying to do her job. I can always find another lawyer, Alfred. But I can't replace family. I hope you've just had a little bit too much to drink this evening. Otherwise, I'll have to consider filing a formal complaint with the club."

The man paled and looked like he was going to be sick. He stumbled through a halfhearted apology and practically ran away. He said something about needing to use the restroom and plowed through the crowd.

I turned to my uncle, prepared to heap praise and thanks on him when I was fully engulfed in a rib-breaking hug. I was stunned. In my previous life, my uncle had little to do with me. When I was on trial, he was nowhere to be seen. He didn't return any of my calls when I needed a shoulder to cry on after my father died. I had no idea what was behind his sudden change of heart, but I had to admit the tight embrace felt nice.

"I'm sorry the first time you asked me for a favor, it turned out like this. I've been waiting for a long time for you to turn eighteen.

I always hoped that you would take the time to make your own decisions about me once you were old enough. I know your father is against any interference from my family in your life, but I just want the chance to get to know you, if that's all right with you."

I was so baffled that all I could do was stare at him with my mouth hanging slightly open. "What if something happens and my name gets dragged through the mud? Would you still want to know me then?" I struggled to reconcile the man in front of me with my memory of the man who wasn't there when I needed him.

My uncle frowned. "I promise I will do my best to be there if you need me."

I frowned, trying to put my past into perspective. Someone from my mom's family found Carlotta when I needed her testimony the most. Someone from my mom's side made sure I had legal counsel. Someone from my mom's side did their best to keep the media out of my life once I was set free. Maybe my Uncle Doyle was behind the scenes all along. I never asked him for help because I lumped him in with the rest of my mom's family, but he might have been different. There had to be a reason he was my mom's favorite when she was alive. And he had gone out of his way to get me into this party without too many questions. The good and bad guys were getting all jumbled up in my mind.

I gave a weak grin and returned the hug. "I'll try to reach out more. Dad is still pretty protective of me, so I have to make sure he's okay with it. But I'd like a chance to get to know you and your husband better, as well. I appreciate you stepping in just now. It didn't seem like anyone would."

He snorted and smoothed a hand over his styled hair. "I tried to get to you before Alfred grabbed you, but that couple wouldn't move out of the way. I finally had to push past them. Everyone at this event thinks they are the most important person in the room. It's so annoying. I can't believe you wanted to come to this party on purpose." His eyebrows lifted. "Didn't you say you were bringing a classmate? Why are you alone?"

THE BEST BAD THINGS

I shrugged and allowed him to guide me to an empty cocktail table now that the commotion had settled down. "He's around. We had different reasons for wanting to attend. I wanted to see you, and he had to take care of something else."

My uncle smiled, and I felt like he could read the hidden frustration and subtext in my words.

"A fundraiser for the local hospital isn't exactly a great date. Other than the free drinks, it's boring. If my husband weren't a club member and on the board of directors for the hospital, I wouldn't be here either. Next time, let's try and find something more entertaining to do. Then maybe our dates won't ditch us."

I chuckled and settled into some comfortable small talk. Before I knew it, we were being ushered into another room for the dinner and auction portion of the event. My uncle kept a hand on my lower back as he looked around for his husband. I fought the urge to text Oscar to make sure he was okay, but as it turned out, I didn't need to ask.

As we were moving rooms, a new scene broke out among the elite as the lawyer with the busy hands suddenly burst out of the bathroom. He looked like he'd been beaten within an inch of his life. His eyes were swollen and his lips were split open. He was bleeding from his ears and his nose. He was holding his wrist and screaming that it was broken. He was wailing that he'd been attacked in the bathroom. Everyone who witnessed the scene looked shocked. After all, there was security, and they were all civilized creatures. Even my uncle looked taken aback. Fortunately, at an event for the hospital, plenty of doctors were in attendance and rushed to help the battered man.

"Well, I guess this shindig is more exciting than I alluded to earlier." Uncle Doyle snickered as security swarmed the area. The bathroom wasn't big, but there was no one inside. They immediately searched other parts of the country club for the attacker. I could've told them not to waste their time.

If Oscar didn't want to be found, he wouldn't be. I had no doubt he was the one behind the violent retribution. For a guy who used to steal cars, he had a righteous streak that ran a mile wide.

Sighing, I turned to my uncle and excused myself. I was done playing debutant. I needed some space to settle myself and figure out my next move with the boy who broke all the rules. My head was screaming at me that it was time to cut my losses and let him go. I understood I was overly attached to him because of the current time slip situation. I didn't want to navigate this weirdness alone. But my heart kept whispering I needed to keep him close. Not because we were both in a tough spot, but because he made me feel safe, no matter how dangerous he was. Out of everyone I encountered between the ages of eighteen and twenty-five, Oscar was the only one who never hurt me, at least not on purpose.

His "don't like me" still stung like a bitch. But it wasn't his fault I was falling for him.

I left the clubhouse and walked back to the valet. I quickly realized I didn't have my keys or valet stub because Oscar parked my car. The young kid who helped him when he first showed up looked embarrassed for me, so I resigned myself to taking off these stupid sparkly shoes and hiking down to the gate. I could call a cab or rideshare and figure out how to get my car back tomorrow when I wasn't emotionally drained.

I only managed to make it a few feet down the manicured drive before my sexy red car pulled to a screeching halt inches away from my bare toes. I blinked in surprise as the passenger door was shoved open from the inside. I bent down and locked eyes with a scowling Oscar.

"Get in."

I slid into the passenger side of my car and let my head flop back against the headrest. I was exhausted.

I closed my eyes as Oscar asked for directions to my house. He planned to drop both me and the car off without a word about what he'd been up to or even a mention of the beatdown he gave the lawyer in the bathroom.

I didn't want to tell him where I lived. I didn't want to be trapped behind another pair of gates tonight. And I didn't want to lie to my father any more than I already had today.

"Just take me to your motel. You can feed me since I missed the dinner we paid a thousand dollars to eat. You can explain to me what you were doing at the club. You're also in charge of making sure my car doesn't get stolen overnight."

He chuckled at my last statement and shot a look at me out of the corner of his eye. "I don't think there are any vacancies at the motel right now. You know how busy the weekends get."

I did. That's when the working girls and boys turned their biggest profit. It was also when the people who weren't from the Point came to the city searching for excitement.

I kept my eyes closed and shrugged. "Then I'll crash with you for the night." I had no more caution to throw to the wind, it seemed.

In my mind, spending the night with him seemed like an easy solution to my current predicament. However, if my eyes were open, and I had seen the look that flashed across Oscar's face, I would've known I was opening the door to all kinds of things that were anything but easy.

I had a lot of questions where he was concerned. That didn't mean I would like the answers.

ELEVEN

SLEEPOVER

My father had given me a curfew before he let me out of the house, and I had to turn off my phone once it passed. I let him know I was going to spend the night at a friend's. He called several times in a row and left a slew of messages letting me know he wanted me home. I knew he'd found out I'd been at the country club rather than a friend's party, but I wasn't in the mood to play the contrite teenager. I did feel bad for lying to him, but I was also frustrated at having to account for my every move. My emotions at the moment were more in line with my actual self. It was hard trying to find the proper balance between who I was and who I thought I wanted to be. In this lifetime, I understood I was going to disappoint others. I also knew that the people who really cared about me, those who loved me with no reservations, would forgive me for not being as perfect as I pretended to be.

When we got to the motel, Oscar surprised me by pulling my car into a locked storage unit in the lot next to the building. There was an old car already in the bay, but this one was in much better shape than the ones he usually tinkered with. It looked like it had all its parts and would actually run once he turned it on. He parked my sports car next to it and led me out of the structure. Once he rolled down the metal door, he chained the lock and even poked a security code into a panel near the entrance I hadn't noticed before. For the Point, these were top-of-the-line security measures. My car might still be around in the morning.

When he caught sight of my curious stare, Oscar lifted a shoulder and softly muttered, "It's Elliot's car. We worked on it together. It's almost finished. He died before he could take it out on the road. Along with getting this damn motel up to code, I'm going to finish this car for him. No one will mess with your ride while it's back here."

I was trying to wrap my head around the sweet and sentimental parts of him he rarely showed when he suddenly moved to take off his tuxedo jacket.

"What are you doing?" I was confused as he reached out to tie the velvet material around my waist.

He moved so that he could crouch down in front of me. He took the high heels I was still holding in my hand and ordered, "Hop on. You aren't walking anywhere in this part of town barefoot. Who knows what you might pick up if you do?"

I blinked a few times and cocked my head to the side as I considered the situation. "You're going to give me a piggyback ride?" He could've just asked me to put my shoes back on. It was only a hundred yards or so to the front of the motel. "Is this so you don't have to explain why you beat up that creep at the fundraiser and why you ditched me?"

"I could just throw you over my shoulder if you don't get your ass in gear. Your dress is pretty short, though. We might end up with a whole new set of problems if you flash your assets to the entire south side of the city." He lifted an eyebrow and looked completely unapologetic over being called out over his actions this evening. "That guy needed to be taught a lesson. He needed to find out what happens when he puts his hands on something that doesn't belong to him. Those entitled pricks get away with too much. Hard to harass the help when your arm is in a cast."

I climbed on and wrapped my arms around his neck. I gasped when he stood up, realizing he seemed even bigger and taller when

I was this close to him. My eyes locked on the black rose tattooed behind his ear, and my nose twitched when I caught a sweet scent lingering against his skin. Oscar didn't seem like he should smell like candy and roses. I was expecting something more abrasive. I guessed he would smell like something that matched his personality, something that hinted at how he spent most of his time buried inside a car engine or underneath the frame.

"Is this your way of apologizing for ditching me at the door of the club? It felt pretty awful when I realized you were using me. I still would've helped you get in if you were straight with me from the beginning. Are you afraid I'm going to try and talk you out of whatever you have planned for the people who killed your brother?"

I held him tighter as he shifted his hold on me. I felt one of his hands slide farther up my bare thigh, and his fingers dug hard enough into my skin that his hold was just shy of painful.

"No." He turned his head slightly, and my lips brushed against his ear. I felt his shoulders tense, and if I wasn't mistaken, he faltered a step as we rounded the corner of the motel. "I'm not afraid you'll talk. I'm afraid that I'll listen to whatever it is you have to say. I almost managed to believe if I stop this place from blowing up this time around, I'm off the hook for how fucked up I let everything get in the first place. You make redemption sound appealing when that's never been something I'm interested in finding."

My arms tightened reflexively around his neck, making him grunt in response.

"I'm not going to get in your way, Oscar. I can't explain why we're here. Maybe you're right, and it's so our fates can untwist. Maybe you're supposed to get locked up, just like you said. I'm not going to stop you." I doubted I could until he admitted my words carried weight with him. "But I don't want to be used by you either. I had enough of being that girl in my last life."

He sighed, and his hold tightened on my legs. "At first, I figured I *could* use you. What did it matter if I was going to prison or end up the same as my brother? We both got a second chance; that was already more than enough if you ask me. But then I realized I didn't want to hurt you again. It's not fair that you were a victim of my carelessness before. I don't want you to inadvertently become my accomplice now. I need your help to get into places a guy like me isn't welcome. I don't want your involvement to go any deeper than that."

He stopped in front of the door to the motel's office and I pushed it open. I breathed out a sigh of relief when I noticed Ms. Nam was behind the counter, not Devon. She was always so kind to me when I first moved here. She was a soft-spoken woman but didn't take any crap from the residents.

After Oscar dropped me on my bare feet, I moved forward and almost grabbed the older woman for a hug. She gave me a weird look when I greeted her enthusiastically, and I realized belatedly that she didn't know eighteen-year-old me. We were strangers. This woman had no idea that she had a hand in saving me when my life was at its lowest point.

"Uh... This is my friend, Vesper. She's friendly. She's not from around here. Where she's from, people hug each other without worrying about getting a knife slipped between their ribs."

The older woman gave a good-natured chuckle and asked if Oscar wanted her to stick around for the rest of the evening since he had company. He shook his head and sent her home. She gave me a look and whispered that she left dinner for him in his room and that was enough for two. It almost seemed like she was happy he brought someone home with him for the night. I even caught her flash Oscar a playful wink on her way out the door.

When it was just the two of us, I tried to turn the conversation back to his plans and why he was trying to keep me out of them.

"Tell me how the country club relates to your brother's death. You don't have to give me everything but give me enough so I can either help you or tell you to go to hell."

He started to unbutton his black dress shirt like he didn't have an audience. He tilted his head toward a door behind the counter that I figured led to an actual office. I walked through it, and I was surprised to find it opened to a pretty similar room to the other motel units. It was a bit bigger and set up more like a two-bedroom apartment. It looked well lived in and surprisingly homey. Well, homey minus the car parts scattered about on various flat surfaces.

When he saw me looking around, he finally offered some personal insight, "My mom took off when I was really little. My dad's family owned this motel for years. When my mom left, they let us move in and agreed to let him run it. Only, my old man was more interested in gambling than taking care of business. My brother was working the desk as soon as he could see over it. We had to do the housekeeping, the maintenance, the bookkeeping, all before we were old enough to drive. Elliot loved it. It kept him focused. He felt like he was giving back to the community and helping people who needed a hand. I always hated it. It felt like a place I worked, not a place I could call home. Now, I guess it's both."

I hummed in agreement and he pointed for me to sit on a bar stool with a cracked leather seat that was tucked under a small breakfast bar.

"I'm learning that things and people are rarely ever just one thing. Good and bad are subjective. Rich and poor share more than most people think. You can't appreciate one without having the other for comparison. Tell me about the fundraiser."

He grunted in agreement and moved to take a handful of plastic containers out of the fridge.

"I already told you that Ms. Nam identified the armed robbers as teenagers. And I told you I know they're not from the Point because of how they handled the robbery and the getaway car. What I didn't tell you is that right before Elliot died, he sent me a strange text message." Oscar closed his eyes briefly, and his hands tightened on the plate he was scooping food onto. "It was something only I would understand because I know cars inside and out. All kinds of cars."

I rested my chin on my hand and watched his face closely. "What did he say?"

Oscar chuckled, but it sounded sad. "Enzo's Cousin."

I tapped my fingers on the breakfast bar, frowning as he turned his back on me so he could heat up the food.

"Are you speaking in riddles? Who is Enzo? And why did your brother text you about his cousin when he was dying?" I liked to think I was fairly sharp, but I was thoroughly confused.

Oscar glanced at me over his shoulder. His lips twitched in a grin. "It's the nickname for a Maserati MC12. There are only fifty of them in existence. They are a true collector's car. Elliot was telling me to track down the getaway car. They're basically a street-legal race car. I figured anyone who has that kind of car has to be a member of that country club. I needed to get past the gates to see if I could find the car."

I tapped my fingers and thanked him for the food. It smelled heavenly, and my stomach growled in response.

"If you knew what kind of car you were looking for, why didn't you tell the police? Let that detective you mentioned track it down. That's their job, not yours."

He snorted and made a face that clearly showed his dissatisfaction. "I did tell the police. It's not enough for them to do anything. There are no pictures of the car on any of the surveillance cameras, and Elliot was bleeding out when he sent the text. It's not real evidence to anyone but me. I told you. When all signs point to the other side of town, no one wants to follow them."

He handed me a fork and I twirled it around in the noodle dish. "Did your little field trip tonight pay off at least? Did you find the car?"

He blew across the steaming forkful in front of him, and his eyebrows quirked upward. "I found it."

I was surprised enough that I paused mid-bite. "You did? Do you know who the owner is? What's the next move?"

"Rich people like to make sure everyone knows how much money they have. They put their name on everything to show off. Finding the owner won't be a problem. The car had personalized plates. It's not the owner I'm after, anyway. Has to be their kid who took the car and used it in the robbery. Fits with everything that went down that night." His gaze went hard, and his mouth tightened. "The car will get me to the person behind Elliot's death."

"What did the personalized plate say? It might be a name I recognize." I put the fork down when I was done eating and hopped up so I could clean up the mess he left in the kitchen. I figured I should do my part since he fed me without complaint and didn't put up a fight when I invited myself to crash at his place.

"WA11-ACE."

I paused as I was dropping the dishes in the sink. "Wallace. The plate said *Wallace*?"

"I guess that's what it was supposed to say. Why? You know who the owner is?" Oscar didn't strike me as guy who was invested in local politics. So, I wasn't surprised the personalized plate meant nothing to him in this lifetime or the previous one.

I debated telling him that he was already closer to his target than he could imagine. Part of me wanted to let him have a go at Rex; after all, the prick deserved it. I had no problem seeing him and his buddies from the swim team daring one another to do something deadly and dangerous in the Point. It totally fits with the reckless, entitled guy I knew Rex Wallace to be. But I couldn't stomach the idea of sending Oscar into the lion's den alone. Rex's family would stop at nothing if they knew he was in danger. Or, more accurately, if they knew the family's perfect image and reputation was on the brink of shattering.

I needed to think things through before I tossed a live grenade in Oscar's lap.

"I might. Honestly, the vague information you have fits more than one of the guys who go to my school. And several of the parents are into exotic cars. Let me ask around and see if I can pinpoint who it might be." I knew it was selfish, but I didn't want to see him do something that would send him to jail. I didn't want to be left in this alternate timeline alone. I couldn't sit by and watch him do something that might ruin his life a second time around.

"Fine. You do your thing, and I'll do mine. I'm going to find them one way or another." He sounded so certain that I had to swallow back the warning on the tip of my tongue. He might not be afraid of anything in the Point, but there were politics and unspoken protocols at play that he didn't stand a chance of going up against on his own.

I shook the soapy water off my hands and turned to look for something to dry them on. I rolled my eyes when he pulled off his unbuttoned dress shirt and handed it to me like it was a cheap paper towel.

Oscar smiled at my expression and shrugged. "It's not like I'm going to wear it again."

I used the black fabric to dry my hands and decided to take it home and wash it. I could consider it a souvenir and a reminder of the date that was never meant to be.

"Do you mind if I take a shower?" A lot had happened in a short amount of time, and I just wanted to wash the entire confusing, frustrating day away.

"Sure. You can crash in my room. I have to keep an eye on the front desk anyway." I guess that meant listening for the little bell over the door to ring. "I'll grab you something to sleep in. That dress doesn't look very comfortable."

I mumbled an agreement and followed him to the small bathroom. It was pretty clean, all things considered. There were no stray car parts on the countertops or in the tub, at least.

After closing the door, I turned on the water and looked at myself in the mirror. The face might belong to a teenager, but the gaze looking back at me belonged to a jaded twenty-five-year-old. I knew Oscar was going to be furious when he found out I not only knew the Wallace offspring but had spent a good portion of my high school days chasing after him like a lovesick fool. I could already picture the look on his face when he realized the bully he saved me from that day in the parking lot of my school was the person he'd been chasing in both lifetimes. He wouldn't want anything to do with me when he figured out how close I was to the person responsible for his brother's death. The thought made my blood run cold and had my dinner sitting like a lead brick in my stomach.

Everything was so complicated. I thought coming back in time meant I could clean up all the messes I made. I had no idea I would be making new ones. All I could do now was minimize the damage and hope I could protect Oscar and my father as the days dragged on.

I splashed cold water on my face, immediately smearing my makeup. I reached behind me to pull the zipper of my dress down, but no matter how far I contorted and twisted, I could only reach the top.

I was struggling and grunting when a soft knock came from outside.

"Are you okay in there?" Oscar sounded like he was holding in laughter. "I brought you a t-shirt and some shorts to sleep in."

I pulled open the door and scowled at him. "I almost pulled something trying to get this dress unzipped. Can you give me a hand?"

He finally let a chuckle out and dropped the bundle of clothes in his hands next to the sink. He put his hands on my bare shoulders and turned me around. Now I was facing the mirror, and he was behind me. The reflection should've looked ridiculous, but I thought we were well matched when I saw the two of us together. We shared a darkness that went beyond our coloring and personalities.

His hands were rough against my soft skin, and since he was still shirtless, his tattooed skin looked like ink against paper next to my paler complexion. I froze when I felt his knuckles drag across the back of my neck and down the top of my spine. Goosebumps lifted on my arms, and shivers shot through my body. For a simple favor, his actions were turning me inside out.

My back felt like it was on fire every place his fingers touched. Since I was so fair, there was no hiding the heated blush that worked its way across my chest and up my throat. My hands curled around the edge of the sink, and my knuckles turned white.

I wanted to ask him why he didn't put a shirt on.

I wanted to ask him why he was still standing behind me.

I wanted to ask him why it took so long for him to get one tiny zipper down.

But what came out of my mouth was, "I thought you told me not to like you."

The husky rasp of my voice shocked me. I didn't sound anything like I remembered eighteen- or twenty-five-year-old me sounding. It was like a strong, sensual stranger suddenly took over my entire being.

Hot lips touched my shoulder, and midnight eyes locked on mine in the mirror.

"I told you not to like me. I didn't say anything about me not liking you, Vesper." My breath stilled in my lungs, and the sound of the zipper finally going down filled the small space. "If you want to run, you should probably do it now."

Once the white dress was in a pool at my feet, and I could hear myself think over the sound of my thundering heart, I met the reflection of those magnetic eyes and told Oscar, "I'm not going to run."

I was going to like him no matter what he did.

TWELVE

VIRGIN SACRIFICE

Once my dress was on the ground and our gazes were locked, unwavering, in the mirror, there was a perceptible shift in the atmosphere between me and Oscar. He had no right to look as hot as he did while his rough hands slid across my smooth skin. Unable to handle the scene's intensity in front of me, I dipped my head and immediately felt my knees go weak when the sharp edge of Oscar's teeth bit into the back of my neck. Who knew my nape was so damn sensitive?

Apparently he did, because his tongue followed the bite with a soothing caress that had me ready to drop to my knees in front of him and pledge my undying devotion.

My experience in this area was limited, but I could already tell the way Oscar touched me, and how I reacted to him, was above and beyond any of my previous encounters. When it came to intimacy, the young girl whose life I invaded was far closer to who I was at the moment than the young woman who originally knew Oscar. I had a moment of panic he would be able to tell just how clueless and awkward I was when clothes started coming off, but he never gave me a chance to get caught up in my insecurities.

I was unable to think straight, so I couldn't worry about much of anything when his long, strong fingers deftly slipped under the fastening of my barely there bra. My undergarments were minimal, considering the dress was white and short. I only had on enough to preserve a touch of modesty. I was practically naked, standing in front of him once the dress was out of the way.

His lips skimmed across the top of my shoulder and up the side of my neck. His warm palm glided around my side and across my ribs, his knuckles lightly rubbing under the weight of my bare breasts. The heat from his bare chest burned against my back, and there was no mistaking the press of his cock once it hardened and lengthened where it was rubbing against my backside. All of it was a hundred times sexier and more seductive than anything I'd experienced before. There was something about the rough feel of his hands, and the soft way he used them to touch me, that was making it hard to think of anything other than falling under his effortless spell.

Oscar's lips nibbled their way up the side of my neck and kissed along the curve of my jaw. I had no choice but to lift my head and look at him once his tattooed hand wrapped lightly around my throat. Our gazes collided in the mirror once again, and I almost moaned when he winked at me. He kept my head locked in place as his mouth moved to my ear, and his other hand slid down my torso and danced against the edge of my very skimpy panties.

My breath caught, and when my eyelids fluttered from anticipation and embarrassment, Oscar used his teeth on the sensitive shell of my ear and ordered, "Keep your eyes open. If you blink, you might miss the good things."

I didn't want to miss anything with him, good or bad. But I'd never been so exposed or vulnerable before. When I was with Rex, everything that happened between us was a blur of desperation and dissatisfaction. It didn't feel real. I could tell he didn't care how I felt, and I was nothing special in his eyes.

Oscar was the exact opposite. Every touch, every word, every look he gave me while he dismantled my defenses showed me that he was as invested in this moment as I was. And it felt, very, very real. It also felt startlingly familiar.

I was overwhelmed. I turned my head to kiss him and get a moment to gather my thoughts. When our lips touched, it was surprisingly chaste and sweet. The kiss was almost innocent, which wreaked havoc on the rest of my senses. The fingers that were lightly touching my lower stomach suddenly dipped much lower. The way he handled me was anything but pure and unpracticed.

His fingertips slicked over warm, damp skin. My entire body clenched. The muscles in my legs started to shake, and I could feel my throat constrict under his other hand. My eyelashes quivered, and I couldn't believe the girl in the mirror was me. I'd never looked so sensual or so close to surrender. It was crazy that the young woman before me was having a life-changing moment because of the person behind her, even though her entire reality was topsy-turvy.

Everything important in my past and my present seemed to be centered around Oscar, so I could only whimper when I felt his fingers glide through wet folds and tender flesh to the unbearable heat inside.

My head jerked, and his teeth locked onto the lobe of my ear. The hand between my quivering thighs was gentle as could be, but everywhere he held me above my neck had a bit of an edge to it. Hard and soft. Sweet and something with more bite. Everything about him was made of contradictions, which made getting a handle on him a challenge.

I arched against him, my head grinding against his strong shoulder as his fingers dipped deeper. He lowered the hand he had wrapped around my neck so he could rub his palm across my flushed breasts. My nipples tightened into painful points, and my heart tried to jump out of my chest. I leaned into his caress and felt my body practically melt around the fingers stroking inside of me.

Guided by nothing more than raw instinct and the desire to make him feel as good as he was making me feel, I worked a pale hand in between our bodies and let my hand trace the hard muscles that I was pressed against. I skimmed the tips of my fingernails over his abs and down the length of the dark trail of hair that disappeared into his dress pants. I sucked in a breath when my fingers touched the warm, smooth tip of his very hard cock. The dress clothes were no defense against his arousal.

Still watching each other in the mirror, I dropped my hand into his pants in a similar way to how he was holding me. His erection was scalding against my palm. The rigid flesh filled my hand, and when I used my thumb to circle the soft head and stroke along the tiny slit at the top, his lean hips kicked against mine, and his fingers that were driving me closer to the brink of something big paused.

I whimpered at the pleasure I was so close to being denied, making Oscar chuckle into my ear at the sound. His lips landed on my cheek in a light kiss as his fingers playfully tugged at a puckered nipple. Once we were both slippery and wet with excitement, and as soon as our ragged breathing matched pace, Oscar suddenly moved to turn me around, so my ass was against the sink, and he was positioned between my splayed legs. I traced one of his bigger tattoos that ran from the hollow at the base of his neck all the way down to his belly button as he carefully helped me ditch the last of my clothing. It was easier to look him in the eye when he straightened because I didn't have to watch myself lose my mind over him.

His dark eyes were bottomless, but the shadowy color was full of life. He looked hungry. Like he wanted to eat me alive. I had no complaints about that plan as he lifted me so I was perched on the edge of the sink. His pants dropped to the floor, the black material a dark pool next to my discarded dress. Oscar reached past me to the medicine cabinet on the wall and pulled out a small, square packet. He gave me a couple of seconds to weigh in on the progression of things. He might've told me my chance to run had come and gone, but the boy was all about consent along the way. I had no idea a man asking for the all-clear could be so damn sexy.

I gave a tiny nod and wrapped my arms and legs around him. His body was lean and cut with defined muscle. He had tattoos in places that looked like they hurt, and some were even in spots I couldn't imagine him letting anyone get close to with a tattoo machine. I was so caught up in looking at him that I didn't see the kiss he aimed at my mouth coming.

His lips touched mine, and he pressed against me so that all the softest and most tender parts of my body touched the hardest and most unyielding parts of his. I wasn't the kind of girl who jumped into bed with a boy because he was pretty, but I guess I was the kind who let a boy fuck her in the bathroom because he said he liked her. Maybe I was too easy where Oscar Osborn was concerned, but I couldn't find any regrets.

We were never supposed to be here like this in the first place. Our fates were not meant to align in such a way. And once he found out I was keeping some very important things from him, like how close I was to Enzo's Cousin, he would go back to pretending like I didn't exist. I wasn't above taking advantage of the current situation once it presented itself.

Only, I forgot something very important. As soon as Oscar used his thumb to press his erection down and lined himself up with my noticeably slick and shiny opening, every part of my body tensed. The barest tip of his thick erection slipped into my entrance, and it felt like I was being torn in half.

I gasped and put my shaking hands on his broad shoulders. My eyes teared up, and I bit my lip as I pushed him back a few inches. Fathomless eyes watched me curiously as I blushed from the soles of my feet to the roots of my black hair.

"I forgot." I waved a weak hand over our suggestive position. "This Vesper hasn't had sex yet. She's still a virgin. I got wasted on cheap margaritas when I was on a graduation trip and slept with that guy you met in the parking lot. Before that, my experience was limited to mostly heavy petting and the occasional oral situation. I was a good girl, remember?"

Oscar blinked at me, and the corner of his mouth kicked up. "You're a virgin?"

I swore at him and smacked a hand on his chest. "Technically." I sighed as he stepped back; some of the heat circulating between us bled out of the room. "That doesn't mean I want you to stop. It just means we might have to move a little slower." I sniffed and gave him a serious look as he gave a regretful look at his latex-covered cock. "I'd much rather give it up to you than that idiot from my school anyway."

For the second time that night, Oscar snorted and moved to pick me up and carry me from one place to another. This time I was wrapped around him like a naked koala as he stepped into his darkened bedroom. It looked like he cleaned it up and changed the sheets on the bed while I was washing my face. He dropped me on top of the dark blue comforter with little ceremony.

"The last time I slept with a virgin was when I was one myself. I don't recall the experience being all that great for her. It sucks you have to go through it a second time. But I know more now than I did back then, so I can do my best to make sure you don't regret doing it with me like you do that other guy."

I wanted to reassure him that I wouldn't regret it. I wanted him in a very different way than I had convinced myself I wanted Rex. They were as opposite as two men could be. Rex represented my previous life, and Oscar was like a prize for surviving the life I'd been forced into when everything went sideways. I didn't get the chance to explain that sex had never been much fun, even after ditching the silly discomfort that came along with being a newbie. What I experienced with him was already heads and shoulders above my previous encounters, and we hadn't even reached the main event.

Once I was positioned on the bed, Oscar crawled over me. It was like he silently decided we needed to start all over from the beginning.

He started by touching me everywhere.

He kissed me from the top of my head to the inside of each knee.

He told me things I never thought I wanted to hear, but each word in his raspy, ragged voice sent tendrils of delight twisting through my blood.

He was softer this time around. He treated me like I might shatter if he made the wrong move. It felt like being worshiped, revered. It felt like being special to someone.

It was everything that had been missing the first time I did this.

There was no rush, no clumsy hands, and no confused kisses. There was no panic or worry over whether I was doing the right thing or not. I didn't hold any profound ideals about virginity being some big gift one person gave to another in my real life. I was thoroughly jaded because my experience with sex and salvation was so skewed by my previous terrible choices. However, being with Oscar made me view it differently.

Being with him, letting him see me at my most vulnerable, and watching him be more careful with me than he'd ever been, seemed like an overwhelmingly important moment between the two of us.

It was give and take. It was sharing something that could only happen once...very much like our weird time slip that couldn't be explained.

He used more than his fingers to drive me out of my mind this time. He put his mouth to work, making sure every part of me felt like it was electrified and alive. I shifted my legs restlessly, wanting more but not sure what to ask for. I missed his candy-colored hair. There was nothing there to hold onto and pull him closer. All I could do was moan his name and arch my back off the mattress. I couldn't string a coherent thought together, but I knew I was on the brink of breaking apart inside. Pleasure lashed through me to the point it was almost painful. When I was eighteen, I'd yet to fully figure out how to manage my own needs, so a full-body orgasm where I blanked out and felt fully satisfied was rare. The looming feeling Oscar was pushing me toward was intimidating. A tiny piece of me was terrified that if I let him shatter me, I wouldn't be able to put myself back together.

There was no holding back the tide when he swirled his tongue around my clit. My insides clenched, and I let out a startled scream. My body bowed off the bed as pleasure bolted through me. My vision went white for a split second, and I couldn't catch my breath.

I thought I reached the pinnacle of satisfaction when Oscar shifted, and I felt him moving between my jelly-like legs. He looked down at me with a smirk, dark eyes glittering.

"Have to make sure you get off at least a little bit, so this first time is better than your last one."

A surprised giggle escaped, but a gasp quickly replaced it as he started to press his thick and heavy erection into my soft, fluttering opening. This time I was ready for the stretch and the feeling of being filled up. My body was pliable from the orgasm, so he didn't have to put too much effort into sliding inside the welcoming warmth. I felt my inner walls contract around his length, and a shiver of delight shot down my spine when he bit out a tense swear word. He touched his forehead to mine and whispered, "It feels like you're pulling me deeper. Like you don't want to let me go."

Once he was fully seated inside, and the minimal discomfort had passed, he gave a look I couldn't read and started to move.

My body tried to mold itself to him. It pulsed and throbbed with his movements, letting him hit places that forced embarrassing sounds out of me. It was good. So much better than it had been before. Some parts of me still ached and felt a bit tender, but those sensations were buried under desire and the need to make this good for him. I wanted him to remember this moment in the way I knew I would.

"I don't think I've ever wanted to fuck someone so well that they're full of me and only me. You do something to me, Vesper. I can't tell if that's a good thing or a bad thing. Hard to think about anything but being inside you."

I didn't need those words, but they were nice to hear. He was sweet in his own unruly way.

One of his hands curled into my side as his hips started to thrust wildly. His breathing grew harsh, and his cheeks turned pink enough it was noticeable even with his tanned complexion. He dropped his face to rest in the curve of my neck, and I felt his teeth lock on the spot where my pulse was rapidly fluttering. A much quieter and more mellow climax climbed through my spent body. It wasn't one that rattled my bones and shook my soul, but it was languid and warm. It felt good in a different, more comforting kind of way. It was the kind of completion that let me know I made the right choice and showed that my body was indeed capable of responding in many different ways to the right partner. My second first time was the one I always wanted. It was more than any young woman could wish for.

My previous self was looking in the wrong direction for the guy of her dreams all along.

Oscar's orgasm followed. He grunted and used the tip of his tongue to lick a long line up my throat. He shuddered against me, his hard body eventually going soft and settling on top of mine. We were sweaty and sticky, but I couldn't recall a moment where I'd felt more satisfied or sleepy.

I was having a hard time keeping my eyes open, but I really needed a shower. Now more than ever.

"It's been a minute since I went through more than one condom in a night." Oscar chuckled as I playfully socked him on the arm. He yawned, which made me yawn even bigger.

I rubbed my tired eyes and sighed. "I still need to take a shower." And to figure out what I was going to do the deeper I got involved with him.

The complications between us seemed to grow by the minute, right alongside our feelings.

THIRTEEN

RUDE AWAKENING

I slept surprisingly well, considering the familiar sounds of gunshots and wailing sirens echoed long into the night. Maybe I was immune to the noise from living here before. More than likely, the sense of security I got when I was around Oscar followed me into my subconscious. Or it could be I was wrung out from hours of intense sexual activity. I didn't know if it was medically possible to fall into a sex coma, but if it was, that's probably why I couldn't remember much after Oscar climbed into the small shower with me and especially after the third or fourth orgasm. One minute I was writhing against the chipped tiled wall while his hands and mouth took me apart. The next, I was wrapped up all cozy and comfy in his bed, trapped under the weight of his tattooed arm.

I rapidly blinked and turned my head, trying to figure out what pulled me out of such a deep sleep. I had to squint against the daylight peeking in through the threadbare curtains while I gathered my bearings. I tried to shift under the weight pinning me down, but Oscar didn't budge. I strained my ears and stiffened reflexively when I realized that it was more than likely the bell above the front door that disturbed my sleep. It was the only sound that didn't fit in with the usual ruckus of being in the heart of the city.

I tapped Oscar on the back and called his name, hoping he was a light sleeper since he was used to waking up at all hours to deal with people checking in and out of the motel.

No such luck. He didn't move, and the arm thrown across my chest, as well as the leg covering mine, seemed to tighten.

"Oscar. You need to get up. I think someone is at the front desk." I pushed against his side and frowned when I thought I heard the door to his apartment open and close. Sure enough, soft footsteps soon followed the sound. "Seriously. Someone is coming. Get up."

All I got was a disgruntled grunt in response.

I didn't know who might have a key to come and go into his place. My best guess was Ms. Nam. And while I really liked and appreciated her, and even though she seemed to approve of my spending time with Oscar, I didn't need her to find me enjoying my very first morning after. Regardless if I was eighteen or twenty-five, there were still some things I needed to learn to navigate maturely and gracefully.

However, I knew the worst-case scenario was more likely.

I had a sinking suspicion Devon was about to burst through the bedroom door, and whatever was going to follow wouldn't be pretty. She was his brother's ex-girlfriend. She said they all grew up together. If anyone was likely to have a spare key, it was her. She'd made her dislike of me clear on several occasions. Devon was in no way subtle with her emotions. I wouldn't have been taken in so easily if Addison was anything like her when we first met. I remembered Oscar telling me he preferred the Point because he liked knowing exactly who his enemies were rather than having to guess. What he said made much more sense to me now.

I stretched my fingers out, trying to grab the discarded t-shirt I never got the chance to put on. I just got a handful of it when the bedroom door opened. The sound was exceptionally loud in the dark and quiet room. I shoved Oscar's arm away and crawled into the soft t-shirt just as my eyes locked with Devon's.

I watched as her pretty face ran the gamut of emotions. She started happy, but her smile quickly turned to a frown when she saw me. Sadness flashed across her features, and anger slowly twisted her expression into something ugly and harsh. She started to shake, and each step she took toward the bed was unsteady.

I sucked in a breath as Oscar finally rolled over and opened his eyes to take in the situation. He looked kind of cute, all sleepy and slow, but his gaze sharpened instantly when he caught sight of Devon reaching for me as she approached the side of the bed.

I yelped in alarm and did my best to scurry out of the way. I hated that I felt like the interloper. Like I wasn't the one who belonged. That might've been true in the sense that the current me shouldn't even know Oscar existed. But the old me might not have made it without him. I owed him so much and wanted to save him more than Devon would ever be able to understand. It didn't matter how close the two of them were.

I still hated confrontation, but I was no longer the girl who cowered in fear when faced with an opponent. I don't know if living in the Point strengthened my backbone, or if it was the cosmic redo of the worst parts of my life that stopped me from being a pushover. Whatever it was, I planned to preemptively end whatever argument Devon wanted to start with me.

I held up a hand and crawled over Oscar so I could climb off the other side of the bed.

"Whatever you have to say is between you and him. I'm not going to be in the middle of it. I know you want me to be the bad guy in this scenario, but I'm not. I don't want to invalidate your feelings. I know you both lost someone very important to you, and there is a long history between all of you. I have no plans to impede on any of that. I'm not a part of whatever is going on between the two of you, so I'm getting out of here before you can villainize me." I pointed at Devon and then cast a look over my shoulder in Oscar's direction. He looked pretty annoyed, but he stayed silent while I did my best to diffuse the tense situation. The vibe in the room was oppressively heavy. I hated it. "And I'm not going to be an easy excuse for Oscar. If he tells you he's not into you because he's into me, don't believe him. I think there are a lot of hidden truths you're both dancing around that need to be addressed, so I'll just see myself out."

My dress was still in a heap on the bathroom floor, and my shoes were God knows where. My car was still locked in the storage unit behind the motel, and I'm sure my dad was livid with me for going radio silent after I didn't go home. None of that was as daunting as getting around the enraged girl who felt slighted and betrayed by the boy she was in love with.

Oscar swore and dragged his hands down his face. He threw the covers to the side and climbed out of bed. He stood and ran his hands over his short hair with little regard to modesty.

"Let me take you to your car." He sounded cold, but it wasn't directed at me, so I simply nodded and scurried around to collect everything I had left scattered the night before while he got dressed.

Devon followed once he came out of the room, but Oscar made sure he kept himself between the two of us. He watched her with one eye and me with the other. I got the feeling he had a lot he wanted to say to both of us and couldn't quite figure out which of us needed the words more. Every time she opened her mouth to speak, he would gesture with his hand, and she immediately quieted down. It was interesting to see that she was scared of him under the right circumstances.

I turned on my phone, and it immediately exploded with notifications. I sighed and waved the device around so he could see it. "Don't worry about me. I have my own problems to deal with." Plus the added one of lying through my teeth to him about Rex last night.

Oscar nodded and told Devon to wait for him as he guided me out of the motel toward the makeshift garage. While we were walking across the parking lot, I noticed the door to the shut-in's room was cracked open. I wanted to run and see if I could catch them, but Oscar was holding my elbow in a tight grip, and my stupid shoes were not made for speed.

"I've told her repeatedly how I feel about her. We're friends. And that's all we'll ever be. Devon just lives in her own little world. If she feels strongly enough about something, it doesn't matter if those feelings are reciprocated or not. She likes me enough that she thinks it'll make up for the fact I don't like her at all. She ruined her relationship with Elliot because she convinced herself she was in love with me. She broke his heart, and just like you said, I became the bad guy." He shook his head as he entered the code to the garage. "I don't mind being a villain, but I hated having my brother look at me like I was in the wrong. I fucked a lot of shit up in my life, but I always tried to do right by him. He was the one good thing I had. He really cared about her. One of the best things about getting to come back and do this shit all over again is that I never slept with her this go-round. I hated myself for a long time for that lapse in judgment."

I cringed, scrolling through the many messages from my dad. He was worried and a bit frantic. I was lucky he hadn't called the police yet.

"Breaking someone's heart doesn't necessarily make you a bad guy. It's far worse to lead someone on. Believe me. I've been there. Your brother understood that. He wouldn't have offered himself up to save you if he didn't see something in you that was redeemable. If you owe him anything, it's making sure his sacrifice meant something this time around. Don't let what he did for you go unappreciated. I know if we went back just a little bit farther, you would've been behind the desk that night instead of him. Something bigger than either of you decided what's done can't be undone, so take that as a sign to live like your brother would've wanted you to."

He looked down at me after the metal door to the bay opened. He gave me a crooked grin and reached out to smooth down a piece of my dark bangs. "When you say stuff like that, it really makes me afraid I'm going to start listening to you. I'm sorry things were crazy this morning. At the very least, I owe you breakfast, and I'll do my best to get my extra key back from Devon."

I lifted up on my toes and placed a soft kiss on the curve of his jaw.

"Do whatever you think is right. I meant what I said. I'm not a factor in whatever goes on between the two of you. I need to get home. I don't remember my dad being so overprotective before. It's sweet but a bit overbearing."

"Be glad you have him around to be overbearing. I'd give anything to get the chance to have my brother be disappointed in my dumbass again." I patted his bristly cheek because he sounded so sad. Oscar was very good at putting things into perspective. He's right. I shouldn't complain about being cared about.

"I'll be in touch. Don't forget to try and talk to the hermit if she shows herself. I think she was looking out her door when we left this morning."

Oscar opened my door and dipped his chin in acknowledgment. I froze when he replied, "You don't forget to keep an eye out for whichever kid at your school filched that car from their parents. I'm going to see if I can get the detective who busted me to run the plates. It might be worth a shot."

I mumbled an agreement, then I couldn't make my getaway fast enough. I felt terrible for not being upfront with him, but not bad enough that I was willing to let him take on the Wallaces and the Hill elite on his own. We may have made it through a massive explosion together, but the inner workings of the incredibly wealthy felt far more dangerous.

I sent a message to my dad, letting him know I would be home shortly. I did my best to put myself together with whatever I had on hand in the car. I still looked pretty ragged, and not at all like a proper young lady. It was definitely the first time my father would see me looking like something the cat dragged in… or like a typical teenage girl who went a little wild on a night out. I always did my best to appear so removed from any of those shenanigans; it was going to be a shock for him to see just how far I'd fallen. That pedestal was long gone in this lifetime.

I'd just pushed open the door and called out a greeting when my phone started to ping wildly once again. Carlotta swooped by, took one look at me, and clicked her tongue. I shot her a bemused grin. I shook my head when she asked if I was hungry, and I agreed with her when she muttered that I should shower and clean up before my dad saw what state I was in. Only a moment later, I couldn't move.

The group chat I used to be in with Addison and all our friends was going crazy. They must've forgotten to remove me from the list. Either that, or they wanted me to see why everyone was going feral. So were all my social media notifications. I got a sinking feeling deep in my stomach, and when the first image popped up, I dropped my phone to the floor.

I never got the chance to put myself together because a second later, my father came flying around the corner looking like the hounds of hell were chasing him. He took one look at me and practically skidded to a halt in the entryway.

"Do you have an explanation, young lady?" His tone was surprisingly harsh, and the expression on his handsome face was one I'd never seen in either lifetime.

I gulped and crouched to pick up my phone. The picture staring at me wasn't totally scandalous, but it was far more of me on display than I ever intended. With everything going on, I forgot that I let Rex Wallace convince me to send him some sexy snaps at one point in time. I was too self-conscious to send full nudes, thank the good Lord. Still, the pictures I did send showed plenty of skin and were in no way appropriate.

"Do you want an explanation for why I was at the fundraiser? Or one for why I stayed out all night? Or how about one trying to explain these pictures and how they got out?" I let out a strangled laugh and let my head drop. "The pictures might be the easiest one to tell you about."

He reached out and grabbed my phone. I tried to protest but realized it would be futile. Any parent would take their kid's phone when pictures like that circulated the internet.

"I sent the pictures to Rex before I came to my senses. I'm sure he's the one who posted them. Or he sent them to Addison, and she posted them. They both have reasons to be mad at me. I know it looks bad, and your PR team is going to have to work overtime, but you have to know I never meant for them to get out." I sighed. "I can't believe I was ever this stupid." I was starting to think I deserved all those bad things I was lamenting about at the beginning of this bizarre journey.

"Do you have any idea how something like this is going to impact your future? These pictures are going to live on the internet forever. Every school you apply to, every job you interview with, they're all going to see you in your underwear. And what about the legal ramifications? It may seem like harmless flirting between teenagers to you, but sending pictures like this can be considered distributing child pornography because you were not eighteen when you sent them. Not to mention the horrors happening with deep-fake technology these days. You might be covered up a bit in these pictures, but that can change in an instant if they fall into the wrong corner of the web. I don't know what's gotten into you lately, but I feel like I hardly know you anymore, Vesper."

I shook my head and huffed out a frustrated breath. "I know, Dad. Things have been weird lately. I can't explain all of it, but some of it is just a byproduct of me growing up. I'm going to make mistakes every now and then. You have to let me fall on my face, so I can learn to get back up and brush myself off. As for the legal end of things, if I get in trouble for sending them, I'm taking down the person who asked for and shared them. That sword cuts both ways." I was reeling on the inside even though my words sounded calm. I thought I would come back to rewrite history, but I had a sinking feeling my graduation and valedictorian title were slipping through my fingers once again. I could deal with the educational stuff backsliding, but I was terrified that the implications of not being able to right those wrongs meant I wasn't going to be able to stop my dad from dying either.

If I had the choice to go back and save him, I would always pick that option rather than moving forward into the unknown, even with my growing, overwhelming feelings for Oscar taking flight. It didn't feel like I had to pick one over the other, but I recognized my dad would never be able to save himself, whereas Oscar was completely capable. My father needed me in a way Oscar never would. Plus, I had serious doubts that my future with the colorful boy from the Point was going to be anything other than dead on arrival after he found out how closely I was tied to the person he hated the most. If I had to sacrifice my own happiness to keep my father from dying, I would do it over and over again. Just like he had done for me time and time again after my mother left us to fend for ourselves.

My father gave me a considering look, followed by a heavy sigh. "Some mistakes are easier to bounce back from than others. If you want to spend time with your mother's family, I won't stop you. If you want to stay out all night, as long as I know where you are and I can reach you, we can come to some kind of compromise. I trust you because you've never given me a reason not to. The pictures are an entirely different issue we need to deal with." He turned and started to walk away. "I'm keeping your phone for now. I don't think you need to see what people are saying about those images. I'm going to have Carlotta take your laptop for the weekend as well. Go get cleaned up and we can sit down and talk about where you were last night and what you've been thinking lately. I'll see what I can do to stop the pictures from spreading further than they already have."

He didn't give me a chance to argue. I had no choice other than to accept the mild punishment.

I kicked off my shoes and headed to my room. Back in my original youth, those sexy pictures had been used by the prosecutor to show how I was acting out and behaving unlike my normal self. They used them to prove further discord in my relationship with my father.

Thinking about the hand I had in my own destruction just served to piss me off even more.

Maybe I should reconsider letting Oscar do whatever he wanted to Rex. The bastard deserved some serious retribution and down and dirty street justice.

FOURTEEN

TATTLETALE

Sure enough, on Monday when I went back to school, I was immediately called into the headmaster's office and told the school needed to launch an investigation. They thought it best if I took a few days off. They tried to frame the suggestion as a way to protect me and look out for my mental well-being, but I could read the room. They were looking for a reason to oust me. The school was still trying to gloss over the whole plagiarism incident, so the last thing they needed was a sex scandal involving their top students. Though it was crystal clear all the accountability was going to fall on me, no matter how much I insisted that Rex was the one who was behind making the pictures public. Without proof, I was the one in the wrong and made the school look bad.

My dad was not thrilled with the outcome. He promised swift and severe legal recourse, but the administration remained unswayed. I was still sent home for at least the next few days so as not to cause a disturbance. It was no secret the sexy pictures had traveled throughout the school's student body, and several other parents had already called to complain. I was the center of attention even more than I'd been following the canceled wedding. With finals coming up, the headmaster insisted it was too distracting to have me in class right now. I agreed to leave quietly for the time being, but I made it known that if my ability to graduate on time and my class rank were in any way affected by the current situation, I would fight tooth and nail to receive the awards I worked for. I got the impression they believed my dad would back down because of the bad press bound to follow the pictures, but they had no clue he cared far more about me than his public image. Because he was so successful, everyone tended to forget he was not a byproduct of the Hill, and that their longstanding protocols couldn't keep him in line.

When I left the school, I could feel the laughter and pointed fingers following me. It was harder to brush off this round of ridicule because I was the one who painted the target on my back. I hated how simple my mind was when I was originally a teenager. Rex didn't even have to work very hard to get me to agree to send those damn pictures. As long as he dangled the carrot in front of me, I followed. I even asked Addison for advice before I took them. She was the one who told me not to send anything fully nude. She insisted it was too basic to send something where everything was on display. She told me boys needed a bit of mystery to stay interested in a girl, and I took her at her word. Looking back, I don't know why she saved some of my dignity, but she was the only reason I wasn't naked in the pictures.

After I pulled out of the gates, I was supposed to head directly home. My dad wanted me to meet with his lawyer and a person from his PR team. I told him I needed to take care of something first. I could tell by his brisk response that he regretted giving me my phone back and returning my car keys.

Regardless of having to face his ire when I got home, I drove through the winding streets of the Hill across the train tracks and into the Point.

Since my destination was the police station, I figured there was a good chance no one was going to steal my car when it was parked out front.

I'd never been in the police station on this side of town. I was alarmingly familiar with the high-tech and ultra-modern station located only a few streets over from my school. When I was arrested, I remember thinking the building looked more like the headquarters of a Fortune 500 company than a police station. The cop shop in the Point was on the other end of the spectrum. It was old and outdated. It looked like it was being held together by duct tape and prayer. That being said, it felt more authentic than the police station on the other side of town. These law enforcement officers were not in the game because they were looking to further some sort of career agenda. They were doing the dirty work because someone needed to do it, even in a place where crime paid more than any other occupation.

I got a few odd looks when I walked in through the heavy front doors. I glanced down at my burgundy and black school uniform and instantly felt out of place. However, the uniform was bound to give credence to the information I wanted to pass on to the detective working on Elliot Osborn's murder.

The cop at the front desk barely held back an eye roll when I asked if I could speak to someone about the robbery and homicide that occurred at the motel on the south end of town recently.

He frowned at me and asked, "How do you know what's on the south side of town? You don't look like you're from around here. We don't have time to entertain you spoiled rich kids just because you're bored and want to see how the other half lives."

I couldn't blame him for his prejudice. The disdain was warranted and went both ways. Why wouldn't they? Those who were economically disadvantaged have been given plenty of reasons to negatively view the well-to-do.

I took a calming breath and wrapped my hands around the strap of my purse. I held it so tightly that my knuckles turned white.

"Can you please point me in the direction of someone who might be interested in what I have to say? I promise I'm not here to waste anyone's time. Do you think I would've skipped school to come down here if it wasn't important? I'm sure you've heard how expensive tuition costs."

The cop looked even more irritated, but he must've agreed with something I said because a moment later, a very tall, very attractive man came through a locked door and gave me an almost friendly smile. He was too big and intimidating to come across as congenial, but his face looked like something gifted by the gods. I wondered if it was payback from the universe that so many of the men who called this crime-riddled part of the city home were so devastatingly handsome. It was so much easier to get away with doing all kinds of wrong things when you made sin and subterfuge look so good.

He was dressed nicely, but not in anything designer. He also had an expensive haircut that looked chic, especially the silver at his temples. He could pass for one of my father's associates any day— the only things distinguishing him as a cop were the gun and badge clipped on his hip.

I was leery of the police after my arrest. I didn't trust them to be fair and impartial, but this guy gave off vibes of being upright and trustworthy. I wondered if I would've been railroaded as effectively if I'd been arrested by someone like him rather than the cops who were more interested in making a name for themselves than the truth.

"I'm Lieutenant King. I can take any information you have to the detective working the case you're inquiring about. Why don't you tell me what brought you in today? Can I get you a glass of water or some coffee?"

His voice was very deep and had a reassuring rumble. I could listen to him talk all day, but there was no missing the sharp, shrewd look in his eyes.

I shook my head and folded my hands together once I took a seat next to his messy desk.

"I'm fine, thank you. I'm sure you can tell from my uniform I go to Hollyoak. I wanted to come in today to tell someone that I think one of my classmates is connected to the robbery and murder that happened at the motel on the other end of town recently. I've heard rumors that a very rare supercar was at the scene. One of the guys

THE BEST BAD THINGS

on the swim team, Rex Wallace, just happens to have access to that kind of car."

I gulped and tried to calm my racing heart. I don't know why I was so nervous, but I felt like I could feel Oscar breathing down my neck and giving me the evil eye from wherever he was in the Point at the moment.

"I didn't think the news about this part of town made it up the hill." The hot cop leaned back in his chair and laced his fingers together under his chin. He had a nondescript wedding ring on his finger, and a series of faint, white scars crisscrossing across the back of his hand. His outwardly elegant appearance was probably misleading, like everything in the Point. All of the beauty here was marred by some kind of imperfection.

I shifted on the hard seat and tried to stop myself from looking away from his probing gaze.

"My father is a writer. He tends to keep his ear to the ground for anything and everything that might be an inspiration for a story. His next project has a criminal element to it. Lately, he's been listening to different police scanners. One from the Hill and one from the Point. He is interested in the different types of crime in the two different suburbs. He told me about the robbery. It stuck in his mind because the man who was murdered at the motel was so young."

I'd worked all weekend on this part of the story I would tell the police since I had no phone or computer. I wasn't sure I was a very good liar since I didn't have much experience twisting the truth. I hoped my innocent expression and demeanor were enough for the cops not to ask too many questions. If Oscar was to be believed, I didn't need much help looking like a lost little lamb on the verge of being eaten.

"Who is your father?"

The lieutenant's questions caught me off guard, so I answered without thinking. "Nelson Bell."

The handsome cop nodded. "I heard he was from around here. He doesn't usually write crime or thrillers, though."

I tried to shrug nonchalantly, but it looked more like a flinch.

"He's trying something new." The lie felt so unnatural as it rolled off my tongue.

The older man stared at me before shifting slightly closer to me. His voice seemed to drop even lower when he asked, "That might explain how you know about the crime, but not how you know there's a possibility of a supercar at the scene. Where did you get the information about the car?" Damnit. The cops in the Point were more perceptive than the cops on the Hill. "The information surrounding the robbery and homicide is limited, and no offense, you don't seem like the kind of young lady who associates with the people who have access to it."

"Umm... I like cars. I'm on a forum that discusses rare cars, and I saw a post talking about a supercar used in a violent crime as a getaway car. A lot of people were saying how ridiculous that was; no one would use a car like that for a petty crime because it's worth more than they would ever get during a robbery. But I know Rex Wallace. He is the type to use such an expensive car to commit a crime. Because of his family background, he's arrogant enough to think he would never get caught."

The cop lifted a dark eyebrow, and the corner of his mouth kicked up in a grin. "You like cars?"

I shrugged again and felt a trickle of sweat run down my spine. I clamped my fingers together on my lap to keep them from shaking.

"I have a passing interest." A recent interest since cars seemed to be at the center of everything Oscar was passionate about.

"So, what kind of car do you think was used in the robbery, Ms. Bell?" It felt like a loaded question, and I regretted coming down here without doing my research first. I was so eager to keep Oscar out of trouble, I jumped into my own pool of it feet first.

"Umm... Enzo's Brother... no, Enzo's Cousin. That's the car."

The cop couldn't hold back a chuckle as he leaned back in his seat once again. "That's not the kind of car. That's the nickname collectors and gearheads use. The forum should've told you the car is a

Maserati MC12. They call it Enzo's Cousin because it looks like it's related to the Ferrari Enzo." He reached out and picked up a cell phone on his desk. He didn't look at me while he responded to a message that pinged in his hands. "There are only a handful of people in this city who would know the exact make and model of a car like that without having to do some digging. One is my little brother. The second works for my little brother. And the last one I can think of is Oscar Osborn. Like me, I'm sure Elliot Osborn picked up a thing or two from his sibling when it comes to identifying specialized vehicles. But I don't believe for one second that you know the difference between a Ferrari and a Maserati."

He put the phone back on the desk, and I noticed whomever he was talking with on the other end made his entire presence soften.

"If you want to prove me wrong, Ms. Bell, tell me what kind of car you drove down to the station today."

I stiffened and gave my head a slight shake. "A Mustang."

"What kind of Mustang? What year? What special features does it have? Did you modify it at all? I can keep going, or you can come clean and tell me why you're here pointing a finger at the Wallaces. Isn't his mother going to run for governor soon? That's a pretty big bear you're trying to poke, young lady."

Realizing I painted myself into a corner and there was no way to lie my way out of it, I sighed and finally unclenched my hands so I could run my sweaty palms over the fabric of my skirt.

"Oscar told me about the car, and I used to have a thing with Rex. When Oscar told me about the license plate, I knew Rex was involved. He would absolutely take his dad's car for a joyride. And he would one hundred percent think it's okay to harm someone he considers beneath him on a dare or as a way to challenge his stupid friends. Oscar said he needed more proof. I just wanted to help him before he does something stupid. If he figures out that Rex is the one with access to the car, there is no telling how far he's willing to go to get justice for his brother. He's going to be so pissed if you tell him

I tried to circumvent him by getting Rex in trouble before he could get to him."

The cop sighed and reached out to pat my arm comfortingly. "Oscar is a handful. He reminds me of my brother. Penchant for taking cars that don't belong to him and all. I knew he wasn't going to sit back and let things slide. I tried to convince him I'm not letting anyone get away with murder on my watch."

I bit my tongue to keep from blurting out that he had, in fact, let someone get away with murder the first time around. I wasn't blaming the cop. He couldn't pull evidence and suspects out of thin air. He couldn't fight the Wallaces with no ammunition. I knew how the system worked now and all the unjust ways it was broken. He might believe he could follow this thing all the way through, but I knew if he was blocked by people higher up with political ties and power, he had little choice but to acquiesce.

"I'm telling you, Rex is involved." I kept my tone firm and tried not to let my rising frustration get the better of me.

"When Oscar told me about the car, I looked into who might own one. I know Barry Wallace, Rex's father, has several exotic cars in his collection. There is zero evidence that the car was missing from the collection the night of the robbery. Both Barry and his wife insist Rex was home resting after practice that night. They swore the car was where it was supposed to be. We have no witnesses, no proof that puts him or the car at the motel that night. I know Oscar is torn up over the fact he was supposed to be at the motel that night instead of Elliot, but he can't go back in time and change that. And if you get in the middle of this, whatever you have going on between you and the Wallace kid is going to be front and center. Tell me I'm wrong, and you two don't have a history together."

Goddamnit. That stupid crush I had on Rex turned out to be the biggest pain in the ass. He might be even worse than Addison now that everything was laid out in front of me.

"How do you know Oscar? That kid has run the streets of the Point since he was in middle school. I doubt he frequents the Hill or Hollyoak very often."

"We had an accident on the same day, and we were in the hospital at the same time. We struck up an unlikely friendship. I felt bad about what happened to his brother. I wanted to help. The guy deserves to have someone on his side." It was much easier to tell him a half truth. Meeting in the hospital was how Oscar and I connected in this lifetime, and that's all he needed to know.

"He has more people on his side than he realizes. But you shouldn't sacrifice for him. He is not the kind of guy who would do the same for you."

I was getting ready to tell him I didn't need Oscar's sacrifice, I just needed him, when something occurred to me. I jumped to my feet, making the cop stiffen, and put his hand on his hip near his weapon. Another detective called for me to calm down as I slapped my hands on the edge of the desk and excitedly asked, "Did you talk to everyone at the motel when you were looking for witnesses?"

The handsome police officer shifted and narrowed his eyes at me. "The cops in charge spoke with everyone who was there the night the crime occurred."

"Even the hermit?"

The cop's eyes widened, and he started to tap his fingers on his thigh. "The hermit? What are you talking about?"

I was almost vibrating in excitement. "There's a woman who lives in the end unit on the top floor. She never leaves the apartment. She's agoraphobic. She never opens the door. She doesn't speak with anyone. She's lived at the motel forever, according to Oscar. If the cops had talked to her about the robbery, they would've had to force their way in. She *had* to be there the night of the robbery. She might've seen the car and the murder. She's your witness."

I saw the cop weighing my words. Something flashed in his gaze, and he patted my arm again. "I'll look into it. If they didn't talk to the woman during their investigation, I'll make sure it gets done now. If I were you, I would keep the information about Rex Wallace to yourself for as long as you can. Oscar will level that fancy school of yours to get to someone he thinks is guilty if he gets the chance."

I pounded the side of my fist on his desk. "He already knows the car owner has a kid who goes to my school. There isn't a lot of time."

The cop stood up, signaling the end of our conversation without words. I gulped when I realized how forceful I was being with someone so scary.

"I can tell you care about Oscar. That's good. Try and talk some sense into him. Remind him there is nothing to be gained if he does something dumb. Elliot was a great kid. He cared about everyone. The last thing he would want is more senseless violence committed in his name. And if Oscar ends up locked up after everything his older brother did to make sure he stayed free..." The man shook his dark head and sighed. "That's not an ending any of us want."

I got the distinct impression he was speaking from experience. But he was right. Oscar saved me plenty of times without me having to ask. I could save him from himself just this once.

Even if it meant he might hate me forever.

My only solace was that I didn't know how long forever might be, because I still had no idea if anything in this world was real or not. I might wake up tomorrow and find all of this gone and realize that everything between me and Oscar was only a figment of my imagination.

The idea of that chilled me to the bone.

FIFTEEN

SCHOOL GIRL CRUSH

"**W**hat are you doing here in the middle of the day? Shouldn't you be in school?" Oscar's voice held a hint of surprise. I was on my way back to the Hill, but I couldn't stop myself from pulling into the parking lot of the dilapidated building when I drove past the motel. Oscar wasn't outside working on his car. I was surprised to see him sitting behind the counter. He had his booted feet up on the desk and was more interested in whatever he was watching on his phone than what was happening outside the dirty windows.

"I got kicked out of school." I rested my elbows on the counter near his feet and looked down at him when he shifted his attention to me. "Today has not been my favorite." I was disappointed the cops didn't have a way to stop Oscar from finding out about Rex before they could do something first.

"What did you get kicked out for? I thought you were an A student and a goody-two-shoes." He dropped his feet off the counter and leaned forward. "I tried to call you this weekend. Figured you were ignoring me after Devon's rude awakening."

I huffed out an irritated breath and rested my chin in the palm of my hand while we stared at each other. "I am a good student, but I was also an idiot. I got kicked out for sexting. The guy I sent

159

the pictures to shared them with the entire school, and because of said scandalous images, my dad freaked out and took my phone and computer away this weekend." I sighed. "I thought I was going to have an easier time graduating in this life. I'm worried that keeping my dad alive just because I stopped his wedding isn't a given, since all this other garbage is happening now."

"You were sexting?" Oscar's dark eyebrows lifted. He held his hand out and motioned for my phone. "Lemme see."

I snorted but handed over my phone and pointed out the chat where the pictures first circulated. It wasn't like he hadn't seen me in far more compromising positions and states of undress. There was little I could hide from him at this stage.

"I was going to call you after school, but since I am now free for the day, I figured I would just come and see you." I looked out the window and frowned at my bright red car. "It should be okay parked out front for a little bit, shouldn't it?"

Oscar was busy scrolling through the message chain. He sounded distracted when he replied, "All someone needs to boost your car is an opportunity. Time of day doesn't matter. You can move it around back if you're sticking around for a while. Ms. Nam is off today. Devon hates my guts at the moment, so I'm stuck in the office all day. You can keep me company."

"I can't stay long. My dad wasn't thrilled with our sleepover. He's pretty tolerant, but I think he's at the end of his patience with me. I didn't provoke him this much when I was a teenager in my first life. I've never seen him frustrated and unsure when it comes to me. I thought things were going to be easier this time around, but it's like all the complications just shifted in a different direction."

Oscar handed me back my phone and reached out to pat my head like I was his little pet. "Maybe there are things in our lives that are meant to be no matter what. Things that cannot be changed because they would ultimately send someone else's fate off course. Just because we want things to be one way doesn't mean that it's right for the rest of the world."

I leaned my head into his hand as he moved his palm down the side of my head to cup my cheek. The rough pad of his thumb rubbed across my lower lip as I sighed heavily once again. "What's the point of all this if we can't change anything from how it was before? I refuse to believe we were sent back here for no reason."

"I'm sure there is a reason. But it might not be the one either you or I want." His dark eyes skimmed over the portion of my body he could see over the top of the counter. He smiled at me, and his expression turned downright wicked as he leaned closer so that our foreheads touched. "I think the schoolgirl outfit is way sexier than the lacy underwear in the pictures you sent to that guy. I think that plaid skirt is my new fetish."

I wagged a finger in the air and let out a soft breath when his lips ghosted over mine. "You do know, the only people who like these uniforms are strippers and people who watch too much porn, right?" I laughed as his teeth nipped at my lower lip. "No actual student wants to wear the same damn thing every single day. The last thing we think these uniforms are is sexy."

Oscar grabbed a hold of the matching plaid tie looped around my collar and pulled me closer. His eyes looked like the night sky; they were so deep and dark. I noticed he had the faintest hint of a dimple in one of his cheeks. He didn't smile much. It was like finding a hidden gem buried away under layers of darkness.

"I think my preference is *you* in the outfit. Since I know you aren't really a schoolgirl, and I know you aren't a stripper, it's kind of like playing dress-up." He wiggled his eyebrows up and down, and the tattoo on the side of his neck moved as he audibly swallowed. "Or like roleplaying. I was never in a position to fantasize about much, but when I see you like this..." he flicked out his tongue, and the tip licked across my parted lips. "It feels like a small dream I harbored away came true. Sometimes I think you're too good to be true, Vesper Bell."

He used his hold on the uniform tie to guide me around the counter until I was standing in front of him. He pressed me back to sit on the desk. It was littered with paper and empty coffee cups. It was clear he'd been sitting at his post for a long time. Oscar sat back down in the chair, and the wheels squeaked as he rolled closer to me. My skin pebbled up, and the hair on my arms lifted when his hands moved down the outside of my bare thighs.

I leaned forward so I could cup his defiantly handsome face between my hands. The softness of his skin never ceased to surprise me.

"I'm not as good as I used to be. This time around, I've done some very bad things." But getting involved with him was the very best bad thing I'd done in either lifetime.

Oscar leaned forward, and I felt his breath against the inside of my knee. It made me shiver.

His words skipped over my sensitive skin as he pressed closer. "Just how bad do you want to be?" It sounded like a dare.

My head tilted back, and I looked at the dirty front window and the bell over the door. This is the last place I thought I would end up today. I knew that door wasn't locked and that anyone could walk in at any minute, but for some reason, those things did not deter me from telling Oscar, "Bad enough that you know I'm real. I'm right here in front of you. I'm not too good to be true. I'm barely good enough to be with you the way I am now. You give me too much credit."

I could feel him looking at me, and I'm sure my words left him with questions. Fortunately, he didn't ask any of them because I didn't want to lie to him any more than I already was.

I gasped when he picked up one of my hands and placed a soft kiss on my palm. The gentleness of the gesture brought a surprising rush of moisture to my eyes. When it came to the two of us, Oscar was the good one. I couldn't find fault with the care he took with me. I was constantly underestimating just how soft and sweet he could be. The fact that all his tenderness and kindness seemed reserved for a select few made the way he handled me all the more special. He deserved more than I could give him at the moment. But if I stopped him from chasing that cruel fate he seemed determined to bring to fruition, I could choke on the secrets I kept until the end.

I leaned back on my elbows and watched with heavy-lidded eyes as Oscar kissed his way up the inside of my leg. His fingers skated along the outside of my thigh, the plaid material of my uniform skirt lifting inch by inch. I wasn't lying when I told him I never found this outfit sexy, but the way he was touching me, and the way his dark eyes glittered, made me reconsider my stance. Anything that made him look at me like he couldn't wait to put his hands and mouth all over me was a keeper. The wheels on the chair made a noise that rang in my ears, but it was hard to hear over the pounding of my heart. Once Oscar's tattooed hands found their way underneath my skirt, I leaned back my head so it touched the higher part of the counter and locked my eyes on the bell above the door. I wanted to care what it would look like if someone suddenly pushed into the small office.

I didn't.

All I could focus on was the rough feeling of Oscar's hands and the heat from his mouth. I suppose I should've made him kiss me before I let him slide his fingers under the soft cotton of my boring white underwear. I had no idea I would end up spread out in front of him like a gourmet meal today; otherwise, I would've dressed for the occasion rather than comfort. Oscar didn't seem to care. I heard him chuckle against the sensitive spot where my inner thigh dipped into the more delicate and responsive skin. My entire body tingled, and I felt my insides clench.

"Lift." The command was growled into the curve of my leg as long fingers hooked under the sides of the basic undergarment.

I used the counter for leverage and lifted myself as he asked. I made a strangled sound as Oscar worked the white fabric down my legs and over my designer boots. We were both more covered than not, but I felt like he was looking right through me. It was hard to hide from someone who saw everything.

"It's quiet around here when the sun is out. The residents who live here work full time during the day, and the kind of people looking for a room for a few hours don't come out until after dark." He was trying to reassure me even though I didn't ask for it.

I found it remarkably easy to throw caution to the wind with him.

"I don't care about them. I care about you." I lifted the hand he kissed and put it on the side of his face. "Locked doors don't keep people out in this part of town anyway."

Oscar hummed in agreement, but his head was between my legs, so the sound disappeared into my quivering flesh. I didn't protest when he used his hold on my leg to maneuver one of my knees onto the curve of his shoulder. The new position forced my upper body to fall back and lifted the hem of my already short skirt to indecent levels. I figured I was all in at this point. There was no turning back. Good or bad, I was in it until the end with this unexpected and unpredictable boy.

I whispered his name when I felt his lips lightly touch my exposed center. It was always when he was at his most reverent and respectful that all my defenses fell. It did something to my heart when he handled me like some*one* he earned rather than some*thing* he deserved. I think that was the defining difference between him and anyone who came before him in our previous lives.

I liked his rough hands and his quiet demands, but when he flipped the script and started to touch me like I might vanish right out from under him at any moment, it scrambled all my good intentions and common sense.

"If you don't want me to like you, you need to stop making me feel like I'm special to you. That's one of the things I like most, Oscar." I sighed when I felt his other hand slide up the inside of my thigh.

His breath was warm on very sensitive spots as his fingers glided through wet folds.

"I don't want you to be special either, but you are now, and you were back then. The last thing I wanted to do was hurt you. That's starting to feel like part of the unchanging fate I talked about earlier. I think I'm going to end up hurting you anyway."

He let out a soft sigh, and it made my entire body pulse in pleasure. A moment later, I felt his tongue flick against my clit as his fingers dipped inside of my fluttering opening. My body tightened, and my head dropped back to thump on the countertop. I closed my eyes and let myself drift on the waves of sensation he was dragging me into.

"You also told me that our fates got twisted up and turned around somehow. So, maybe in this lifetime, I'll be the one who hurts you." My heart throbbed painfully at the truth behind the words. No one expected the lamb to bite the wolf, even if it was to protect the predator from the shepherd. I had a gut feeling that the betrayal, when it was uncovered, would burn twice as badly. I felt like I owed him a warning at the very least.

Long, thick fingers moved skillfully within my body as his quick tongue swirled around the small spot that made my insides quake and drip with excitement.

Oscar pulled back, and I felt his eyes watching my expression as I writhed in the palm of his hand quite literally.

"You can hurt me, Vesper. I might like you even more if you do. It makes it seem like this thing happening between us, whatever it is, might be possible. Don't people say that pain is how we know something is real? If we can't feel it, how do we know if it's there?"

I didn't have an answer for that. Pain lingered much longer than most other feelings; he was right. Maybe it wasn't always a bad thing.

I stopped being able to think straight when his head moved back to the spot where his fingers were still stroking through gathered wetness and rubbing against pleasure-sensitive spots inside of me. This time when his tongue touched me, I felt like I was going to come out of my skin. I shivered under the erotic onslaught and locked a hand on the back of his head to have something hold me in reality.

My legs shook on either side of his head as I felt the scrape of his teeth on my clit. He was far too good at this. If I didn't know he had more experience than the average twenty-one-year-old because of the time slip, I might be alarmed at *how* freaking skilled he was. It was easy to feel in over my head when he touched and tasted me.

His fingers curled at the same time his tongue swirled. I saw white spots and felt my breath catch in my lungs. I would've locked my thighs around his head if one of his hands wasn't still holding my leg in place on his shoulder. I felt like I might come apart in his hands. I was overwhelmed with all the things he made me feel, not just desire and delight from how he manipulated and maneuvered around my body, but also the growing feelings I developed the more time I spent with him. I was no longer attached to him because we were in the same odd boat. I wanted to be around him and keep him alive because I cared about what happened to him. I knew it was a very short jump from the like I felt toward him to something closer to first love. He would be my true first love in either life. I'd never felt so strongly about anyone before.

I whimpered and moved involuntarily, my body following his touch in search of more pleasure. When he switched his attack, I called his name at an embarrassingly loud volume. Oscar used his tongue to lap and lick at my damp center, and his thumb moved to apply steady pressure on my clit with deliberate strokes. My head felt like it weighed a thousand pounds. My heart was racing, and I couldn't catch my breath. When he used his fingers to carefully pluck and tug my clit. I didn't know if it was possible to pass out because something felt so damn good, but I was on the brink of finding out.

My nails raked across the back of his head, and my hips lifted of their own accord when his tongue reached inside of me as deeply as it could go. It felt like being savored and enjoyed like an expensive delicacy. He never failed to make me feel like I was somehow better than I actually was.

It didn't take long for the new assault to send me over the edge. I shouted when my body suddenly released in a flood of satisfaction. The sounds his mouth was making as it moved over and within me were enough to tip the scale over to completion. I heard him grunt when my fingernails dug even deeper into his head, and when he chuckled lightly, the orgasm I was spiraling through sent little aftershocks of pleasure shooting up my spine and through my limbs. It seemed like every time I opened myself up to him for a new experience, the parts of me that were broken from my experiences in my original life didn't seem as sharp and jagged. The edges were still there, and so were the lessons that painfully lingered. But they no longer cut into me and made me bleed when I brushed up against them.

The fact that Oscar liked those parts of me better than the polished, smooth pieces that came from living a privileged life made me appreciate them much more.

I jerked when he let my leg slide back down as he stood up between my thighs and bent over to drop a wet kiss, one that smelled like seduction and sex, on my cheek. He smiled against my heated skin. There was no way I wasn't going to blush beet red after what had just happened on his check-in counter.

We both looked toward the dirty window when the alarm on my car suddenly started blaring.

My gaze locked with Oscar's as he quickly straightened and started to make his way around the counter toward the door.

"I guess it's better to be interrupted by someone trying to boost your car than the bell over the door." He gave me a crooked grin, and the elusive dimple in his cheek popped out. "Give me a minute."

He pushed out of the door as the alarm continued to shriek. I took a deep breath and climbed off the ledge. I looked around for my underwear and couldn't find them. Apparently, they were still with Oscar.

I shook my head and wondered what in the hell I was doing. Being bad with him shouldn't come as effortlessly as it did, yet here we were.

He said all someone needed to steal something was an opportunity. It felt like Oscar had a prime moment right in front of him to make off with my heart if he decided he wanted it. I would more than likely surrender it to him. If only I knew what he would do with it once it was in his hands.

What had me worried was if he planned on destroying it after he found out I was standing between him and his revenge. I wasn't sure I could, or should, stop him.

SIXTEEN

BLAST FROM THE PAST

Oscar saved my car, minus a few scratches and a broken steering wheel column, which he fixed for me before I headed back up the Hill. I told him there was a high probability my dad would confiscate my phone once I got home. He told me not to worry about it. If he needed to talk to me, he would find a way to get to me regardless. His assurance made me feel a bit better. When he kissed me goodbye before I drove away, it felt like I was getting closer and closer to falling into a dangerous kind of love with no safety net.

When I got back to my house, my father was fit to be tied. Surprisingly, he was more furious at the school and the blatant sexism of sending me home and threatening my future— while the party who asked for the pictures and was most likely the one who shared them faced no repercussions—than at my disappearing act. He had already mobilized his formidable team. I was shocked to hear he was looking into hiring a specialized computer security expert named Stark. They assured my dad that the secretive computer hacker could find the origin of the shared pictures and proof of the culprit who instigated the whole ordeal in no time. The guy was hard to find, though, and didn't work for just anyone. But according to the source, he had an innate sense of justice and hated politicians. Since Rex was the son of a future governor, my case might interest him enough to help me out.

I didn't think my father needed to go so far as to get involved with some shady hacker, but he was determined that Rex would be punished for what he was putting me through. I had no idea my creative, eccentric father had such a streak of vengeance within him. He was a formidable opponent when he wanted to be. If anyone could take on the Wallaces and win, it might be him.

I spent the rest of my suspension studying for finals, should I be allowed to take them, and finalizing college applications. I narrowed down the schools close to home, but still far enough away to snatch a little bit of my independence back. Originally, I knew I wanted to be able to visit my dad whenever the opportunity arose. Now, there was an inkling in the back of my mind that I wanted to be close to Oscar as well. We might not ever be able to define our complicated relationship, but all I cared about was the fact there *was* a relationship of some sort.

My dad and I spent a lot of time together. It was nice and weird. For him, we had all the time in the world to be with one another. He had no idea that I'd grieved for him to the point it felt like the sadness might crush me. He had no clue that I wanted to soak up as much of his time and attention as I could just in case the future was unwilling to let him live. I appreciated him and all the wonderful little things that made him such a great dad, more now that I knew what it was like to be without him. My father took my new desire to bond with him in stride. He always liked my company, and now that I was slightly more self-aware and had a bigger view of the world, our conversations were enlightening and lively. I tried to absorb everything I missed in the previous timeline.

When the middle of the week rolled around, and I was supposed to go back to school, my dad became further outraged when the school decided to extend the suspension until the following week. It wasn't only my father's legal team who was putting pressure on them. Other wealthy parents wanted me expelled and even charged with anything from child endangerment to pedophilia. It was a big mess, and I was caught in the middle of it.

I agreed not to fight the suspension as long as the school let me turn in my assignments and kept me up to date on all the study material I needed for finals. The headmaster assured me they would collect what I needed and send everything digitally to my house.

Since I'd been stuck at home for so many days, I jumped at the chance to go with my dad to a book signing a few towns over. I thought a change of scenery might be nice. While I hadn't lost my phone privileges, my dad watched my every move, so I hadn't been able to make it back down to the Point since my last rendezvous with Oscar. He was better about texting me back these days, but he still didn't say much in his replies. I wanted to see him. So much. Yet, I forced myself to stay away. I didn't want to annoy him by being clingy and needy. I didn't want to like him more than he liked me. It all sounded so silly when I thought about it. However, Oscar always had the upper hand. I thought it made sense that if he liked me more than I liked him, it evened out some of our more drastic differences. That train of thought made me realize a little space might do both of us some good.

The bookstore where my dad was set to sign was nice. The city it was located in wasn't as affluent as ours, but it was closer to the water and had a more laid-back, beachy vibe. The crowd that gathered to see my dad speak was impressive. There had to be at least three-hundred people gathered in the space.

I asked my dad if he was nervous. He shook his head and told me, "You should've seen the crowd at Comic-Con a couple of years ago. This is nothing." He laughed and waved good-naturedly as an older woman screamed his name like he was a rockstar.

"I have to go find the organizer and get ready. Do you need anything?" He handed me some cash and told me to find the café if I wanted anything to drink.

I shooed him off to be his famous self. I wandered up and down the different aisles looking at all the beautiful books. I wondered where my current story fell. Was it science fiction? Was it fantasy? Was it time-travel? Or maybe it was a romance since I spent as much time thinking about Oscar and how he made me feel as I did the predicament of being blown back in time. Both felt otherworldly and unreal. Both felt improbable and inexplicable.

I was muttering to myself while I picked a graphic novel off the shelf when a tiny battering ram plowed into my legs. I had to grab hold of the shelf to stay on my feet as I looked down at a tiny little girl who was grinning up at me with a wide smile that was missing several teeth.

"Hi. You're pretty." The little girl spoke with a bit of a lisp, but that's not why I was struck dumb. Even though she was seven years younger and barely out of her toddler stage, I recognized Tobi. She was a smaller, younger version of my favorite neighbor.

I returned her smile and crouched down so we were eye to eye.

"Hi. You're very pretty, too. Do you know who I am?" Tobi was friendly when I first met her, but she knew better than to run up to a stranger and hug them. What were the chances that she remembered the past me and recognized her in the current me?

"Don't know you. I like comics. Can you read to me?" She wiggled her body side to side and blinked big eyes at me. She was a happy, fearless little girl. I hated that all of that had been taken from her by the time I met her.

"Where are your parents? You shouldn't be wandering around such a busy store alone." I didn't want to be bitter, but I remembered how careless and inattentive Tobi and Jordan's mother was when she lived next door to me. The woman was constantly drunk and acted like her small children should be able to care for themselves. I had a big problem with her parenting style and overall attitude.

"October Grace! Tobi! Where are you?" A woman's shrill voice followed my question a moment later as a heavily pregnant woman came waddling around the end of the aisle. Her face was red from exertion, and she was breathing heavily. She put a hand protectively over her round belly and looked at me where I was kneeling in front of the little girl.

She hurried over and grabbed her daughter's hand. "Sorry if she was bothering you. She slipped away while I was on the phone. I'm not as quick as I usually am."

She panted the words out and looked anxiously around the bookstore.

I climbed to my feet and gave her a hard look, trying to see if she recognized me at all. The woman showed no signs that we'd ever met before, but she acted very differently from how I remembered.

She didn't look haggard or like she had a drinking problem. She seemed very concerned about her daughter and looked downright terrified when Tobi was out of her sight.

I flipped a hand nonchalantly. "No problem. We were just talking about comic books. We both like them."

The woman nodded, her head still swiveling around like she was on alert for something. "You're not here to see Nelson Bell? I thought everyone was here for him."

I laughed and shook my head. "No. I didn't come to see him. But I am a big fan."

The woman nodded. "Me too. I wanted to get a book signed, but..." She trailed off as a man suddenly stormed around the corner and marched down the aisle.

"I told you to keep an eye on her. What were you thinking?" The man reached for the woman's arm, and the way she flinched away from him was telling. "Let's get out of here. There are too many people."

"I want a new comic book, Daddy." The little girl who was smiling so happily a moment ago looked like she was going to cry, and so did her mom.

I felt a pang of regret. I judged the woman so harshly for her failings. I thought she was a terrible mother and that Tobi and Jordan deserved better, but I never once stopped to consider why she lived in the Point with her two kids. I never thought living in the motel was better than wherever they might've been previously. There was clearly a story about why the small family hit hard times, and I wish I'd been sympathetic enough to ask for it.

"You have enough damn books. Grab the kid and meet me in the car. If you're not out in five minutes, you can find your own way home. You're both a pain in my ass." The man grumbled and griped as he walked out of sight. I heard the woman sigh in relief as she reached for her daughter. When she moved, I noticed her wrist was encircled with a ring of bright blue and purple bruises.

"Sorry again. Thank you for being so nice to Tobi. She can be a handful." The woman sounded like she was going to cry.

Before she could walk away, I held out a hand and almost shouted, "Wait a minute." When mother and daughter paused, I fished around in my purse for a piece of paper so I could write my number and Oscar's number down. "If you ever need a place to go, if you need to get away for any reason, just call one of these numbers and ask for Vesper. I know a place where you'll be safe." Maybe she would reach out before she started drinking so heavily. Maybe she would leave before she was hurt so badly that she stopped caring about anything, including her kids. "If your husband asks about the number, tell him it's someone who can get you a signed copy of a Nelson Bell book. I have connections." I winked at Tobi and tried to smile reassuringly at her mother.

I wanted so badly to help them get on a better path than they had traveled previously. I only wished the mom recognized me so I could know she knew exactly how bad things would get if she didn't get herself out of her current home situation.

The mom didn't say anything, and she curled the scrap piece of paper up into a ball in her fist. I didn't know if she would toss it, but I tried to help. It was all I could do without sounding like a raving lunatic, which I knew wouldn't help anyone.

Tobi turned around and wiggled her fingers at me. I gave her a wink and turned to lean against the rack of books as I fished my phone out of my pocket so I could text Oscar.

~ Do you remember the woman and two kids who lived in the room next to mine?

It took a few minutes for him to respond.

~ I do. You brought them food from the diner all the time.

I nodded even though he couldn't see me.

~ I just ran into her and her daughter. She is currently pregnant with the little boy. Neither of them recognized me from before. It really is just you and me who came back after the explosion and remembered everything from the future.

~ Are you sure she wasn't just playing that she didn't know you? I remember that woman being hella shady.

~ She's married to a jackass. I don't think she was always shady. I think circumstances forced her to become that way. I gave her your number and told her to call if she needed a safe place to go.

~ You think sending someone to the Point is safe?

I could practically hear him chuckling through the message.

~ I think sending her to you is safer than staying with her husband. Just give her a room if she calls, okay?

~ I'll keep an eye out for her. If you think we're the only two who remember the future, does that mean you're done stalking the hermit?

I blew out a breath that sent my bangs fluttering over my forehead.

~ No. I still really want to talk to her.

Not so much for the time slip anymore. I wanted to know if she could put Rex at the scene of Elliot Osborn's murder. She might not hold the key to why we went back in time, but she would be instrumental in making sure Oscar had a future.

~ She still hasn't come out of the room.

~ She has to eventually. I'm at an event with my dad. I'll talk to you soon.

He sent a thumbs-up emoji, and I was a little crushed he didn't bother to ask when he would see me next or ask when I would make it back to the motel. I always felt like I wanted to see him more than he wanted to see me. Calling him names under my breath, I collected a couple of graphic novels that looked interesting and made my way to the checkout. There was no getting through the crowd. People crowded into every available nook and cranny to hear my dad speak before signing their books.

I was proud of him. Before, I never took the time to appreciate how hard he worked or how difficult it was to stay relevant and creative in such a difficult career. He still loved to write and still loved love. Even if his experiences with the latter had been harsh and unforgiving, my father persevered and he stayed true to himself. I was so glad I stopped him from marrying that woman who would have ruined him.

But now, I needed to find him one he could grow old with. One who wanted to protect him and cherish him the way my mother did when she was still with us. He needed a partner who appreciated him for more than his money. He needed someone who valued his heart above all else. It was a shame Ms. Nam was in her sixties and already married. She would be a good candidate for the role.

Snickering over my thoughts, I started when my dad suddenly mentioned my name.

"People ask me all the time what inspires me. They want to know how I can bring my characters' emotions to life. The answer to both is my daughter Vesper." He didn't point me out or signal to me in any way, but his gaze found mine through the crowd, and a lot of people followed the movement. "She's my greatest inspiration. I do what I do because I want her to be proud of me. I want a legacy to leave for her when I'm gone. I want her to be surrounded by the words I leave behind and the characters I created to keep her company when I no longer can. I write about the love I felt for her mother and the kind of love I hope she finds for herself in the future. I started writing full time early in my career so I could stay home with Vesper when she was a baby. I always had a huge imagination and loved to tell stories. I figured if I could make money and stay home with my kid, that was the best option. It's still the best option, even though she's almost ready to head out into the world on her own."

The entire crowd seemed to let out a resounding "awwww..." and then they clapped wildly. My dad followed up, answering questions about his work-life balance and the timeframe he usually worked within.

I used the side of my knuckle to wipe a tear from the corner of my eye and clutched the books closer to my chest.

Coming back to this point in my life had a lot of benefits. One of the biggest ones so far was hearing things like what he just said with the understanding and compassion that came from losing him. I wanted him to live forever, or at least longer than he had before. But if fate refused to bend, and he was bound to go as he had previously, this time I got with him now would help soften the blow.

Every moment mattered...it shouldn't have taken a bizarre catastrophe to bring me back and make me see it.

SEVENTEEN

THE ENEMY OF MY ENEMY IS MY FRIEND

I stared at Addison through the iron gate at the end of my drive-way. I couldn't believe she dared show her face at my house af-ter everything she'd done. She had obviously intercepted the per-son the who was supposed to bring me my assignments and study guides from school. When she texted that she was outside the gate and wanted to talk, my first instinct was to refuse. But I needed the homework, and I had to admit I was curious why she suddenly want-ed to talk. So, very begrudgingly, I agreed to walk down to the gate to meet up with her. Keeping the iron bars between the two of us gave me a false sense of security as I reached out a hand for the bag she'd stuffed everything into.

"Danika was never going to bring this stuff to you. It would've ended up in the trash if I didn't stop her from tossing it all in the closest dumpster." She scoffed and lifted a hand to wrap it around the filigree of one of the bars between us. "The headmaster had to know what she was going to do with it once he asked her to make sure she got it to you. They don't want you in that school any more than they want me there."

I cocked my head to one side and clutched the bundle of books and papers to my chest. "Why did you intervene? I figure I'm the last person you want to help."

178

Addison looked as confused as I felt. She used her fingers to tuck a piece of long, blonde hair behind her ear.

"I don't know, maybe because I want to be the one to ruin you. Or maybe because you've been through enough lately." She frowned. "I can't explain it. I keep thinking about what you said the other day. If I put my mind to something that matters, I could succeed based on my effort rather than following my mom blindly from man to man. No one has ever said anything like that to me before. It doesn't matter that I'm always at the top of the class, or that I consistently get amazing grades. Everyone always thinks I'm nothing more than a pretty face. My mom has always drilled it into my head that I need to look good to get what I want in life. Not once did she encourage me to work hard. Ever since my dad, she's bounced from one man to another. Each one was richer than the one before. She figured I would follow in her footsteps. I was honestly looking forward to her marrying your dad. I thought all the scheming and manipulating might finally be over. Your dad is like the ultimate catch in this town, after all."

I shifted my weight and narrowed my eyes at her. "He is a good catch, but he's worth more to your mother if he's dead. She didn't want him. She wanted his estate."

Addison looked confused. She lifted a hand to tug on her lower lip. "But his estate belongs to you."

I shifted again and drilled her with a glare. "It belongs to me unless someone tries really hard to get me out of the way. Your mom convinced you to tank my chances at getting into the school I want, and she also convinced you to trick me into spending every cent of my inheritance. Don't underestimate your mother's greed. You always told me your dad just disappeared from your life one day when you were young. Have you ever pushed your mom for more details? You know better than anyone how devious she can be. Why would you take her word for what happened back then? As I said, you're too smart for whatever your mom has planned for you."

She tilted her head to match mine. A serious look passed over her pretty face as she appeared to contemplate my words.

"Are you saying you think my mom did something to my dad?"

I shrugged. "I don't know. But I can guess she hasn't been totally honest with you about the situation. I'd have plenty of questions to ask if I were in your shoes."

"You mentioned something happening to your dad. Can you tell me what you meant? My mom is an angel until she gets a ring on her finger. I don't remember her ever doing anything to hurt your dad. She definitely wanted me to try and get close to your dad and gain his favor, but she never said anything to me about hurting him."

I huffed out an irritated breath and moved the books to my other arm. "It's hard to explain, Addy. All I can tell you is that I'm positive that if I hadn't stopped the wedding, my dad would've ended up dead, and your mom would've done anything and everything to make sure I was out of the way so she could take over every inch of the estate. It's more than a gut feeling."

We stared at each other in awkward silence for a long moment. She finally broke the standoff with a big sigh. She pushed a hand through her hair, and I realized this was the most frazzled and unkempt I'd ever seen her. For once, she looked like any other pretty teenage girl just trying to get by.

"One more thing before I go." She frowned and looked down at the toes of her sneakers. "I had nothing to do with those pictures Rex shared with everyone. He's going crazy trying to keep his parents off his back. They're beyond pissed he screwed things up with you and, by extension, your father. If he can't bully his way back into your good graces, he's going to do whatever he can to discredit and embarrass you. He wants to ruin you so that his parents stop trying to force him to win you back. It takes a lot to freak me out. He scares me, Vee. You need to watch your back around him."

I took a step forward and clutched at the bars between us. "Did Rex tell you he sent the pictures to everyone?"

She sighed again and lifted her gaze to mine. I was shocked to see a hint of remorse when our eyes locked. "It was my idea. When he asked how he could get you kicked out of school, I remembered the pictures you sent him. I didn't think it would be too bad since you weren't naked or anything, and I'm still bitter you got me expelled. But once I saw the pictures, I realized how dirty I felt. No one should have their privacy violated against their will like that. I haven't talked to him since."

"Can you tell the headmaster that you know Rex was behind the picture leak?" There would be no way they could heap all the blame on me if they had a witness who could verify Rex was involved. I knew it was unlikely Addison would stick her neck out for me, but I still had to ask.

I was stunned when she told me, "I already did. They told me my eyewitness account didn't mean much since I'm no longer a student at the school. Rex must've given them some song and dance about me being a scorned ex-girlfriend. The school didn't want to hear anything I had to say. I think they're happy to have both of us out of the way for the rest of the school year."

"That's bullshit." I practically growled the exclamation as my blood started to boil.

"I agree. Your pedigree is just as good as Rex's. The only difference is your gender and the fact he's an athlete. It's a bunch of sexist nonsense." She shrugged her shoulders and turned to look out at the view, her gaze skimming over the Point to the water beyond. "I'm going to transfer to a public school so I can graduate on time. I think I'm going to take a gap year and travel. I need some space from my mom and this lifestyle she's been chasing ever since I can remember. Without her influence, I need to figure out what I want and who I am. If you hadn't destroyed the wedding the way you did, I don't know that I ever would've woken up from the nightmare my life had become." She looked back in my direction and gave me a small smile. "I lied when I told you that no one likes you. I liked you a lot. I never met anyone who could see the good in everyone they encountered before. I thought you were dumb, but the longer we were friends, I realized that you were just genuinely nice and unassuming. You didn't have an ulterior motive, and I had no clue what to do with someone like that. I thought being good all the time made you boring, but it didn't. It made you unique and so much better than most kids who go to that damn school. It made you better than I've ever been. I hope you manage to keep that part of yourself as life goes on. Me and my mom are far from the worst people you're going to encounter. Everyone is going to want a piece of you. Your money. Your name. Your connections. Your face and your body. Be smart about who you decide to share any of it with."

I fell back a few steps and nodded. "I'm going to make good choices from here on out, not just easy ones. And Addy," I waited until she turned back to look at me. "If you ever get in any serious trouble, let me know. I don't think anyone in this world deserves to be completely alone. I want you to have an escape route if you need one." Those damn good intentions. It seemed like I couldn't get rid of them no matter how hard I tried.

"I appreciate the offer, Vesper. I think I'm going to look into what happened with my dad. It's well past the time my mom is honest with me about things. Regardless, I'm not following her into her next relationship. I'm sick of being her pawn. Take care of yourself."

I watched her until she disappeared. I was baffled by our conversation. Whatever I expected Addison to say to me when we met up again, *this* wasn't it. It didn't feel exactly like burying the proverbial hatchet. It was more like she pulled out the knife she'd shoved in my back. The wound was still there, but it didn't hurt as much as before.

Contemplating what I would do if the school didn't let me come back to graduate, I walked back up the long drive to the massive house up on the hill. I passed Carlotta on my way inside. She paused to give me a one-armed hug and told me dinner was in the oven. My dad was working on his next book in his office, so she reminded me to let him be unless there was an emergency. He got incredibly cranky when his process was interrupted. I promised her I would make sure he ate something, but I knew if he was on a roll, he might work through the night, and it would be morning before he made an appearance.

I jogged up the winding staircase to the level of the house where my room was. I pushed open the door, planning to toss the armful of books on my bed, but I stopped short when I realized that space was already occupied.

I felt my eyes pop wide as my gaze traveled over Oscar, who looked like he was making himself at home in my bedroom. The books slid to the floor as my grasp loosened, and I jumped when they banged loudly against the wood. I shot a frantic look around the room to make sure there was nothing overtly embarrassing on display and asked, "How did you get in here? How did you know which room was mine?" This house was huge. There were eight bedrooms and five bathrooms scattered on different floors. Not to mention the study, my dad's office, the theater room, and so on. Plus, my dad's security system was top of the line. He didn't take any chances after more than one zealous fan tried to break in.

Oscar had his ankles crossed and his hands tucked behind his head. He looked at me like I shouldn't ask questions I might not want the answers to. He seemed very out of place in the professionally decorated and expensive-looking space. I'd never had a boy in my room before, so it was a little jarring to have this place, and my youthful memories of it, invaded.

"I told you I would find a way to talk to you if you didn't answer your phone. I've been calling you for over an hour. As for knowing which room was yours," he lifted his dark eyebrows and smirked at me, "I recognized this room from your sexy photoshoot. This house is too fucking big for only two people."

I walked closer to the bed. My phone was on the mirrored nightstand. I forgot to take it with me when I went to meet Addison. I was so surprised when she showed up, I wasn't thinking straight.

"Why were you trying to call me? I had to grab some school stuff from a classmate. I forgot to take my phone." I pointed at it and let out a gasp when he grabbed my hand and pulled me down on the bed, so I sprawled on top of him.

It felt forbidden and naughty to have him in my room. Similar to what went down on his front desk, the probability of someone walking in on us was high, making all the feelings and emotions I had toward him triple in intensity. Our heartbeats paused, then picked up a similar rhythm. It was uncanny how our bodies managed to keep time so effortlessly for two people who lived out of sync with one another.

"I called because I finally got a name to go with the license plate. I want you to tell me everything you know about a guy named Rex Wallace. His dad owns the Maserati from the night of the robbery."

I blinked and quickly tucked my head under his chin. He had a name, but he must not have found a picture of Rex. Otherwise, he would recognize him from that day in the parking lot. I doubted Oscar would forget the face of the guy who claimed to be my boyfriend, or the fact that he'd punched him.

"He's a big deal at my school. His family is a big deal in this part of town. Big money. Big connections. His mom is probably going to be a state representative in the near future. He's not someone you should take lightly just because he goes to private school."

Oscar smoothed a hand down my hair and muttered, "What's your connection to him?"

I tried to keep myself from freezing. I closed my eyes and curled my hands into the fabric of his plain white t-shirt. "My connection to him is complicated. Why didn't you look him up once you got his name?"

"Hmm... because I knew once I saw the face of the person who killed my brother, I wouldn't be able to control myself. I would've hunted him down like a dog. That's the old me—the one who could never see the forest for the trees. The new me has a cute little lamb who keeps whispering in my ear that I need to be smarter about things this time around. She says I need to make the second chance I've been given count for something. I might only get one shot at the guy. I'm not going to waste it."

"I..." the words trailed off. There was so much more I needed to let him know, but the words felt lodged in my throat. I wanted to protect him, but I was running out of time, and so was Rex. "I don't want you to get in over your head. This isn't the Point. The people who break the law here have resources that ensure they never get caught. If Rex killed Elliot, his family will do everything in their power to make sure it never comes to light. I don't think you understand what you're going up against."

"Don't underestimate me, Vesper. Anything that stands in the way of getting justice for Elliot is collateral damage. I'm not scared of the rich and famous. They should be scared of me."

I swore under my breath and decided we needed to change the subject before I gave something away. I let my fingers creep under the hem of his t-shirt and scratched my nails over the lines that carved out his abdominal muscles.

"I can't believe you broke into my house. My dad would lose his mind if he knew I had a boy in my room. It makes me feel like I'm really eighteen again and doing something wrong." His skin was warm and taut under my fingers. His stomach tightened, and the hand stroking my hair moved to hold my face up for a kiss.

"No use in feeling guilty unless we're doing something scandalous. Wanna make some trouble with me?" His voice was enough to seduce me, and the question was a no-brainer. When he kissed me again, his tongue twisted around mine and flicked enticingly against the roof of my mouth. It was wet and needy. It was a kiss that made up for the one he skipped when he devoured me on top of his front desk. The heat from his lips made me dizzy, and the rasp of his hands on my skin let me forget about everything I wasn't telling him.

I never thought I would be back in this room.

I never imagined getting the chance to live my life differently or the chance to make a difference.

I sure as shit never anticipated a boy like Oscar showing up and turning everything upside down.

The unexpected parts of this timeline were so much better than the unfortunate events of the previous one. They said the road to hell was paved with good intentions. It was hard to deny I was well on my way.

EIGHTEEN

DON'T GET CAUGHT

I kissed Oscar for a long time.

Partly because it felt so good and made both of us breathless, but also because I wanted to apologize to him for being less than truthful. I couldn't use my mouth to say the words just yet, but I could use it in other ways to show my sincerity. I always felt like my moments with him might be the last. I needed to make the most of them and show him where my heart was, even if my actions proved otherwise.

I already stripped him of his t-shirt and was licking down his tattooed neck when he asked, "Isn't your dad home? It's been a long time since I had to sneak into a girl's bedroom." His dark eyebrows lifted as my hair dragged across his chest and down his abdomen as I kissed and nipped my way toward his belly button.

"He's working in his office. It's on the other side of the house. When he's in the zone, he isn't aware that the rest of the world still exists." I blew out a soft breath across his stomach and watched as the strong muscles contracted enticingly. "He won't come up here unless there's an emergency. But keep quiet, just to be on the safe side."

Oscar snorted, but it turned into a soft moan when I started to work his heavy leather belt open.

"I'm not the loud one. That would be you, little lamb."

I flicked the tip of my tongue over the ruddy tip of his erection as it peeked eagerly out of the waistband of his black boxers. If we were somewhere else, I would waste no effort to make his inner wolf howl, but the last thing I wanted was to arouse my father's suspicions. There was no way I could explain who Oscar was, how we knew each other, or why he was in my bed that would make sense to the man who still saw me as his sweet and innocent little girl. I'd rather avoid the two of them crossing paths for as long as possible.

I pushed his pants and boxers down just far enough to free his cock. It bounced a little at the force, and I giggled when it tapped against my parted lips with no help from either of us.

Oscar grunted and reached out to rub his thumb across my damp lower lip. "Looks like my body has a mind of its own where you're concerned. I knew you were going to be trouble from the minute I first laid eyes on you."

I wrapped a slightly shaky hand around the base of his length and bowed my head over the hardness. I used the very tip of my tongue to lick along the sensitive slit and around the tapered head. I felt his body heat and pulse in my palm as his muscles tensed even more.

"I was too scared to look at anyone when I first ended up in the Point. I missed seeing a lot of things back then." How would things be if I saw him back then? Would my life be easier or harder if I noticed him noticing me when I was at my lowest? I don't know that I knew what it was like to love someone back then. I was so caught up in myself, and my failures and losses, love was a foreign concept. He was pretty much all I could see these days. It was alarming how important he'd become to me in such a short amount of time. Eighteen-year-old me was definitely in the thrall of first love. The twenty-something who inhabited my soul was preparing for the first real heartbreak that was bound to be on the horizon. I was very aware that our tenuous relationship would be the causality of my choices to keep him in the dark. I mean, if it took time travel for the two of us to be together, it was probably never meant to be from the start.

However, I had no intention of letting those dour realizations ruin this moment. It was fun pretending to be a normal girl, fooling around with the boy she liked, and hoping she didn't get caught. The old me would never be so daring. I had too much to lose to let any sweet and sexy moment with Oscar slip through my fingers.

I parted my lips and took as much of him as I could into my mouth. I swallowed reflexively and looked at him from under the fringe of my bangs when he growled my name as quietly as he could. One of his hands grabbed a handful of my hair and pulled it away from my face; the other curled into the fabric of my comforter.

I sucked hard until my cheeks hollowed out and used my tongue to outline every ridge and divot that traveled his impressive length. His hips arched the smallest bit, and his long legs shifted restlessly underneath me.

I felt his body react to my mouth and hands. It felt like he grew even harder, and I could taste how turned on he was the longer I licked at him. I lapped at the leaking slit and slid my hand along the wet trail my mouth left. I could feel his body throbbing and the way his cock kicked in response as I loosened and tightened my hand around him.

Oscar grunted and used the hold he had in my hair to move my head in a rhythm I wouldn't have found on my own. The motion was a bit harsh and made my eyes water. I dug my fingernails into his sides and swallowed as the tip of his cock tapped the back of my throat. This wasn't the first time I attempted to give a guy head, but it was the first time I was as invested in the act as my partner. I didn't know it was possible to get turned on by simply giving someone else so much pleasure. Every sound that escaped his lips, every shift of his big body, every drop of silky, salty fluid that touched my tongue made my insides tingle. My nipples tightened into hard points, and my skin started to feel too tight. I wanted to rub against him like a cat.

One of Oscar's hands found its way under my shirt, and his fingers danced up my rib cage. He only got so far before our position prevented him from getting his hands on anything good. His fingertips felt like little points of fire everywhere they touched. I was getting dizzy; I don't know if it was because I forgot to breathe while I had a mouthful of rigid flesh, or if I was simply that weak and eager for his touch.

Oscar swore under his breath, still trying to be quiet and not alert my dad. He pulled me up and over the top of him. He pulled off my oversized t-shirt and the stretchy black shorts I was wearing with hasty hands. Since I'd been stuck at home as of late, I didn't bother to wear anything underneath the casual clothes. He got me naked much faster than I got him partially unclothed.

Before I threw his jeans on the floor, he motioned for his wallet. I was at a loss when he handed me a condom and watched what I would do with amused eyes.

I took a deep breath and tried to recall the very basic sex education private school offered.

Things slowed down while I fumbled through, getting the protection situated correctly. It was uncanny the way he made me feel like both my old self and new self at the same time. Oscar brought out both parts of me without even trying. Sometimes I felt wise beyond my years when I was with him, and other times, like right now, I really reverted to an unsure teenager experiencing big things for the first time.

I leaned over so I could place my lips over his. It was a deep kiss. It was an intense kiss. It was an important kiss. I felt like far more than our lips were connected when his mouth moved under mine. He told me he liked me, and I could tell how much by the way he kissed me back.

His hands skimmed up my spine and across my shoulders. He pulled me closer, and I felt his hardness rub through the wetness that was gathering between my legs. The way I was arched over him was incredibly intimate and open. It was always hard to hide anything from him. I don't know how I'd kept the truth hidden for so long.

One of his hands covered my breast. He slid his palm across my pebbled nipple and caught my gasp of pleasure with his mouth as the kiss turned wild and wet. I rocked my hips forward and felt the tip of his straining erection drag through sensitive folds. I was already wet and ready from driving him out of his mind with my amateur blow-job skills. The head of his cock knocked purposely against my clit, and the sensation was so intense I forgot to breathe for a moment.

"If you want it, you have to take it, Vesper. This is your show... your turf. I don't make the rules up on the Hill."

I moaned and rocked against him again, forcing his hardness against my softness. It felt so good. But it wasn't enough. I wanted him inside me. I wanted more.

"You don't make the rules anywhere, Oscar. But you sure have no problem breaking them all over the place."

He chuckled, and his dark eyes glimmered brightly. "I only break the ones that get in my way."

"Spoken like a true thief."

"When you have nothing that's yours, it's easy to convince yourself that it's okay to take things that belong to someone else. But, when you finally find something... or someone... who belongs to you and only you, stealing suddenly seems a lot more wrong than it once did."

My heart squeezed at his words, and I had to close my eyes because I was sure he could see every unvarnished feeling I had for him clear as day.

Instead, I reached between our heated bodies and wrapped a hand around the stiff flesh poised at my opening. Oscar muttered my name as I slowly sat on his rigid length.

The press of his body into mine made my eyes flutter closed. I braced my hands on his chest and started to move. It took a second, and his hands on my hips, for me to find my rhythm. Once I did, I bounced up and down on him like he was my favorite ride. It was fun to feel in control and in charge of how fast or slow we found our pleasure. I panted and moaned until he put a hand over my mouth and looked at me with a knowing smirk. He put a finger to his lips and silently reminded me how bad it would be if we were interrupted.

He pressed his thumb against my lips until I sucked it in and locked it between my teeth. I swirled my tongue around the digit and watched as the sensation made him grind his teeth together. He retaliated by catching one of my nipples between his fingers and relentlessly pulling at the hard point. The rough caress made my breasts feel heavy and sent pleasure shooting right to my core.

I moved faster and more frantically on top of him. The only noise in the room was our heavy breathing and the slick, sexy sounds of our bodies moving together.

I was certain I would send Oscar over the edge first if I kept sucking on his finger and grinding against him for all I was worth. He changed the dynamic and regained the upper hand when he slipped one of his hands between my legs and gently rubbed his fingers over my clit. It wasn't a sneak attack since I watched him do it, but the sensation that washed over me was unlike anything I had felt before. I was blindsided by pure bliss. It felt so good; it almost hurt.

I came around a strangled shout and fell forward in a boneless heap as a powerful orgasm rippled through my whole body. While I was draped over the top of Oscar, he caught me around the waist and rolled us over so that he was on top. While I was passive and pliant, he moved inside of me, rough and fast, until he found his own hurried release. There was always something a touch desperate and needy about how we went at each other. Kind of like we both realized that being together went against the natural order of things. We held each other like we were afraid the other would disappear at any given moment.

Unfortunately, we didn't get the chance to bask in an afterglow. As soon as we separated, I heard my dad calling me from somewhere nearby. He wasn't outside my bedroom door, thank God, but he was close enough I nearly kicked Oscar off my bed in my haste to climb back into my clothes. I ran to the hallway, shutting the door firmly behind me as I raced to the top of the stairs.

I was panting and trying to look like I hadn't just had sex while asking, "Are you looking for me? I thought you were working, so I planned on leaving you alone for the rest of the night."

"Have you noticed anything unusual in the last couple of hours? The security company called and said a couple of the outdoor cameras stopped working. They're sending out a tech to take a look. I was engrossed in what I was writing, so I didn't hear or see anything. I wanted to check with you, and I'm going to call Carlotta to see if she noticed anything before she left." He tilted his head and gave me a concerned look. "Are you feeling all right? You look flushed. Do you have a fever?" He took a step toward the stairs, and I waved my hands in front of myself to stop him.

"No. I feel fine. I was just following some dumb workout trend on TikTok. I haven't seen or heard anything weird other than you leaving your office while you're deep in deadline mode."

He laughed and shrugged. "Guilty as charged. I think I'm going to go walk around the house and check things out just to be sure."

I panicked because Oscar was still in my room and needed a way out of the house. If my dad was wandering around, and then the security company sent a tech out, his window for escape was going to be incredibly narrow.

"I think you should just wait for the security company, Dad. What if it's another obsessed fan? You pay for security, so why put yourself at risk?"

He tapped his chin and nodded after thinking it over for a minute. "You make a good point. I guess I'll eat something since my flow was interrupted. Did you already eat?"

I nodded and put a hand over my thundering heart. "I'm good. Let me hop in the shower real quick, and I'll come down and join you. I don't want you to eat alone."

He smiled at me and turned in the direction of the kitchen. "Take your time. I still want to call Carlotta, but I would appreciate the company."

Once he was out of sight, I dashed back to my room. I was prepared to rush Oscar out of the house with a hurried apology, but my room was empty. I checked the closet, the bathroom, and even under my bed. Oscar was nowhere to be found. I could almost convince myself I dreamed the entire encounter if there wasn't a torn condom wrapper peeking out from under one of my pillows.

I called his name as softly as possible, but he was gone. He'd slipped out just as suddenly and quietly as he came in. I wondered why he didn't stick around to say goodbye or leave a note when I noticed that my phone was glowing with a notification.

Plain as day, Rex's name was in the sender field. Even if Oscar had only glanced at my phone when it pinged, he would've seen Rex's name, and he would know I lied about knowing the owner of the fancy car.

"Fuck me," I swore as I picked my phone up and read the message.

~ Are you ready to play nice yet, Vee?

Instead of replying to Rex, I sent a message to Oscar.

~ I can explain. I promise whatever you think it is—it's not.

There was no response, and my dad was calling for me to hurry up if I planned on keeping him company while he ate.

I took a super-fast shower and ran down the stairs, still clutching my phone. My dad frowned when he saw me, and once again questioned if I felt all right. I guess I looked a little pale, and my hands were far from steady.

I tried to text Oscar a few more times, and the longer it went without a response, the worse I felt. It was like Rex had the uncanny ability to make every bad situation worse. His timing was impeccable.

I ended up being a lousy dinner date for my dad, and he quickly returned to work after I offered to clean up.

I got another message, and my heart sank when I saw it was from Rex, not Oscar.

~ We should talk, Vesper.

~ I have nothing to say to you.

~ I have a lot to say to you.

I swore and knocked the corner of my phone against my forehead. The last person I wanted to have a conversation with was Rex Wallace. However, if I met with him, maybe I could get him to admit he was the one who shared those sexy pictures. And maybe, just maybe, I could get him to confess to the part he played in Elliot Osborn's death. He still had no idea that I knew how evil and entitled he really was.

~ Fine. Let's talk, but it will be the last time we have anything to do with each other.

~ We'll see about that.

The threat was clear, but so was my determination to finally bring the asshole down. I was not going to lose Oscar in vain, and I would not let Rex ruin any more lives in any timeline.

NINETEEN

SNEAK ATTACK

I agreed to meet Rex at the same coffee shop where I picked Oscar up for our pseudo-date. At first, he tried to convince me to meet him somewhere alone, but I knew that was a terrible idea and flatly refused. Once Rex realized he could no longer threaten or cajole me into getting his way, he relented and agreed to a meetup in public.

I was nervous. I knew Rex had a lot to lose, and he'd more than likely already murdered someone just for the thrill of it. He scared me more than Oscar ever had. There was something about a very bad guy hiding his evil intentions under a veneer of civility that made my skin crawl and had every warning bell in existence ringing frantically in my head. I knew it would be a long shot to get Rex to admit that he was behind the robbery and that he killed Oscar's brother, but now that Oscar knew I lied about knowing Rex, I also had nothing to lose.

I threaded my way through the tables and around customers to a small table in the back of the upscale shop. Rex looked as comfortable as could be tucked away in a corner with an expensive tablet propped up in front of him. He was smirking at whatever he was watching on the screen and leisurely sipping from a white mug. When I sat down across from him, the way his gaze gleamed at me in unspoken triumph sent chills down my spine and made my stomach turn.

I put my small purse on the table in front of me and curled my hands together to keep them still.

"You wanted to talk, so talk."

Rex chuckled and set his coffee mug down. "Are you enjoying your suspension? Wouldn't it have been so much easier if you just pretended to be my girlfriend like I asked? If you played along and got that money back from your dad, the entire town never would've seen you like that."

I sucked a breath in between my teeth and steeled myself from lashing out. I had a bigger purpose than letting Rex know what an asshole he was. I needed to keep him talking, not push him to the point where he got angry and walked away.

"Who cares if the whole town has seen me in my underwear? You act like I have to stay here for the rest of my life. You seem to think a mistake I made as an impressionable teen will define me for the rest of my life. I know that isn't true." I shrugged indifferently. "And who knows. I might be able to prove you're the one who shared those pictures. If that happens, both of us are to blame."

Rex laughed again. He reached and pushed my purse to the side, which made me tense. I ordered myself to calm down and tried not to react any further as he flipped the tablet around and showed me the video he was watching before I sat down.

"Sure. Maybe you can outrun some harmless, sexy pictures, but I don't think the same is true if this video starts making the rounds. It'll ruin you. And I'm sure it will have a pretty big impact on your father's business and reputation as well." His smirk turned outright malevolent as his eyebrows lifted mockingly. "Go ahead and hit play."

I watched him with trepidation. I didn't want to give him the satisfaction of watching whatever had him feeling so smug, but my curiosity got the better of me.

I regretted the impulse immediately. As soon as the video came to life, the black screen switched to a very x-rated image of a woman who looked alarmingly like me, having some seriously hardcore sex with multiple men. It was a high-quality porn movie, and I seemed to be the star. Only, I never, and would never, put myself in that situation. I was all for sexual liberation and for a woman owning her own body, but I had my dad to think about. After all, he was a public figure, and he did have a wholesome and heartwarming brand to consider.

I watched my doppelgänger handle three men with ease and didn't look away until someone sat down at the table behind me.

I hurriedly clicked the video off and stared at a grinning Rex across the table. "I'll ruin you if you don't give me what I want, Vee. Planning your downfall has been so much fun. It's a shame your dad called off the wedding. I could've helped Addy and her mom get their hands on his entire estate. You've thrown a wrench in all my plans since that day. It's so annoying. I miss the old you who did whatever I asked without question. This 'new' you sucks."

I hissed a breath between my gritted teeth and stared at him through a veil of rage that clouded my vision. It never occurred to me through my arrest, the trial, the time I spent locked up that anyone other than Addison and her mother was behind what happened to my father and me. I always believed, down to my bones, that Addison's mother married with the intent to murder my dad and get her hands on his money. Rex's revelation made my mind spin. I knew he had a hand in setting me up when he testified against me, but I was stunned his machinations went so much farther than that.

"It's a deep fake. You digitally imposed my face on that woman's body. My dad warned me you might do something like that." I sounded calm despite the fury I was practically choking on. "I can prove it's not me."

"Sure. You have experts dissect the video and declare you innocent, but how long will that take? How bad will your reputation be by then? What will your future prospects be with even a hint of this in your background? The internet stretches out endlessly. You can leave the Hill, but I can make sure this video follows you anywhere you go."

My nostrils flared, and I could feel blood heating my cheeks and throat. I was sure the flush crawling across my skin looked as furious as I felt.

"What do you want, Rex?"

He leaned back in his seat and crossed his arms over his chest, looking every inch the victorious villain.

"I want your dad to repledge that money to mom's campaign. No, double it. I want him to endorse her. I want him to publicly say she impacted him; he was willing to back her. I want you to talk to the other side of your family and get my mother a meeting with your grandparents. If they endorse her, I'll make sure that video never sees the light of day. I want you to play the doting girlfriend whenever I ask. I want you to follow me to college, like the lovesick girl you're supposed to be. We're going to be the perfect, young political couple. If you step out of line even a little bit, I'll drag you and your dad to hell with no qualms."

We stared at each other in tense silence for a long, drawn-out moment. I think he expected me to cave the minute I saw the video. He had no idea that my backbone was no longer made of glass. It wasn't brittle and breakable. My future self infused it with steel and tempered it against threats like these. It took a lot more to bring me to my knees than it used to.

I braced an elbow on the edge of the table and crooked a finger in his direction to draw him closer. When he leaned in, I whispered, "You might ruin my reputation by putting that video out in the world, but I can put you behind bars if people find out you're a murderer. What are you going to do to me from behind bars, Rex? And what are your parents going to do to you when they find out that you robbed a motel and murdered a young man for no reason? My dad's public image is nothing compared to your family's manufactured facade. No one cares about saving face as much as the Wallaces."

He blinked a few times, and a furrow dragged his golden eyebrows down in a deep V. It was his turn for his nostrils to flare and his face to flush a beet red.

"What in the fuck are you talking about, Vesper?" He pounded a fist on the small table. The motion bounced the tablet to the floor. Both of us ignored it as we glared at one another.

"You might think your money will keep the people in the Point quiet. You might think you covered all the bases and destroyed all the evidence, but there are eyes everywhere in that part of the city. People know how to hide and how to leverage information. That's the thing about rats, Rex; you can never get rid of them. You're not the only one who can drag someone to hell. I already know the way, and I guarantee I can get us there faster than you ever will."

He pulled back, and his scowl deepened. "You're full of shit. Do you think I'm dumb enough to buy that you're suddenly an expert on the Point? I don't care if you're fucking some scumbag from the slum. I know you've been hanging out with that asshole who punched me in the face. Someone saw you pick him up the night of the fundraiser. But you don't understand how that place operates. If someone has enough money, anything that happens in the Point can magically be rewritten. There is no history in a place like the Point. Nothing is solid."

I snorted at his ignorance and prejudice. "You are so wrong. Nothing disappears in the Point. The injustice lingers forever, and no one ever forgets how the rich get away with murder. It makes them angry and bitter, and most people who call the Point home can't wait to turn the tables. You don't have to believe me, but I know your dad's fancy car was at the motel that night. Someone saw you go into the office. Your parents can do their best to cover it all up, but I know everything, and I have no plans to stay quiet about any of it." I was stretching the truth since I had no real proof. As long as I got Rex talking and possibly lead him to a confession, I would play mind games with him all day long. "The young man you and your friends killed was barely older than us. He had his whole life in front of him and a family who loved him. You deserve to rot in the worst prison the Point has for taking a life for no reason at all. You're worse than any of the criminals there who are forced to do what they do because they have no choice. You have all the opportunities in the world, and you chose callously to take everything from someone else. You're the worst kind of person there is. Someone who does bad things because they can, not because they have to."

I gasped as one of his arms shot out, and his hand clasped the back of my head. He yanked me forward, almost like he was going to kiss me, but his lips landed near my ear. Rex whispered, "You have no idea just how bad the things I can do to you are. If you think I'm capable of killing for no reason, just imagine what I can do to you if you provoke me. Stop pushing your luck and be a good girl."

I struggled to get free. I grabbed my purse and stood up. I didn't get a confession, but I had enough that he wouldn't get away with the revenge porn, and maybe enough that the police could bring him in for questioning. Even that was more than they could do in the first investigation. It probably wasn't enough to get Oscar to forgive me or get him to back off, but it was something.

I turned and walked away from my former crush, cursing that young girl who tried to be perfect. Had I known how dangerous that desire to please would end up being, I never would've let myself be such a proper young lady. Who knew a streak of rebellion was the key to saving me every ounce of heartbreak I'd experienced?

I hurried away from the coffee shop. Once I got to my car, I pulled out my phone and hit the button to stop the voice recording. It was a crude way to trap him, but it was the best I could come up with on short notice. My dad had many different recording devices disguised as everyday objects so he could stealthily record conversations when he was looking for inspiration for banter for his books, but I didn't want to explain the odd reasons why I needed to borrow one.

I was scrambling, using shaking fingers to upload the recording to the Cloud and text the conversation to Oscar, just in case something happened to my phone, when the driver's door was jerked open. I forgot to lock it. Bad things really did happen to dumbasses, because I could've driven away. Rex grabbed my phone out of my hand and smashed it on the ground. How had I not remembered all the silly mistakes I made that led me to my ruin the first time around? This was history repeating itself in the worst way.

I yelled at Rex to stop, but it quickly turned to a scream of pain when he caught my arm and wrenched me out of the car. I hollered for help, but everyone on the sidewalk or passing by turned a blind eye. It was amazing that people who lived on the Hill could be as blind to wrongdoing as the people in the Point.

"Let go of me, Rex!" It was unbelievable that a boy who grew up with nothing and made his own rules was so much more reliable and trustworthy than the boy born into a golden life. "You will never get away with whatever you think you're doing. My dad will be the least of your worries when people realize I'm gone. The brother of the boy you killed at the motel knows who you are. He's coming for you. He already knocked you on your ass once. Imagine what he's going to do now that you've provoked him." I tossed Rex's words back at him, hopefully distracting him enough I could twist free. I figured Oscar wouldn't mind saving my ass once again, even though he was really mad at me at the moment. I stubbornly believed that Oscar was a better man than Rex had ever been.

He didn't answer as he pulled me across the street, his fingers digging painfully into my arm. I tried to dig in my heels. I struggled the whole way, but he was bigger and stronger than me, so my efforts were futile. It was like the situation in the school parking lot, but this time there was no Oscar to intervene and save me. I was more terrified of what Rex might do to me now than I'd ever been walking home at night from the diner.

He dragged me to a car I didn't recognize. I tried to bite his hand. I wiggled around so I could kick him. My purse fell to the ground, but it went ignored like the tablet from earlier.

I was calling him every name I could think of. I was yelling for help at the top of my lungs. I thought it was impossible for Rex to abduct me or hurt me in the middle of the day in such a populated area. Oscar was right, all a criminal needed was an opportunity, and I'd given Rex plenty.

Somehow he managed to get the door of the fancy sports car open while still controlling my movements and preventing my escape. I couldn't see what he was reaching for when he shifted toward the open door, but a moment later, my entire body froze and then collapsed as electricity zipped through all my nerves and muscles. I couldn't control my body. The pain and shock from being hit by a Taser was unlike anything I'd ever experienced before... which was saying a lot, since I'd been blown to kingdom come in another lifetime.

Rex grunted as I collapsed against him like a boneless jellyfish. I was struggling to breathe through the agony that coursed through me. I was like a ragdoll and offered no resistance when he shoved me mercilessly into the car. My head knocked against the window, and I fought to keep my eyes open. My hands spasmed, and my lungs felt like they had forgotten how to work.

"You need to remember that whatever happens next is all your fault, Vee. I gave you a way out. You refused to take it. I don't know what you think you know, but I'm not taking any chances. My dad loves this car as much as your father loves you. They're both going to grieve over what they lost." He sounded sickeningly satisfied with himself over whatever he had planned for me and the ridiculously expensive car.

I wanted to argue, wanted to say anything that might defuse the situation, but the next thing I knew, his fist was flying at my face, and everything faded out as my vision turned black and my ears started ringing. Before I fully passed out from the pain and the sucker punch to the face, my last thought was that I should've learned how to save myself.

All those years in the Point and the redo of my life up on the Hill, and I still couldn't keep myself safe. I wasn't a hero or a villain; I was forever caught up in the clash between the two.

TWENTY

RACE AGAINST TIME

I fought to get free as a fistful of bitter pills got shoved into my mouth. I tried to spit them out, but Rex clapped a hand over my face and blocked my nose. The only option I had was to gag down the dry, powdery residue. My hands were bound together in front of me, and I was strapped into the driver's seat by a tight and complicated seat belt system. It was different from the kind found in an everyday car. It locked me in place so tightly I could barely move. Rex was leaning down into the low-slung sports car, forcing a second mouthful of pills down my throat.

There was no telling what he was giving me, but my head already felt foggy and as heavy as a bowling ball. My breathing was choppy and uneven, and my heartbeat felt like it had crawled to a snail's pace. I felt like I was dreaming, but the threat, and Rex's plan to get rid of the Maserati and me, all at once, was plain as day.

The hill where we lived wasn't the only small mountain in the area. There was another section of the terrain that was steeper and harder to traverse. It was home to many popular hiking trails and typically filled with nature enthusiasts during the daytime. At night, the rough, unpaved roads that snaked down the side of the mountain became a very dangerous racetrack. High-powered sports cars and earth-rattling muscle cars zipped through the curves and often skidded off course and down into the ravine on either side. It was a deadly game with few winners. Rex was going to make it look like I was driving and lost control of the supercar, causing it to run off the road. Sadly, I knew it would be easy for him to convince anyone that I went along willingly with him. He could say we went for a nice drive to work out our recent differences. The way I fawned all over him before I came to my senses was going to haunt me forever. All he had to do now was put the car in neutral and give it a good push. Gravity and inertia would handle the rest. Especially if I was too stoned on whatever he drugged me with to react.

I couldn't lift my feet off the floorboards, and my head drooped heavily on my neck. I struggled to keep my eyes open as he situated me where he wanted me.

"This car is insured for so much money; my dad will eventually forgive me for getting rid of it." Rex hummed under his breath and forced my head up so I could look him in the eye with a finger under my chin. "I should've taken care of this loose end the night of the robbery. But it's such a nice car. I hated to destroy it."

My stomach twisted and my numb fingers twitched. He was remorseful over the loss of the car but could care less about the young life he'd ended. How could I have missed how sick and twisted he was? How had I not seen how morally corrupt his entire family seemed to be?

"Thanks for the heads up about the witness that night. I was pretty sure I covered all my tracks in the slums, but now I know there is a bit more cleaning up to do." Rex sighed and dropped my head. It flopped forward in a lifeless manner as my ears started to ring and it became even more difficult to breathe.

"Why?" I barely got the word out. It was more an expulsion of air, but Rex heard me.

"Why? Why did me and my friends rob the motel? Why did I shoot the kid behind the counter? Why was I ever there in the first place?" He chuckled, but it was a dark and broken sound. "Because I was bored. Because I'm tired of trying to be who my parents want me to be all the damn time. I'm sick of perfection. In the Point, you get to be as bad as you want, and there are very few consequences. I wanted to see how that felt for once. As for killing that kid, I couldn't leave a witness. He just had the bad luck of being the one behind the counter that night. I would've shot whomever was there." He sighed and flashed a wicked grin that made my skin crawl. "Watching him bleed and beg for his life was the most fun I've had in I don't know how long. I look forward to his brother coming to find me. I'm happy to send him off into the void as well. Someone like that can't be a threat to someone like me. You should know that better than anyone, Vee."

He moved to slam the door, but he looked down at me one last time before it closed. He reached out to free my hands. He tried to brace them on the sleek steering wheel, but they fell into my lap a second later. I had no control of my limbs or this fucked situation.

"You're different. It'll be fun to see how unhinged everyone becomes when they find out you're gone. I wonder if they'll praise you for being the fucking uptight prima donna you've always been, or if they're going to remember the annoying, self-righteous bitch you've become. I can't wait to watch your dad suffer. I hope you feel terrible for all that you're about to put him through, Vesper. You are such a selfish and self-righteous daughter."

Of course, I wanted to refute everything he said. I wanted to scream and vent. I wanted to punch him in the face and kick him in the balls, but the pills in my system turned me into a zombie. Every single part of me was numb and immobile. I felt like I had to throw up, but even that took more effort and stamina than I had.

I heard the car's tires start to crunch over gravel as it slowly rolled forward. Everything in my lethargic body screamed at me to put my foot on the brake and grab the steering wheel, but I couldn't move. Out of the corner of my barely open eye, I caught the reflection of Rex happily waving to me as the car started to pick up momentum and roll faster and faster down the incline. It was a straight shot for the first hundred yards, but the first turn on the hazardous road was a hairpin. Even fully awake with functioning reflexes, the drive was harrowing. This time, there would be nothing to stop the car from barreling over the edge into the deep valley below.

I started to cry. At least, I think I did. It was hard to tell what was real and what was my imagination as the drugs moved faster through my system because of the heart-racing fear I was experiencing. I felt like I was watching this scenario happen to another person. It seemed as unreal and inexplicable as waking up on my eighteenth birthday after the explosion at the motel. I couldn't figure out why every reality was so deadly. But at least it wasn't going to be my dad who died in this version. I was super pissed at myself that I had the wrong bad guy in both lifetimes and that Rex was going to get away with murder all over again. It was disgusting how much pleasure he took in the suffering of others. He was so much worse than anyone I encountered in the Point. All over again, I realized I'd missed so much by refusing to look at anything going on around me after my father passed away in my first life.

The car started to shake, and the windows rattled as the speed increased and the road became more uneven. I could see trees and the sky whizz by at an alarming rate. I was so mad I didn't get the chance to tell my father I loved him and give him a proper goodbye yet again. My heart twisted painfully when I thought about Oscar finding out I was gone so soon after losing his brother. I knew he was going to feel guilty, and everything I'd done to keep him from throwing his life away would be for naught. Rex was a master at creating the most damage possible with his calculated attack.

The car started to veer off to one side. A cloud of dust flew up and blocked out the brief glimpse of what was flying by outside. The vibration rattled my teeth, and my fingers flicked and spasmed where they rested uselessly in my thighs. I ordered my feet to follow my commands, but it was no use. A minute later, I was thrown to the side so violently that I was pretty sure I heard something inside my body pop and snap. The extensive seatbelt system caged me in as the world rattled around me.

I finally let my eyes shut and sent up a silent goodbye to those I was leaving behind. I wanted to ask for another chance to do everything all over, but what were the chances that I wouldn't screw that one up as well? I resigned myself to my fate. Enzo's stupid Cousin and I were going out in the most dramatic way possible. At least this time, there was someone who would miss me when I was gone.

Just as I was fully ready to give up, the sound of metal grinding on metal and the tinkling of broken glass filled my fuzzy ears. The collision jerked me in the opposite direction, and the car shrieked in protest as the forward momentum was abruptly brought to a violent stop. I could smell gasoline and blood. It felt like my brains were scrambled, and my entire body was bruised. I heard another loud *pop* as my bones took a beating. I could feel tiny bits of the shattered windshield on my face and in my hair.

I was still caught in the three-point harness and limp as a doll with no stuffing. I was also hanging upside down, my hands dragged over the interior of the roof. It was super dramatic and scary, but I couldn't do anything other than dangle there.

I was bleeding from somewhere. Blood trickled down my face and into my eyes. The metallic scent filled my nostrils as the scarlet liquid started to soak my hair. I have no idea how long I stayed trapped upside down while all the blood rushed to my head, but I could feel that I was on the verge of losing consciousness when the mangled door pressed against me was pried open.

I tried to open my eyes, but I couldn't. And even if I did, there would be no seeing through the veil of blood that covered my face.

I vaguely heard a deep voice swearing up a storm as the harness of the seatbelt was popped open. The smell of spilled fuel and smoke got stronger as someone pulled me roughly from the totaled supercar. The bones that snapped in the collision screamed in protest, but I didn't make a sound.

Frantic fingers peeled my eyelids back, and I was stunned to see Oscar looming over me. He was as bloody and messy as I felt. I heard him call my name over and over again, but I couldn't answer.

I blacked out for the second time that day as the pain overwhelmed me. I was honestly grateful for the narcotics in my system. If I hurt enough to lose consciousness with all those pills in my bloodstream, I doubted I would survive the agony of the varied injuries while sober.

When I came to, I was on my back on the ground looking up at the sky. Someone was holding my hand, and I could hear sirens off in the distance. I still couldn't move very well, and I hurt all over, but I managed to turn my head enough to see Oscar sitting on the ground next to me. His clothes were torn. His face was covered in blood, some of it dried in places, and he looked beaten down and exhausted.

When he turned his head to look down at me, I could see places on his red-stained cheeks where tears had rolled down his handsome face. Our eyes locked, and his hand squeezed mine tightly.

"Hold on a little bit longer. I called in the accident, and the paramedics are on the way. They couldn't get up the mountain, so I had to carry you down."

I tried to ask him how he found me and stopped the Maserati from going off the road, but the words wouldn't come out.

He reached down and picked a piece of my bloody hair off my forehead. He smelled like candy and motor oil.

"I put an AirTag on the Maserati the night of the fundraiser. I've known where it was since that evening. When it showed up on the mountain, I knew something was wrong, and when I heard the voicemail you sent..." He shook his head and let out a breath that made his whole body shudder. "That was smart of you, by the way, trying to trick him into confessing. But I knew you were in trouble when you didn't answer me when I called you back. I grabbed Elliot's car and raced up here to confront Richie Rich. I ran head-on into the Maserati as it was coming around the curve. Luckily, I stopped it before it went off the road." By stopped, he meant he'd crashed into it. Oscar swore and looked down at me with his too-soft heart in his dark eyes. "I could either stop the car or go after the dickhead who shot Elliot. I could see him standing at the top of the mountain, watching the car lose control like it was a damn movie. I had a bad feeling you were stuck in the car, so the choice was easy. I'm glad I picked you. So you have to hold on and be okay, Vesper, because I gave up everything to save you."

His shot at taking down Rex. His beloved brother's car. His revenge. The indifference about what happened to him as long as he made someone pay for what happened to his brother. He gave up everything that mattered to him so he could save me.

Oscar stroked his thumb over my forehead, clearing a spot so he could drop a kiss on my face without getting a mouthful of blood. It was a sweet gesture and one I would take with me when everything faded away around me.

"Now I have even more reason to put that guy in the fucking ground," Oscar growled just as help arrived. I went from looking at him to looking into a little light that was flashed in my eyes as a uniform-clad paramedic buzzed around me.

I vaguely heard someone ask Oscar if I was a known drug user. Whoever it was seemed more concerned about my blood pressure and labored breathing than the fact I had several broken bones and was covered in blood.

I lost Oscar's reply in the buzzing that started to fill my head and the immense weight that seemed to crush my chest.

"Vesper!" I heard Oscar call my name, but he sounded very far away. My eyes drifted closed again, and I wondered if I was ever going to open them again. There was a deep sense of dread swirling through the darkness that engulfed me. Whatever was happening to my body was a hundred times worse than being blown up. It hurt so much more.

Vaguely, I recognized more sirens, and a familiar voice called Oscar's name. I couldn't place the deep growl, but whomever belonged to the stern voice was keeping Oscar from fighting his way to me as I was loaded into the back of an ambulance. They ordered him to calm down and asked him to explain what was going on. He was fighting hard to get to me, as if he knew once he could no longer see me, I would be gone forever.

Oscar quieted when the other deep voice told him he had news he needed to share. It was all happening in a haze, so I couldn't tell if it was real or not. At some point, I was pretty sure my mind separated from my body, and I was looking down at myself dying as I lay on the stretcher below me. There was so much blood, and I was so cold and still. The girl was as white as bone, and her dark hair dripped with crimson liquid.

What a tragic character she was destined to be. I couldn't help but feel sorry for her.

I wanted to thank Oscar for saving me—all those times—and giving me a fighting chance.

I wanted to apologize for lying to him. I wanted to tell him I more than liked him and that I would do everything in my power, and use every ounce of my privilege, to help him bring Rex down. I desperately wanted the right words to tell him how much he meant to me and how much better I was as a human after having him in my life, both then and now. Our relationship, whatever it was, made me appreciate our differences and realize how powerful our similarities were.

But all I could do was slip away as breathing became impossible, and the pain launched into the realm of unbearable. This ending was bittersweet, maybe because I saw it coming and there was nothing I could do about it.

I knew one thing for sure: I was tired of my life slipping away while I still had so much I wanted to change and so many things I wanted to experience.

Maybe, just maybe, the third time I got to restart my life would be a charm.

TWENTY-ONE

THE USUAL SUSPECTS

"The head-on collision caused several fatalities. The remote location was difficult for rescue crews to access. Authorities aren't saying if it was illegal racing gone wrong, but the age of those involved and the types of cars at the scene indicate racing as a high probability. Local governments from both sides of the city have promised to address the dangerous road that is the scene of frequent accidents and fatalities. This has been Madison Martin reporting live from the crash site. I'll be back at ten with more details and information for the evening news. Thank you for choosing Channel Thirteen, first in facts as the story breaks."

The cultured, pleasant voice broke through the steady beeping that was echoing in my head. The void of blackness I was swimming through suddenly burst like a bubble and I was thrown into a blinding white light. It was so intensely bright that it hurt. I tried to suck in a deep breath close my eyes against the glare, but the brightness was everywhere. It engulfed me like a living thing. It burned my eyes. It crawled across my skin and pumped through my blood. Every place the light touched, I was acutely, achingly aware of it. Pain crawled all over my body. It was a dull throb that seemed to fill me up from head to toe. I felt like I'd been run over by a semi-truck and been buried alive.

"There she is. I've been waiting for over a month to see those pretty gray eyes of yours for myself. Your dad was right; they are special." A young woman came into view as the white light slowly faded away. She sounded cheerful and friendly, and her hands were incredibly gentle as they moved over me and around the machines making loud noises. "My name is Addison. I'm the nurse who has been in charge of your day-to-day care while you've been with us. We've spent a lot of time together over the last month. I feel like we're best friends even though we've never officially met. You can call me Addy when you're ready to start talking."

I couldn't speak, my mouth tasted foul and bitter, and I could hardly keep my eyes open. I must've looked toward the TV because the blonde nurse chuckled and reached for a remote to turn off the news. "Try not to move too much, and you won't be able to speak until your throat heals a bit. You were intubated for a long time." She sighed and offered a change of subject seamlessly. "My last name is actually Martin as well. Madison Martin and I are not related. Since our names are so similar, I sometimes get her mail and have crazy fans show up at my apartment thinking I'm her." The nurse laughed and shook her head. "I usually watch the news on a different station because she weirds me out, but it's been on in your room because your dad seems to like her." I felt soft fingers brush my forehead and push my bangs to the side. "I'm going to let Dr. Nam know you're finally awake. She's good. She told your dad it would be any day now that you would come back to him. She might be as excited as he'll be that you finally rejoined us. I'll be right back, Vesper. Just try and relax. Everything will be fine."

I blinked, and it took every ounce of strength I had. My eyelids felt like they weighed a thousand pounds each. My throat was on fire, and my mouth was as dry as the Sahara. I had no idea what was going on or how long I'd been unconscious in the hospital. The nurse, who looked *exactly* like Addy, said she'd been waiting a month to see my eyes, but I couldn't make sense of it. Addison already knew what my eyes looked like, and she definitely wouldn't ever ever go into healthcare. Also, Madison Martin wasn't a newscaster—was she? I was having a really hard time making my mind work the way it was supposed to. All my thoughts were cloudy and wispy. I couldn't land on anything that felt solid. Everything felt like vapor floating all around me, slipping through my fingers whenever I tried to grab onto a memory.

The confusion intensified when the nurse brought the doctor in to check on me. Dr. Nam was a small, older Asian woman who was also incredibly familiar, but not in the way I remembered.

She smiled and poked and prodded me from top to bottom. Occasionally she hummed in either approval or disappointment, but through it all, I got the overwhelming feeling that this woman had done her very best to take care of me. She was truly my guardian angel in whatever role she played in my life, in whatever version of my life she appeared.

"I know it hurts to move and to talk. You'll get tired very easily for the foreseeable future, and I'm sure you have a killer headache. I won't go over everything that happened to you or go in-depth about your diagnosis until you're up to it. It would be best if we wait for the more serious questions and concerns until you can communicate. For now, blink once if the answer to my question is yes, twice for no. Do you think you can manage that, Vesper?"

I blinked once, but now that she mentioned my head hurting, I realized I was in agony. It felt like there was an ax lodged into my skull, and a million angry bees were buzzing around the inside. Every time my heart pumped a beat, my brain pulsed painfully. It made me want to rip my head off my shoulders.

"Do you remember how you ended up in the hospital?" Dr. Nam asked the question softly while running her hands over my head. Her manner was identical to the woman I remembered from the motel. Her kindness saved my faith in humanity when I was at the end of the emotional rope. The machines beeped angrily as I tried to respond. I forgot I couldn't talk, and the words caught in my throat forced me to choke and cough, which made my head want to explode even more.

Everything hurt. Really, really hurt.

I blinked twice. I thought I was in the hospital because of a car accident, but I couldn't be sure. Between her and the nurse, who was Addison's twin, I was very bewildered and lost.

"Okay. Don't worry too much. You suffered a traumatic brain injury. Memory loss is to be expected. The severity can be assessed when you feel a bit better. You have a lot of healing to do, but your vitals are strong, your body is on the mend, and the human brain is a miraculous thing. I think you'll be back to normal in no time. You have to be patient with yourself." She picked up one of my hands and gave it a soft pat. It was such a familiar gesture, but still felt totally foreign. "Your father has been here with you the entire time. He refused to leave your side. No one believed that you would bounce back more than him. I can't wait to tell him that you're awake. I know you're in a lot of pain. We'll try and help with that. Sit tight."

The nurse who looked like my former best friend, and the doctor who looked like the woman who took me in at the motel, bent their heads together and started talking in low tones. Another nurse, who looked a lot like the superfan I encountered when I woke up after the explosion, messed around with the drip line hanging somewhere over my head. While everyone was occupied, I took inventory of my battered body.

There were a plethora of wires and tubes attached to different parts of me. One of my arms was immobilized in a cast, there was a brace around my neck, and one of my ankles was wrapped up like a mummy. Something itchy ran across my forehead, which I assumed was a healing wound. Every ragged breath made my chest and ribs scream in protest. And my entire brain felt like it had been used as a punching bag. I couldn't believe how bad just blinking my tired eyes hurt. Even without the full picture, I could tell I was one hell of a mess.

All I wanted to do was fall back into the void where even a time slip seemed more plausible than whatever I'd woken up to. I couldn't remember anything, and everything I thought I knew seemed to be wrong or misplaced. It was very scary and super hard to process on top of the pain wracking my body. I closed my eyes and silently asked to drift back to oblivion, but the small reprieve was interrupted by a harsh, raspy voice calling my name. I couldn't turn my head to look in the direction of the sound. A moment later, a man I would recognize anywhere was hovering over me. He was crying, his tears landing on my skin as his fingertips traced over my face.

My dad looked exactly how he'd looked the last time I saw him. Though now he was wearing casual jeans and a familiar, faded flannel shirt, instead of something fancy and designer. His dark hair was styled away from his face. His eyes were still kind and intelligent. His elegant and distinct features, which had aged so well, clearly showed his sorrow and worry for me. His structured facial hair was now scruffy and speckled with gray, making him appear a bit older than I recalled, but it didn't matter because he was in one piece and looked strong and healthy. He was in far better shape than I was at the moment.

My dad started crying in earnest as he lifted my hand that wasn't in the cast and held it to his face. The wires and tubes coming out of the back looked horrifying, but I guess they had kept me alive, so it could be worse.

"I knew you were going to wake up. You've always been a fighter. You would never give up." His breath caught, and he squeezed my fingers hard enough to hurt. "Dr. Nam told me you can't remember why you're here. She told me your memory might be touch and go, along with some other basic functions. You've been in a coma for nearly a month. As long as you're awake, I know you can overcome anything. You're so strong, Vesper. So brave. I love you so much." He took a deep breath and rattled out an excuse that seemed to roll off his tongue as if he used it so often it was second nature. "Your mother would be here if she could. I hope you know that. She's trying to get better, and having you in the hospital for a month while she's stuck in her house, unable to leave because of her condition," he shook his head and looked apologetic, "it's another tragedy. Her agoraphobia is out of control, but it shouldn't stop her from being a mother. I know she feels awful that she can't be here when you need her the most."

My dad kept crying while I turned the new information over in my foggy brain. Was I in a coma? But how did I end up there? What was the cause of all these damn injuries? Wasn't my mom gone? Didn't she leave me when I was little? Could those memories be real? Was she really the recluse from the motel? She was the one I was always trying to catch a glimpse of... the one I was sure had the answers I needed? How could that be?

Everything inside of me erupted into chaos. I was sure I was still unconscious, and all of this was just another hallucination. I was pretty sure I'd gone crazy and my mind had splintered into a million different realities. How would I ever know what was real and what wasn't?

Was there an explosion? Or a car accident? Was my ending and beginning something else entirely? My reality seemed liquid and undefinable. My past, present, and future blended into a kaleidoscope of fantasy and uncertainty.

What was real?

My dad cleared his throat and lifted the hem of his shirt to wipe his face. "I don't want to overwhelm you since you just opened your eyes. I will tell you that you had an accident, that's how you landed in the hospital. You took a nasty fall down the stairs. You broke your wrist. You tore a muscle in your neck. Your ankle has a nasty sprain. You broke a few ribs and punctured a lung. But the most serious injury was to your head. You cracked your skull wide open, and your brain bounced around inside your skull really hard. It swelled up and started bleeding. You had to have several surgeries to get the situation under control. You're a very lucky girl, but you've got an ugly haircut at the moment. The day you fell, your stepmom stopped by your place to pick up the dishes you took home for leftovers when you came over for your little brother's birthday. If she hadn't found you and called for help..." he trailed off and choked up. "I know you don't get along with Pearl, but she saved your life. She's brought Tobi and Jordan to see you every single day you've been here. The kids have been as anxious for you to wake up as I was. They love you so much."

Stepmom? Jordan and Tobi? The kids I saved, the kids I adored without a second thought—did I know them from somewhere else? What on earth was going on?

My dad put my hand back on the bed as delicately as if it were fine china. He patted my arm and let out a shaky breath.

"Dr. Nam needs to run some tests, and she said your head probably hurts something fierce. Your visitation is limited for the time being, so I'll bring the kids to see you when you're feeling better." He sighed and reached out to stroke my forehead. I realized my bangs were gone. I wondered exactly how much hair I'd lost while they were fighting to save my life. "There's someone else who has been dying to get in here, but he has to wait his turn. And don't be surprised if a detective comes by to get a statement from you. They want to talk to you about what happened the day you fell. Your roommate, Devon, keeps saying it was an accident, that you were the only one at home. But Detective King seems suspicious of her. I trust that guy. He's sharp as a tack."

Devon? As in my love rival Devon? How was she my roommate? And was she terrible enough, demented enough that she could've pushed me down the stairs? It was too much to take in. My banged-up brain hit the limit it could tolerate in this state.

I let out a deep, uneven breath and let my eyes close. This time, there was no black oblivion, and the stark pain followed me into the darkness. I heard the medical staff moving around me and felt my IV move as the line attached to my hand jiggled. A moment later, the pain dulled to an almost bearable level. I still hurt all over, and I was disoriented and unclear about who was who and what was what. I wondered if I was losing my mind or had already lost it.

Nothing felt real or concrete.

I wanted to sleep and wake up in a world that made sense, but there was no rest to be found. I was trying to piece my life together through a haze of doubt and heavy painkillers. I wasn't even sure of my own name until my dad used it. I wondered if I would be in an entirely different life when I opened my eyes again. I was falling through time with nothing to grab onto and nothing to stop me from crashing into all the questions needling me and making me doubt my sanity.

I couldn't tell how much time passed. I had no idea who I was. I never felt so lost and alone.

It was all a fog of discomfort and confusion. But sometime after my hospital room quieted down, and the visits of doctors and nurses started to be less frequent, heavy footfalls brought someone to the side of my bed.

I pried my eyes open, but all I could see were shadows upon more shadows. It didn't matter. I would recognize Oscar in any situation, through any amount of haze and hardship. He was the one thing that felt genuine and tangible. He was the one thing that seemed unchanged. He was the only person I didn't question or wonder who he was to the current me. He used his knuckles to brush my cheek, and the familiar scent of candy and cigarettes wafted to my nose.

He was mine.

And I was his.

It didn't matter if it was before, after, or right now. The role Oscar played in my life was unchanging. His importance, and the truth of my feelings for him, remained unshifted on very unsteady ground.

"You look like hell, little lamb." Those rough fingers brushed over my other cheek and across my dry, chapped lips. "You aren't allowed to scare me like this ever again. You have to promise. I'm going to get in trouble for sneaking in to see you when you aren't supposed to have visitors. I might have to hurt someone if they try to keep me from you."

He was my Oscar. Everything I remembered, from the sound of his voice to how he spoke, and how his hands moved reverently over my face was the same. He still did sweet in his own special way. I would recognize it anywhere. Nothing about him scared me or made me feel like a lunatic.

"Your old man told me you might not remember me. I think he was hoping you forgot all about me. He will never like me. But I dare you to forget me." He let out a low laugh, but I could hear how strained and scared it sounded. I fought to bring his uniquely attractive face into focus, but the drugs the doctors had me on were too strong. He was just a dark blur that probably should've scared me instead of offered comfort.

His voice was ragged, and he sounded like he might cry when he told me, "I'll make you fall in love with me all over again if I have to. It was fun the first time, and I can fix everything I always screw up if I get to do it all over again. You can't get away from me that easily, Vesper. I have no intention of ever letting you go." He bent over me, and his lips touched that itchy spot right in the center of my forehead. It magically started to feel better. Sometimes an ouchie needed a kiss to make it stop hurting. Knowing Oscar was still here, and still a part of whatever life I was living now, was like some kind of cosmic balm to my tattered and torn soul.

He pulled back and whispered, "Rest up, little lamb. Get better, so you can come back to me. I've missed you."

Before he moved, I tried to grab his hand. I was too clumsy and uncoordinated, but he knew what I wanted and curled his fingers around mine.

I couldn't tell him anything. I couldn't ask him to stay. But I reached for him because that's what I always did. And he held onto me because that's what he always did.

That was the only reality that mattered.

TWENTY-TWO

WHAT A TANGLED WEB WE WEAVE

I may have woken up, but I was far from out of the woods.

I stayed in the hospital under a doctor's care for another two weeks, followed by several months of physical therapy. My fine motor skills and memory were affected by the brain injury. My mind reminded me of a big block of Swiss cheese. There were holes everywhere, some shallow and faint, others so deep I wondered if I would ever see the bottom of them. It was frustrating that I gained control of my fingers, toes, and overall mobility before everything in my mind and memory straightened out. I was also going to have a full head of hair before I could recall my past in full. Right now, I had short, dark stubble all over my head. It looked an awful lot like the shorn hair Oscar sprouted in the long, wildly detailed dream I had while I was unconscious.

My father was incredibly patient with my endless questions and recovery. He walked me through my childhood, my teen years, and filled me in on the basics of my current status as a young career woman. According to him, I was fresh out of college and had just started my dream job as a childhood speech pathologist. I guess my injured mind still recognized my desire to help kids from all walks of life, and that's why I imagined myself going to school to be an advocate. I wasn't a teenager or in my mid-twenties. I was in the middle of both.

But all the parts of my past and future life I imagined so clearly after my fall down the stairs seemed to have some basis in my real reality. The worlds I built while I was unconscious pulled from parts of my normal life, even if I couldn't remember any of those moments.

My dad really was a writer. Not one as successful and well-known as his imaginary counterpart, but he was skillful enough to support our family. He didn't write romance, but rather novels that focused on time travel and sci-fi. One of his books had even been adapted to a short-lived TV series. He told me it was my favorite of all his books, but it was too niche to find a following. It was about a young girl who could travel through time and how her actions in one timeframe drastically affected those in other realities. She was based on me, so of course, she was my favorite, and some of that story found its way into my injured mind. And while he made a decent living, we were not filthy rich. I don't know why I imagined my past self to be wealthy. We lived comfortably, but our house was not up on the Hill overlooking the ocean; it was at the bottom of the embankment, situated much closer to the train tracks. It was a modest home, and I had a very normal upbringing. There was no private school or plot to murder my father for his money. There were no school uniforms or fancy sports cars. I'd never been locked behind gilded gates in my youth. Maybe I had some unresolved envy over growing up in the shadow of such lavish lifestyles. And maybe I was acutely aware of how easy it would be to slip just a tiny bit and become a resident of the crime ridden part of the city. Again, reality was somewhere in between all the things I imagined myself to be.

I was already out of the house when my father remarried. And just like in my wild dream, I deeply opposed his wedding. I didn't protest to stop the rushed event, but I hadn't been very supportive or happy for him. He couldn't tell me why I never clicked with my stepmother. And I didn't remember that they'd been together for many years. I wasn't a fan of the relationship from the start, and it caused a lot of friction between my father and myself. I couldn't remember any of it, but it all sounded eerily like what happened in the life I lived while I was unnaturally asleep in the hospital. My father took on Pearl's two kids as his own as soon as they met, and I embraced them as my siblings from the get-go. Whatever forgotten reason I had for disliking Pearl, I didn't transfer that animosity to her kids. I adored my step-siblings and was a very active participant in their lives. I loved it when Jordan and Tobi came to visit me now, but I could see it scared them silly when I asked them questions they thought I should know the answers to. They were a touch too young to understand what was going on with my faulty memory. So, I let them rub my nearly bald head to distract them and assured them I would be back to normal any day.

My mother was alive, but I hadn't seen her since I was very young. On top of her agoraphobia, she struggled with various other mental health issues, one of which caused her to nearly drown me when I was a toddler. This part of my dream was true as well...her family was incredibly wealthy; they lived on the Hill and really belonged to the country club. They pretty much locked her away in an exclusive assisted living complex in lieu of her going to jail for child endangerment after she tried to kill me. My father told me I hadn't seen her or had contact with her since she was sent away. My father did keep me away from that side of my family for most of my life because he was scared they would use their money to take me away from him. My Uncle Doyle was also real. My dad told me I had limited contact with him because he lived overseas with his husband, but he paid for me to go to a good college, and if I ever needed anything my father was unable to financially provide, my uncle stepped in to help out. He even came and for a visit to see how I was doing once I was up to having visitors for longer than a couple of minutes at a time. He seemed nice enough, but he was obviously hurt by the fact I could remember very little about him. There were tangled threads of truth woven within the complex web of figments of my imagination my mind weaved together while I was unconscious.

Surprisingly, it was the familiar hot cop who came to talk to me once I could sit up and speak who filled in some of the biggest gaps. Detective King looked exactly how I remembered him from my imaginary visit to the police station in the Point. His gaze was just as sharp, and his voice just as deep and mesmerizing. He was very patient and gentle when he questioned me about the fall and my relationship with my roommate Devon.

Apparently, the pretty girl with the wild, curly hair was the first friend I made when I went to college. We studied in the same field, so we shared a lot of classes and were pretty much inseparable. We lived together from the time we were allowed to leave the dorms until just recently. I was planning on moving out of the house we rented together to live with Oscar. The detective verified that information with Oscar. My boyfriend told the police that Devon and I were at odds lately, not just because of the move. I'd been selected for a job we both applied to. According to him, jealousy played a big part in the current tension between us, and it wasn't only career related. Oscar told the detective my roommate had made several moves on him and then tried to convince me that he was unfaithful. She'd had designs on him for quite some time, but only got aggressive when he and I planned on moving in together. It sounded like the police didn't think I fell down the stairs on my own, judging by the questions they asked. They thought I was pushed, just like I imagined had happened to my father. It was more fragmented slivers of truth laced throughout the fiction I believed was real.

I couldn't verify the suspicions of either Oscar or the police. I didn't remember anything about Devon or my relationship with her. I only knew the angry and sad girl from my dreams. I hoped the fall was an accident, but I wasn't going back to live with her under any conditions. Just to be safe. When I was first released from the hospital, my dad wanted me to come to stay with him, but it was too stressful trying to convince the little kids everything was fine. Plus, I was super awkward with Pearl. I don't know why there was so much tension there, but I had bigger holes in my recollection to worry about before I tried to tackle unraveling that particular relationship. Maybe I knew she had a drinking problem when I lived with them. Maybe she was scared from leaving an abusive relationship and didn't trust me. There was a high probability both those things were true, and I hadn't made an effort to be understanding and open with the woman when I had the chance. Obviously, we didn't trust each other and simply made concessions for the other people in our lives who loved both of us. I carried that resentment into my unconscious state in a big way. I was very aggravated by Jordan and Tobi's mom in my dream. But now, I felt like I saw a bigger picture and could work on understanding the woman and everything she'd been through.

Since I was planning to live with Oscar before the accident, I decided to follow through with that decision once I was cleared to be on my own for longer than a few hours. Out of everyone in my life, I remembered the most about him. Maybe because he seemed to be the closest to my fictitious version of him. His hair looked like candy. It was baby blue at the moment. And his dark gaze was as unwavering as always. The way he dressed, and the way he carried himself were exactly the same as the make-believe version of him. The crows inked into his skin were still stark and black, and I liked them more than any real bird I'd ever seen. His prickly and defiant personality comforted me in a way all the kindness from others couldn't touch. He still wasn't the nicest guy I'd ever met, but he was bluntly honest and upfront about everything. I didn't have to guess how he felt about me. I didn't have to pretend I was fine for him, because he didn't fake anything for me. When he was scared, he showed it. When he was frustrated, it was clear on his face. When he was hurt or sad because I couldn't recall something he thought was important, he didn't try and cover it up. And when I made him happy, he never hesitated to let me know. I trusted him implicitly.

Whenever Oscar came and sat with me while I was in the hospital, or when he attended one of my physical therapy sessions, I felt like I was more productive. If he reminded me of something, I had an easier time filling in the blanks. His deep, no-nonsense tone resonated with me. He was the key to unlocking everything I needed to know. I was sure of it.

I might not remember the exact moment I fell in love with him and started to lean on him, but unlike everything else, there was no question that he was the person in charge of holding onto my heart.

Oscar's place was on the other side of the train tracks. He was a boy from the Point through and through. In any lifetime. He wasn't a car thief, but he worked for a former one at the busiest and most popular garage in the city. His boss was a notorious former criminal, and there were whispers that the garage operated an illegal chop shop during off-hours. Oscar loved his job as a mechanic and car customizer. And while he didn't break the law on a regular basis, I was certain he came far closer to the line more often than he let me know. I think if we hadn't gotten together, there was a good chance he would've become the guy who wasn't scared of death or prison in my imagination.

Oscar's job was how we met.

My car broke down late at night when I was driving through the Point on my way home from my dad's house. It was a scary situation because I was alone, in the dark, in the Point. That was all real fear that translated while I was out like a light. Fortunately, Oscar was on his way to his place after leaving the motel his family owned and stopped to help me get my car started. He chased off a couple of guys who were lurking in the darkness, waiting for me to get out of my car. He lectured me for over fifteen minutes on being in the wrong part of town and making myself an easy target. He really did see me as a lost little lamb from the start.

I had to convince him we could be together once I realized how much I liked him. I was the one who chased him, just like in my fantasies. I was the one who wouldn't let go, even though we were very different and didn't have much in common. I had to prove to him that I wouldn't be scared away from who he was, and where he was from, if he let himself love me. Fortunately, I won him over. My persistence paid off. Those battles were more than my imagination.

The struggle was real.

So was the motel. And his older brother was in charge of running it. Only, there was a fire not long before my accident, and the entire building burned to the ground. Oscar's brother was seriously injured and landed in the hospital for even longer than me. His injuries were extensive, and he was still learning to live with the scars. He nearly died, and it had deeply affected Oscar. My mind turned the fire into an explosion and pulled Elliot out of Oscar's life because he acted like he lost his brother for a long time. I remembered smelling smoke on him, and wiping ash off his face when I met him at the hospital. He looked like he had barely escaped an explosion, even though he barely got near the burning building when he arrived as the first responders were rescuing his brother. Oscar still blamed his father for not being a responsible enough person to look over his legacy, and he was really angry that his brother was at the motel by default. Some of our history together was starting to fight its way through the fog that swallowed most of my memories.

"What are you thinking about so hard?" A glass of lemonade was plunked down on the table in front of me. I looked up at the sound of Oscar's voice and past him toward the water just beyond the industrial shipping part of the Point. His condo was nice enough, but there were still car parts in places there shouldn't be. It even had a small balcony with a table and chair set he thrifted form somewhere. I couldn't remember spending time in this spot, but it felt right. It felt familiar and soothed the anxious parts of me that still felt rattled when I tried to remember something that I just couldn't catch a hold of.

I grabbed the drink and ran my fingers over the condensation on the outside of the glass. I leaned into Oscar's palm as he cupped the side of my face. As soon as we were alone and I could talk without complications, I told him all about my fantasy self and our fabricated relationships. About how I was a rich kid with everything when I was young, and how the older me lost everything and gave up on life. I explained that he was with me through both versions, and how he assured me he would still love me no matter which girl I was. I told him that he saved me and taught me how to save myself. He was so important no matter what was real and what was fake.

Right now, I was a twenty-two-year-old young woman who fell somewhere in the middle of the different versions of myself I let run uninhibited while I was unconscious.

"I was thinking about the parallels between my dreams and reality. Everyone I encountered and thought I knew had made an appearance in my life, for the most part." The odd man out was Rex. I'd yet to encounter the blond golden boy, which was probably a good thing. I wasn't sure how I would react to seeing any version of him after everything that happened in my imagination. Even if he was a good guy in the real world, I would never trust him. "There are a few things I still don't know where I got the inspiration from. I want to know why they played such a big part in my subconscious." Like being on trial for murder and going to prison. Or the struggle to graduate and get into college. I guess the fight for graduation could've been a manifestation of getting a good job in my desired field. I wasn't sure. Nothing in my real life mirrored those events.

Oscar bent down and pressed a light kiss on the top of my head. I knew he really loved me because he didn't even blink at the sight of my shaved head or the scar that marred my scalp. It wasn't pretty, but I wouldn't be alive without it, so he told me it was beautiful at least once a day. His thumb rubbed the side of my face as he tugged me to lean into his side.

"Cut yourself some slack. Not everything that happened while you were asleep has to be tied to something in your real life. You suffered major trauma. Who knows what your brain was doing to cope with all the injuries? Didn't Dr. Nam suggest that you try hypnosis in a few months if you still don't have your memory back? There are options we can explore."

I sighed and let him take most of my weight as I slumped against him. "I know I shouldn't obsess over it, but everything seemed too real. I honestly thought we slipped through time together. I was trying to make things right, so that makes me think there were things I did wrong before I got hurt."

"You weren't perfect before the fall. I'm sure you did do some things the wrong way before. Everyone does. You're harder on yourself than you need to be. Especially now." He brushed some of my hair back and used the tip of a finger to trace the outside shell of my ear. The soft caress made my whole body shiver. "Did you remember anything else today?"

I didn't feel pressured when Oscar asked. Probably because most of my returned memories centered around him. Whenever my father asked the same thing, I felt terrible that I couldn't recall our moments together. The puzzle pieces were starting to fall into place, but I still couldn't determine what the picture was supposed to be.

I tilted my head backward and smiled up at the blue-haired boy. "I remember our first date."

Oscar snorted. "It was a disaster. There are much better memories for you to get back than that night."

I giggled and lifted a hand to pat his tight stomach. It was a disaster. The worst date I'd ever been on, which explained why the memory came back so bright and vivid.

For some reason, we went to one of the most famous and expensive fine dining restaurants on the Hill. I was a broke college student, and Oscar hated everything that had to do with wealth and entitlement, but we'd been out to impress. He wore a suit much like the tux from my dreams. I wore a white dress and heels. We barely spoke throughout the dinner, and I think we both figured it would be our first and last date. It seemed like we had nothing in common, and if we'd dressed to impress, both of us failed.

"You looked good all dressed up, but I still prefer you dressed down." No one rocked torn jeans and faded t-shirts the way he did. Every day, I'd take his tattoos and scuffed boots over a bow tie and cufflinks.

"I still don't understand why you have to pay more for less food in places like that. Fine dining is a bunch of bullshit."

I chuckled because I remembered him saying the exact same thing the night of the date. What won me over and made me realize I wanted to be with him no matter what was when he stepped in when a waitress was being harassed by a customer. I liked that he didn't care about making a scene and had a clear idea of right and wrong. He always looked out for those who couldn't look out for themselves. Just like when he rescued me when my car broke down.

The confrontation happened much like the showdown at the country club in my dream. Only, Oscar was protecting the girl, and I witnessed it when he punched the unruly customer with the busy hands in the face. All three of us ended up permanently banned from the restaurant, but I didn't mind. Oscar was right—it was too expensive, and the food was too small.

As we walked back to his car, he pointed out the name and type of all the luxury cars we passed. He got excited over a few of them, but when we passed a red car he called Enzo's Cousin, I remember that his dark eyes lit up like a kid on Christmas. He even took a picture of it. I pretended to care while he explained how it got its name and the similarities between this supercar and the other one it resembled.

The details my brain latched onto when injured were weird. But each one was a building block I needed to repair my fractured thoughts. And now that dumb car was everywhere. Aside from the news report I woke up to when my brain decided to restart, talk of the crash on the mountain road was everywhere. Maybe because of the mystery, or because more than one person had died in the crash, people were intrigued. You couldn't turn on the TV without seeing something on the local news about the accident. There was even a petition going around to close access to the mountain road. Politicians on both sides were taking a stance on whether the road was too dangerous, and whether the city needed harsher laws around illegal street racing.

Since my head was tilted toward him, he bent down and dropped a kiss on my parted lips. It was quick and not enough to start anything more risqué.

One of the things I was dying to find out was if my imaginary lover was as amazing in real life. Oscar was very respectful that my body needed time to heal alongside my mind. I appreciated his consideration, but I was also starting to get frustrated by all the PG interactions. I wanted to experience sex with him for the first time all over again.

He was and would always be my first love and the best I'd ever had. It didn't matter what life I ended up in.

"We're supposed to meet my brother and his new girlfriend, Carlotta, for dinner. You've only met her once before, so you don't have to struggle to recall anything specific. She's nice. I'm so glad he found someone who doesn't make him self-conscious about his scars; I'm ready to welcome her into the family without knowing anything else about her."

I frowned and rubbed the spot on my brow where my head throbbed as I tried to remember. "What does she do for a living? Is she a housekeeper?"

Oscar looked at me with an expression I was getting very familiar with. It was part confusion and part approval. "She works as a personal assistant for some big shit up on the Hill. She's basically an overpaid babysitter, but that includes taking care of the house and kids. How did you know that?"

I laughed, but there was no humor in it. "I have no idea how I know anything." What I remembered and what I didn't seemed to have no rhyme or reason.

I was slowly getting back to my life before the fall. I was spending time with my family. I was trying to reconnect with friends. I was falling back in love with my boyfriend, and eventually, I was going back to work. They were baby steps, but I could feel myself getting closer and closer to having all the pieces I needed to put myself back together.

Even without a time slip, I got a second chance to do everything over and live a better life. I was a lucky lady. I could take lessons from my past, present, and imagined future and use them to be the very best version of myself.

I let Oscar pull me to my feet and followed him back into the condo. I told him I needed a minute to fix my hair and touch up my makeup. He grunted in agreement and started scrolling through his phone while he waited for me to get ready.

I messed up the wing of my eyeliner when a loud, "Holy shit!" came from where I left him. I scowled and tried to clean up my face when he burst through the bathroom door, holding his phone in front of my face.

"Remember the Maserati from our first date?"

I elbowed him out of the way and went back to work on my eyeliner. "Enzo's brother?"

I got it wrong so that I could watch his eyes get big and a cute frown pull at his excited face. Real Oscar was more open with his emotions than my dream version had been. There were a lot of improvements in the genuine version.

"Enzo's Cousin. But yeah, that car."

"I remember." I would never forget that stupid car for so many different reasons.

"The big crash out on the old mountain road involved that Maserati. It's the car that ran the others off the road. Rescue crews finally pulled it out of the ravine. Guess who it belongs to?"

I dropped the makeup in the sink and turned around to stare at him. I lifted my eyebrows and asked, "A famous politician?"

Oscar's jaw dropped, and he looked down at his phone and back to me like I'd grown a second head. "Uh... yeah. Senator Wallace. She's saying she has no idea how the car got up on the mountain, but the street racers are all pointing fingers at her son. He's some washed-up college athlete. They aren't happy he ran their friends off the road and caused those fatalities. No way is this getting swept under the rug." He swore under his breath. "The car deserves better than that. But how did you know that's who owned the car?"

I shrugged, wrapped my arms around his waist, and gave him a tight hug. "Lucky guess."

He rested his chin on the top of my head and asked, "Do you know the senator or her son?"

"I honestly don't remember." And if I did know Rex in the real world for any reason, I was determined to keep him out of my life this time around. "It doesn't matter if I do; it sounds like he's in some serious trouble and will get what's coming to him. Maybe this will even be enough to derail the senator's career."

Oscar chuckled and squeezed me. "You're vicious now. I like it."

I breathed in his sweet scent and whispered, "I think I'm going to be a lot of different things I've never been before. Promise me you'll like all of them."

He laughed again, and this time when he kissed me, it lingered and felt anything but innocent. "I promise that I will always love all the things about you, even the bad things."

I looked at him and swore an oath from the bottom of my soul that echoed what I'd told him when I fell in love with him all over again in the void.

"I'll be the best bad thing that ever happened to you, Oscar. Don't give up on me."

"Never." He said the single word in such a way it was impossible not to believe him.

Good or bad. Here or there. Now or then. Rich or poor. Predator or prey. We were meant to be. We found each other in every timeline. When I was on the brink of death, I followed him home through the darkness. I came back so we could be together. I remembered what it was like to be loved by him because he made it impossible to forget.

I was no longer a lost little lamb, because the wolf found me and kept me safe until I could get back to my flock.

Epilogue

Birthday Wish

"Are you positive the person who pushed you down the stairs the day of your accident was Rex Wallace?" I couldn't blame the hot cop for questioning my credibility. I'd gone from months of not remembering anything about that day to everything becoming crystal clear.

I cleared my throat nervously and shifted on the hard chair next to his desk, exactly as I'd done in my dreams.

"Rex Wallace is the father of one of my step-siblings. My dad married his ex-girlfriend several years ago. Rex was horribly abusive to Pearl and both of her kids. My stepmother risked her life to get all of them away from him." I rubbed the spot on my forehead that was throbbing with pain. "Senator Wallace and her team, including Rex, came by the center where I work for a photo-op before my accident. I have several pictures of me and my younger siblings, as well as a full family photo, on my desk. I didn't know Pearl had left Rex and was in hiding. I had no idea she was terrified of him finding her and the kids. She was convinced Rex wouldn't stop looking for them and that he would kill her because she took his son away from him. She was also worried Senator Wallace would use her connections and political influence to take Jordan, my younger brother, away from her. Rex saw the pictures in my office and started stalking me, hoping I might lead him to Pearl. At the time, I didn't know I was being followed. I was dealing with my own issues." Namely, my feud with my former friend and roommate, and the emotional fallout from the fire at the motel after Elliot nearly died and Oscar became unhinged. It never occurred to me that a wealthy and famous heir to a political legacy lurked in the shadows. I was oblivious to any danger that didn't come from the Point. I was disgusted by the fact that I previously had a bit of a crush on the handsome heir to the Wallace fortune. Before Oscar, my type apparently ran toward the upper crust. When I was younger, I had a lot of Cinderella fantasies that stared Rex as the handsome prince. No wonder he was such a looming specter in my imagination, and I had so many conflicting feelings about him when I was unconscious.

"Rex must've gotten impatient with the waiting. I was busy at the time and didn't go home to my dad's place. Plus, my stepmom and I never really got along, so there was a lot of tension in my relationship with both my dad and Pearl." I think that's why I was so concerned about appreciating my father when I was in la-la-land.

I wanted to get back to when things were effortless between us. I subconsciously felt bad for letting our relationship fracture when he clearly loved his new wife so much.

Now I understood that Pearl always kept me at arm's length for my own protection. She was worried anyone she got close to might befall the Wallaces' wrath. No wonder she played so hard to get when my father started courting her. Falling in love with him was a huge risk. It was no wonder she started to drink more than was healthy to deal with her heavy emotional burden.

I laughed, but it held no humor. I met the detective's gaze and told him, "It's that damn car." That fucking car was at the center of everything. "The rare Maserati. It was everywhere I went for weeks, and I bet it was parked somewhere near my house the day of my accident. I remember answering a knock on the door because I recognized the man on the other side. I thought Rex was at my house for something to do with the speech center. I foolishly thought people with his status and visibility were harmless. Plus, I live in a busy subdivision. What could possibly happen?"

I frowned harder and lifted a hand to rub my temples. "I was an idiot." Both when I was unconscious and in real life. "He pushed his way into my house. He threatened me and demanded to know where Pearl and the kids were. I think he was worried she would leak the abuse allegations before his mother's election. He was screaming at me and grabbed me. He hit me. Hard." All he needed was an opportunity. I sighed and shook my head. "I called for help and tried to run away from him, but he chased me up the stairs. I don't know if he pulled me backward or pushed me, but I know Rex Wallace is why I almost died. I'm sure you can find evidence that he followed me, and I bet he left fingerprints if you look closely at that house."

The detective nodded and got up to get me a bottle of water. "Have a drink. You don't look too good, Ms. Bell." Once he sat down, he gave me a serious look and told me, "The house has already been rented to someone else, so I don't think anything we find there will be much help. Rex Wallace is already looking at vehicular murder charges and a slew of other offenses for street racing. Not to mention the entire Wallace family is being dragged through civil court for damages from the crash. I don't know that mucking up the narrative without solid proof will benefit the cause."

I was appalled. Of course, money, power, and prestige kept someone like Rex Wallace insulated from the full force of law and order.

"However, if your stepmother wants to come in and talk about the abuse he put her and her kids through, we might be able to do something with that. Especially if she documented the situation. I know it's frustrating to hear that we can't always punish a bad person for all their crimes, but sometimes that's just how the justice system works."

I scowled at him and climbed to my feet. "The system sucks."

The cop nodded in agreement. "It often does. I appreciate you coming in and telling me your story. I'll let you know if I can do anything with the info moving forward." He got to his feet and shook my hand. "Oh, and I hope you have a happy birthday." He chuckled at my surprised look. "I'm a good cop. I remember the details."

I thanked him, left the police station, and headed home to the condo I now shared with Oscar. It was dark when I parked in the garage and took the elevator up to the unit. I'd spent most of the day with my dad and the kids. Pearl even made cupcakes for the occasion. I was doing my best to make amends and live without regret.

The only reason I knew about her tragic history was because, just like in my fantasy caused by the fall, Tobi was a chatterbox and filled me in on her past with Rex Wallace. The little girl was so straightforward about the abuse and horror she'd been through, I couldn't help but soften toward my stepmother. It was nice to be around the entire family without the tension that was always there. I hoped I could get close enough to her that she might listen to me when I encouraged her to tell the hot cop about what Rex had put her and the kids through.

When I walked into the condo, the lights were dim. A soft glow came from a handful of candles on a big birthday cake in the center of the kitchen table. The cake was lopsided, and the frosting was uneven. It looked like it was about to slide onto the table with a *splat* any second. Oscar had clearly baked the monstrosity himself. Black and silver balloons covered the ceiling, and messily wrapped presents were stacked in a sloppy pile on one of the chairs near the table.

I smiled at the sight and walked toward the small balcony where he was waiting.

"I thought we agreed we wouldn't do anything special for our birthdays this year. Especially with anything involving flames." Why tempt fate?

I wrapped my arms around his lean waist and rested my cheek against his strong back. "You didn't have to go through all of this trouble." Fortunately, I got him the fancy rims for his current rebuild he'd been hinting at wanting. I was glad I wasn't the only one who splurged on this birthday.

Oscar grunted. "You don't remember most of your birthdays from before the fall. I want to make sure you have a whole new set of memories from here on out. I'll make each birthday better than the one before it, so you won't miss the old ones."

Damnit. He still did sweet better than anyone else when he put his mind to it. I didn't imagine that. "How was your visit with the cop? How much of what you told him was the truth?"

I snorted in response and held him even tighter. "Does it matter? He doesn't think I'm reliable, regardless of if I lied about what I do and don't remember from that day."

Overall, about eighty percent of my memory was back. There were still holes here and there, but they mostly made themselves known when I was trying to look farther back in my life. But some recent events were still foggy, like the situation with Rex. He really had shown up at my house that day, demanding to be let in. But I couldn't remember if I opened the door for him or not. At least I now understood how Rex and the trial were tied to my delusion when I was in the coma. My mind was trying to tell me who the bad guy was all along, and my imagination was far richer and more layered than

I ever expected. So were my morals. "Are you worried that if I can lie to that detective with no problem, I might start lying to you?" I had no intention of doing that, but I wanted him to know I was far from perfect and could bend the rules just like he did when need be. While I hovered on the brink of death, all my biggest fears and insecurities played out in front of me like a motion picture. I wanted to be with Oscar no matter what. I didn't want our differences to come between us. He could be the hero for me, and I could be a villain for him.

Oscar turned around and wrapped me in a rib-crunching hug. He kissed my forehead and grinned at me as our eyes met.

"No. Others might not be able to tell when you're lying, but I always can. I can see how uncomfortable playing with the truth makes the good girl you've tried to bury since the accident. You can't hide her from me."

I sighed and looked toward the cake that really was going to fall over any minute. "You're right. I can't lie to you. I'm sure you worked really hard on that cake, but it looks inedible." I wrinkled my nose to really drive the point home.

He chuckled and grabbed my hand to pull me inside. "It's gross. I think I mixed up the salt and sugar. But the frosting is awesome." He stopped next to the table and dragged a finger through the white cream that covered the surface. I opened my mouth, expecting him to pop his finger inside, but instead, he dragged the frosting over my parted lips and then bent down so he could lick it away. I finally got a taste when his tongue dipped between my lips and flicked across the roof of my mouth.

It was sugary and sweet enough to make my teeth hurt. There was no way anyone could eat more than a small bit of it.

Still, I wanted to praise Oscar for the gesture and let him know how wonderful I thought he was, but he didn't stop kissing me after the quick taste.

His tongue swirled around mine, and his teeth scraped across my lower lip. His hands started tugging at my clothing, and he moved us so that I could lean against the table with one of his legs inserted between mine. I braced my hands on the flat surface and kissed Oscar back with everything I had. He tasted like dessert, but every part of him pressed against me was hard and strong. It was a deadly combination and one of the main reasons I always found him so irresistible.

Once Oscar had me naked from the waist up, he let me breathe. He smiled at me with wicked intent as he leaned past me to collect more frosting. The position pushed his bent knee into the apex of my thighs, and it rubbed roughly against my most sensitive spots.

A moment later, the white frosting was smoothed along the side of my neck, and a little dollop was laid on top of each nipple.

I often felt like Oscar wanted to eat me up. Tonight, he was showing just how hungry a wolf could be. And just how sharp its teeth were.

I gasped in delight as his mouth moved down my throat and across the curve of my breasts. He didn't miss a spot as he licked me clean. The top part of the cake slid off with a plop, but the candles remained glowing as they rapidly melted into the squishy confection. I moaned and wrapped my arms around his neck as he lifted me to sit on the table's edge.

He helped me pull his t-shirt off and let me work his belt loose so I could open his jeans. I giggled when he lifted my legs into the air so he could pull off the rest of my clothing. It was playful and fun, but simmering heat still burned below the surface.

I pulled him closer so I could tug on his ear with my teeth, and I buried my fingers in his denim-colored hair.

"I don't know that this table can withstand whatever you have planned." I sighed the warning as his hands skimmed down my sides, his thumbs pausing to circle my pebbled nipples.

"If we break it, I'll buy a new one." His voice was husky and impatient as he stepped between my legs. I felt his hardened erection nudge against the part of me that was trained to respond to his littlest movement. My insides got hot at record speed, and my body fluttered in excitement. I smoothed my hands over his broad shoulders and let my head fall back as he spread my legs wider. I felt his gaze trace over my flushed skin like it was a physical touch.

"I'm so glad you came back to me, Vesper." He used the tip of one finger to outline a heart on my chest. "I don't know what kind of person I would've become if I lost you. I love you."

I whimpered when I felt the tip of his erection slide through the quivering folds surrounding my waiting entrance.

"You'll always be a force to be reckoned with. Regardless if I'm around or not. You walk the line of being good and bad better than anyone I've ever met, Oscar. I want to be just like you." The words trailed off because he started to push into me. That first breach of my body was always tight and made me tingle from head to toe. The way my body automatically adjusted to accommodate him made my heart soft and sent butterflies dancing in my belly.

"You can be like me with everyone else. I like it when you're the good girl with me. I want to take care of you. I'll be the one who does bad things so you don't have to. Okay?"

I moaned as he forcefully sank all the way inside. I hugged him close and let him kiss me stupid as I tried to catch a thought to answer him.

"Not fair. You know I'll agree to anything when you're doing what you're doing." I really was weak for him. No wonder most of the memories I retained were related to him.

"You know me well enough to know that I never play fair. I play to win." He jerked me closer to the edge of the table and bent me back farther. His teeth nipped at the pulse pounding on the side of my neck. One of his hands covered mine, and I wrapped a leg around his hips as he started to thrust in and out with significant force.

The table rocked underneath me, and the rapidly dying candles on the wobbly cake sent eerie shadows dancing across the walls and my skin.

I was gasping and panting as we vigorously fucked. I couldn't catch my breath long enough to tell him that if there was a winner in this relationship, it was definitely me. Oscar was the constant in my life. He was the person who pushed me forward or dragged me back when things were too close to the edge. He was the one who showed me where I was supposed to be.

His teeth bit into the top of one of my breasts, and I knew there would be a bruise there tomorrow. He was a bit rough when he lost control of himself, but I wasn't complaining.

I squeezed my thigh muscles to hold him tighter and moaned his name when he started to move even faster.

Birthday sex was the best. He was the best present I could ask for.

"I love you. Happy birthday, Oscar." The words were ragged and uneven as my body quaked violently around his hardness.

"Happy birthday, little lamb."

I knew I was about to come. I could feel pleasure pulsing throughout my body. Coiled tension circled the base of my spine, and my extremities started to feel heavy.

I put a hand on the back of Oscar's head and moved to kiss him. He growled my name against my lips, and our eyes locked. It felt like an electric current passed between us, and both of us stopped breathing for a painful moment.

Suddenly, it felt like a cool breeze moved through the condo. The candles on the cake went out, and the balloons floating innocently against the ceiling looked like they were alive. Oscar and I froze as time seemed like it stood still.

"Since the candles went out, you better make a wish before something weird happens." Oscar's voice held a hint of strained humor, but I could tell he was as weirded out by the shift in atmosphere as I was.

What was it about our birthday that turned the world end over end?

"I only have one wish." And he already made it come true. As long as he could find me and love me wherever we ended up, in whatever version of reality we found ourselves, I couldn't ask for anything more.

The End

AFTERWORD

You might be wondering: Jay, how did we get here? What even is this weird-ass book?

Lol... I asked myself the same thing several times.

The answer to that is threefold. First, one of my most favorite things in all of literature is an unreliable narrator. There is something so unique and engaging about a storyteller whom you can't fully trust. The unreliable narrator is typically found in thrillers, mysteries, and suspense novels. Very few romance novels have a hero or heroine who is untrustworthy throughout their book. And when we do see one, their unreliability is often based on some sort of personality disorder or mental health struggle. I wanted to try my hand at writing my own version of a questionable lead, but not in the usual way. Having a heroine who can't tell fact from fiction, and who can't tell real from imaginary was a thrilling challenge. If you noticed instances of inconsistency and continuity, I assure you that was deliberate. I wanted the reader to be as confused as Vesper was. This is also why we spend the entirety of this story inside Vesper's broken mind. This type of story wouldn't work with one person having full control of their world and perception and another not knowing anything.

Second, the Point is my favorite fictional place I've created. I know that series isn't as beloved by readers as some of my others, but to me, those books are where I really shine as a writer. I desperately wanted to revisit the gritty streets and vague morals of the Point. And since it is a make-believe place, it fit in perfectly with a heroine who can't tell if anything around her is real or not. Fun fact: I actually toyed with the idea of making the city a figment of Vesper's imagination, and all the books that take place there a part of her coma-induced hallucination. In the end, I couldn't wipe my favorite place off the map so easily. Plus, there is a certain character from the very end of that series who has found his way into my new series about the Marked Men kids, so he has to be real. And for the extra perceptive crew, if you noticed the difference between 'the Point' vs 'The Point', I did that on purpose for this book. In The Point series, the city is a main character. It lives and breathes just like all the people who inhabit it. For this novel, I tried to make the city more of a background player. I'm not sure I succeeded, but making the small change to how I referred to the city helped me keep the magic and mystery of what was happening to Vesper as the main player.

And lastly, I'm sure if you follow me on any social media platform (other than TikTok because I have no clue how to use that one), you know I love k-dramas and webtoons, and a common theme in a lot of entertainment from Asian countries is rebirth and reincarnation. I've been reading a lot of transmigration (which is basically a normal person getting sent into an alternate world or reality) books lately, which takes the idea of being reborn to a different level. I find the premise so fascinating. The idea of getting to live as yourself in a perfect world or in a world where you get to undo any injustice you suffered in the past really appeals to me. I feel like we all have before and after parts of our lives that define who we are. For example, my life before and after I published *Rule*. One press of the *publish* button really changed everything in my life so drastically. But...what if I didn't publish? Where would I be now? What would I be doing? Who would my friends be? What would I be passionate about? It's such a layered and nuanced idea that I was dying to see how I could integrate it into a romance novel.

If you couldn't tell, *The Usual Suspects* is one of my all-time favorite movies. For years, I've wanted to write my own Keyser Söze type of character. Things just fell in place for that to happen when I started working on this book. I knew the ending before I even started the beginning. That never happens to me as I write very linearly when I work.

I think I did a good job tucking all the bits and pieces together... but you never know until your book baby is out in the world and the opinions start to roll in.

I've had a hard time connecting to anything over the last couple of years. I'm sure it was pandemic fatigue on top of some general burnout. I've written a minimum of four books a year, every year, until 2020. I wasn't very inspired or invested in anything. That sucks as a creator and artist. I wrote books, but they were not easy ones. They were not light and fluffy. They took a lot of work and every ounce of concentration and skill I possess. When I got the idea for Vesper and Oscar's book, it felt like a light bulb moment. I knew the premise was weird, and not necessarily something my audience would gravitate toward. I didn't care. I finally *wanted* to write with every fiber of my being. I let myself run wild and had a great time while doing it. I feel like this book helped me get a little bit of my footing back. There is no denying my creativity is alive and well on these pages.

If you love this book, or hate it, I appreciate you giving me the space to find my way back to myself with these words. I wrote this book for myself, but I am very happy to share it with all of you. It's bound to be an experience!

If you want to drop a review to warn others of the weirdness, I would be extremely grateful.

ACKNOWLEDGEMENTS

Big thanks to each and every reader. Always and forever. It doesn't matter if this is your first book you've read by me or the thirty-fifth. The time and attention you pay to my books are greatly appreciated. There are a lot of authors and choices out there. I know taking a chance on my words is never a guarantee because I march to the beat of my own tambourine and truly only write what I want. So, I appreciate those of you who are willing to jump into my words and worlds blindfolded. I always say this is an adventure we are on together, and I wouldn't pick any other group of readers to travel this road with.

I can't believe it has been ten years since I started writing professionally. Being a *romance* author was always my dream job when I was younger. I specify romance because that is the genre in which I have always wanted to work. Romance novels were my favorite thing in the whole world long before I started writing them. I honestly had no clue they had such a stigma to them in the literary world until I worked in this field. But I can definitely say, with utmost confidence, romance novels are still my favorite even after a decade of living and breathing them.

I really need to send a special thank you to my assistant Melissa Shank. She has always kept me on track and has been my biggest cheerleader. She is full of southern sweetness but takes no shit from anyone. It's a combination I find delightful. She adjusts to my workload being either feast or famine better than I ever do. Since I do nothing in moderation, she either has nothing to do for months and months or has so much to do in just a few weeks that it would send a weaker woman running for the hills. She is the best, and I don't know what I would've done all this time without her. She's been my

PA for almost as long as I've been writing. I just adore her and appreciate her so much.

Huge shoutout to my spectacular beta team. They are smart, fearless, insightful, and more helpful than one can imagine. They roll with whatever I toss at them. And I have yet to find their feedback on my raw and unfiltered work anything but helpful. They make my books better. They make me better. Anyone willing to give up their time and ability to help someone out with minimal reward is a special type of human. I adore these girls, and I can't ever thank them enough for all their help. Alexandra, Sarah, Teri, Pam, Kelly, Karla, and Cheron... you ladies are the best. Thank you for suffering through all my ugly as hell first drafts so we can make something beautiful together in the end. <3

Speaking of beautiful, I bow down to Hang Le and her stunning design work. I counted it up the other day, and we've worked on over twelve covers together. She has made the cover for every book I've self-published. I adore that I send her vague, often abstract, ideas, and she never fails to pull off my vision perfectly. It's hard to make some of the dudes I've had on my covers look better than they already do, but Hang managed to do it each and every time. I appreciate how good she is at her craft and admire her artistry.

The same goes for both of the editors I repeatedly work with. I think they do miraculous work. I publish both with big-name publishing houses as well as on my own. I say with no malice or artifice, the editors I handpick to work on my independent stuff bring a little something more to my work than the trad editors do. It's like comparing apples and oranges. Trad editors are looking at what will sell the best and appeal to the widest audience. They have to consider rules and regulations about what certain sales outlets allow on their shelves, so I don't think they get attached to the work the way indie editors do.

When I send my work off to Elaine and Beth to polish up and make it as pretty as can be, I know they are looking at what the story will be. I know they are all about the vibe and keeping my voice and storytelling skills as sharp as possible. They focus on providing the reader with the best experience rather than what is most marketable. I feel like they treat my books as art the same way I do. And that comes across in their thoughtful and precise edits. Like with my covers, Elaine and Beth are the team I turn to when I put out self-published books. I've worked on over ten with them. Thanks for being badass no matter what I throw at you ladies. And Beth, thanks for teaching me more about prepositions and prepositional phrases than I ever learned in school!

You can find all the information/websites for my professional team at the front of any of my self-published books, including this one. Trust me when I say their services are worth all the dollars.

Thank you to my super-agent, mostly because I haven't said it in a while, and I want her to know how much I appreciate her.... Stacey...you rock. You're the best at believing good things will happen for me. You're the best at believing in me when I am so ready to give up. I think you managed to manifest all the amazing opportunities that have come my way... from the beginning to the end. I know I wouldn't be where I am now if it wasn't for you and your unwavering faith in me and my talent.

As always, I want to shout out my most awesome reader's group, Crownover's Crowd. They are just the chillest, most encouraging group of readers on the interwebs, and I'm so happy we have a safe place to gather and interact regularly. If you haven't joined, I highly suggest you do.

Below is a list of all the places you can find me:

Facebook.com/groups/crownoverscrowd
Bookbub: bookbub.com/authors/jay-crownover
Website: jaycrownover.com
My store: shop.spreadshirt.com/100036557
FB page: Facebook.com/AuthorJayCrownover
Twitter: twitter.com/jaycrownover
Instagram: instagram.com/jay.crownover
Pinterest: pinterest.com/jaycrownover
Spotify and Snapchat: Jay Crownover
Email: JayCrownover@gmail.com

ABOUT THE AUTHOR

Jay Crownover is the international and multiple *New York Times* and *USA Today* bestselling author of the *Marked Men* series, the *Saints of Denver* series, the *Point* series, the *Breaking Point* series, the *Getaway* series, and the *Loveless, Texas* series. Her books have been translated into many different languages all around the world. She is a tattooed, crazy-haired Colorado native who lives at the base of the Rockies with her awesome dogs. She can frequently be found enjoying a cold beer and taco Tuesdays. Jay is a self-declared music snob and outspoken book lover who is always looking for her next adventure, between the pages and on the road.

OTHER BOOKS BY JAY

Marked Men Series
Saints of Denver Series
Forever Marked Series
Welcome to the Point Series
Breaking Point Series
Getaway Series
Loveless Series
Standalone Books

Lightning Source UK Ltd.
Milton Keynes UK
UKHW012233060223
416577UK00003B/253/J